Tempest,
Take Me Home

The book fondly known as *Butt Pirates*

Charlie Knight

TEMPEST, TAKE ME HOME

www.cknightwrites.carrd.co

Santa Fe, New Mexico

ISBN: 979-8-9924393-0-4 (Print)
ISBN: 979-8-9924393-1-1 (e-book)

Cover Image and Formatting by Makeshift Miscreants (www.makeshift-miscreants.com)

First printing editing 2025.

This book is dedicated to everyone
who needs to explore to find their home
and their family. You'll get there,
and it'll be worth the journey.

And to my monkey. I didn't know
what family was before you.
I love you, and I like you.

Preface

While this story is not particularly dark, there may be some things on the following pages that could be upsetting, surprising, or triggering to some readers. Please read the following list of content warnings before continuing, and please take care of yourselves.

- Attempted kidnapping
- Kidnapping
- Attempted and actual assault of a disabled person
- Child abuse and neglect (mentioned/remembered)
- Extreme poverty (mentioned/remembered)
- Transphobia/enbyphobia (mentioned/remembered)

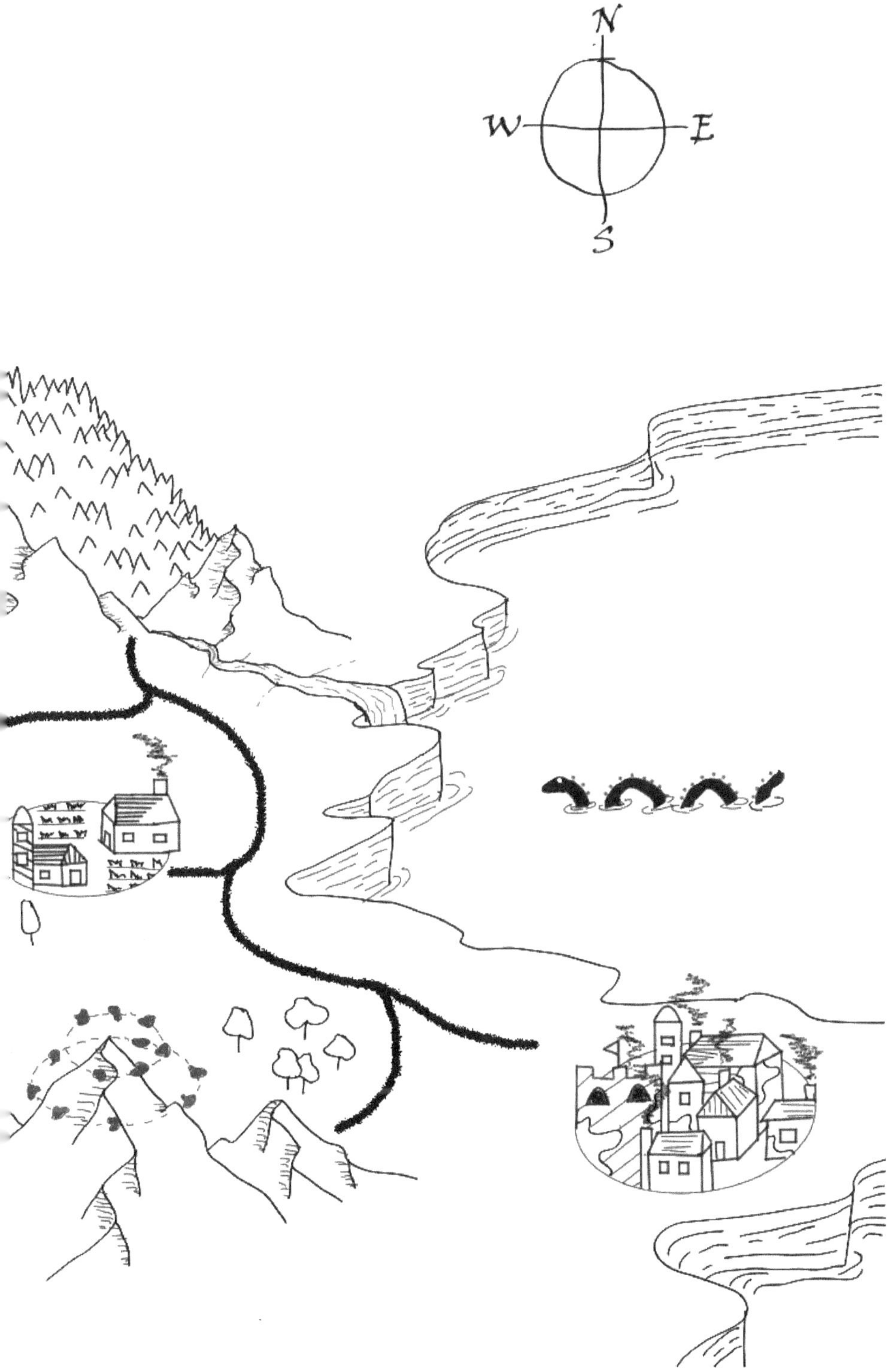
N
W
E
S

Chapter 1
Eli

I fucking hate the smell of magic.

I've been told dozens of times that it doesn't have a smell or a taste or anything else identifying. I've heard it from magic users and regular folk like me. As a kid, I thought those people were screwing with me. Turns out it's probably just further proof of my screwed-up brain.

But whatever anyone else says, magic has a smell so strong that I can taste it. It's like licking rocks that got covered in something slightly sour. And it always tastes cold. Makes no sense even to me, but there it is. Even fire magic—cold. And with the magic around us tonight, it's not just the smell that my overworked senses have to deal with.

Stone makes everything echo; the waves following us into this cave are creating an absolute cacophony. The high tension while we wait for a signal and an opportunity has the hairs all over my body standing, and each breeze off the ocean feels frigid. I don't move, don't react. Our map said this is where we need to be, and I'll be damned if I fuck this up for my crew just because my own body seems to be working against me at the moment.

Further inside this cave is the treasure we came for and the creature guarding it. Griffin are nothing to be fucked with, and approaching one like this is widely considered a death wish. Treasure hunters are widely known for our death wishes.

I've wedged myself into a too-small space between a rock and hard place, using the natural growth of mosses and slippery plants I can't name to further hide my shape and scent from the winged beast. Yenvyl has managed to squeeze herself into an even smaller spot, and she's under order not to move or give up even if I get caught; one of us needs to get what we came for. We planned our arrival before high tide will threaten us in here, but we're already seated in puddles of water cold enough to make my balls scream for their lives and send them retreating in my stomach. With her tiny form, barely any meat on her, I have no idea how Yenvyl isn't giving us away with chattering teeth.

We're not far enough in to see the griffin; I'm generally of the belief that if I can see something, it'll be able to see me, and I don't care to be a plaything for those lion claws or the eagle's beak on the monster we're here to steal from. Well, steal back from. Seriously doubt the griffin will take a second to care for the ethics, and it's not like I can blame an animal for acting like one. Especially since we're invading its territory. But even though we can't see it, we're close enough to hear when it starts moving. Fuck, I hope it's moving because the rest of my crew is on their task, not because it caught a whiff of me.

A rustle of feathers makes my heart jump into my throat. I don't dare breathe. The distinct click of claws on stone has my stomach in my boots, and a screech nearly shatters my eardrums. But I can't even wince, can't cover my ears. Can't risk it. It's not until the griffin is tearing out of the cave, wings strong enough to blow the water around and splatter my face with icy droplets, that I catch the scent of smoke. Fire. Wood burning. The griffin is leaving to protect the island that it calls home from fire—exactly as planned. If only the smoke could get rid of that magical stench.

I make eye contact with Yenvyl just long enough to nod, and we both climb to our feet. Well, she just pops up all nimble and lithe and elfy. I have to grab onto a handful of rock-attached slimy moss to lever myself up and nearly fall backward when my legs protest after crouching for so long. "Doesn't pay to be oversized," she stage whispers at me. Probably don't need to whisper, but considering where we are and that we'll have no real warning before the griffin comes back, it seems wise. I've never claimed to be wise, though.

"Doesn't pay to be a smartass," I retort, then catch Yenvyl by her upper arms and jerk her sideways like I'm going to toss her off the rocky cave floor and back into the water. She yelps and contorts herself impressively to cling to me. It'd at least make sure that I have to go in with her. "I give! My balls have had more than enough cold water, thanks."

"It pays to have those if you're in the right line of work." She then snorts at her own joke, and I can't help laughing with her. We're supposed to be professionals at this.

We do manage to get moving further into the cave. It's colder outside the water, with the wind constantly moving through here. Griffins are the size of large houses, and they're covered in thick, water-proof feathers, so it's probably a cozy home for that beast. And hopefully a cozy one for the little beasts—there are four eggs in the nest.

"Oh. I didn't realize they make actual bird nests," Yenvyl admits. When she stands just outside the nest, the border made obvious by a ring of carefully chosen branches, leaves, and animal bones, it's almost as tall as she is. "Okay, maybe bird isn't the right comparison."

I laugh, joining her in climbing over the side of the thing. "Just a good thing they don't hoard like dragons."

While dragons will collect anything and everything, including people if a person makes the mistake of being interesting enough, griffins are only interested in shiny stuff. They're more discerning, so I know the pile of gems, jewels, and jewelry we need to search through isn't as bad as it could be. Or at least that's what I'm going to tell myself while dealing with the reality that the griffin could come back and kill us at any moment.

"Remember, it's blue."

"I know what color sapphires are, *Captain*."

"Oh, pardon me. I forgot I was speaking to a lady of class."

That gets me nailed in the face by what I hope is a handful of moss. I refuse to look at it and find out. I don't care about it at all when I spot what we're looking for. It's a deep, rich blue, it's nearly the size of my palm, and it's been expertly crafted into an oval shape. I don't know if this thing is in the shape that the people who lost it remember, a few scratches on the surface that don't look like rich people would like them, but they only paid me to find the thing—not polish it.

I grab it, take one more second to be certain that this is what I need, and then shove it into my pocket. If the griffin does catch us, we'll have a better shot at survival if it doesn't know for certain that we stole from it because it sees the damn gem.

"You don't want me to do anything to the nest, right?" I frown at Yen, and she glances at the nest, the eggs, then wiggles her fingers at me, sparks flying from the tips, just above her pink-painted nails.

"Nah, I don't want to kill the thing—just needed it distracted. Let's get the fuck out of here while it is," I tell Yenvyl, and she does not need to be told twice. There are a lot of other gems in the nest that we could sell for a pretty penny, but our current job has a damn nice payment attached, and wasting time in this place is just foolish. We're treasure-obsessed, sure, but we aren't fools.

"Did you see how big that thing is?" she asks as we make our way out, sticking to the walls where the water is shallower and we can stand instead of swim. "I'm gonna brush my hair in the reflection on it. And I wanna sleep with it tonight. Gods, I wanna bathe with it."

Treasure-obsessed. I don't fault her for any of that. At the moment, I envy her.

I wanted to come here, wanted to get the treasure. There's a high with chasing after something, especially when we have it to steal it out from under—literally—a beast so powerful and so magical that the smell is now clogging my throat. Now that we're on our way out, though, now that I have the thing in my pocket, now that it's almost done...I have to wonder if this was worth it. Not the risk—the delay.

We took this job because of the payment attached. A little bit for the reputation boost of getting to say we took treasure from a griffin's nest. As captain, the jobs that we take on is my call, and I agreed to this one because it's good for my ship and my crew. But this job took me in the wrong direction. It took me further from Max.

We've known each other since we were kids, I'm fairly confident we've both been in love for almost all of that time, and technically, we've been living together for six years. But since getting *Tempest* and setting sail as captain and professional treasure hunter three years ago, I feel like I've barely been home at all. We were supposed to be home now, taking a break to visit and to give me the time with Max my soul needs to feel less fractured. Instead, I'm ducking through hanging vines that smell like fish and salt on the way out of the griffin's cave to bring treasure back to my ship. And after this, I'll have to bring it to the client.

When I'm missing him so much that my stomach hurts and I can barely sleep, the high of the hunt and the rewards don't feel worth it. When I know I won't get to share even the stories of what we've done for the last three months with Max for another two weeks, it doesn't feel special or important that we completed this hunt. Hard to care about anything else when I haven't been home for more than a week straight in over a year, even if that's because I've built *Tempest's* reputation so well.

The griffin is flying overhead, screeching its anger and panic, using its wings to try and snuff out the fire that my crew started when Yenvyl and I reach the little dingy that we left among the rocks. I untie it while she climbs in, and on the moonlit water, I can see the other dingy heading back toward my ship. My Tempest. The place I've always wanted to live, the ship I fought to make mine for most of my life. But now, rowing back to her, I know I'll feel empty.

I want to go home.

Chapter 2

Eli

"I fucking hate the smell of magic." Feels good to say it out loud.

"It doesn't smell like anything!"

Dava and everyone else whose said that to me seem to have functional noses otherwise. But I know for a fact that they're wrong. Magic has a smell—a smell of cold and vinegar and something totally unnatural—and the big blue orb Tevin is tossing while we walk is soaked in that stench.

"Have you ever told Max you think he smells terrible while working?" Tevin teases, grinning at me the second I look up at him. At least part of the grin is because the angle we're at does force me to look up at him; even though he and Dava are orcs, I'm one of the few humans tall enough to meet their gaze. Mostly. In heels. Except for now when Tevin is walking up on the curb and I'm in the street. I shove up next to him, making us almost even again, and he laughs. "Don't get mad at me. I just don't think Max would appreciate your opinions about the smell of magic—that's all I'm saying."

"Max never smells terrible, thank you," I argue. "His magic must be special."

"Sure, that's it." Tevin laughs again when I roll my eyes at him, the deep sound rolling through the crowded market street ahead of us and turning a few heads.

We don't generally get to pick where we meet our clients, not if we want them really happy, but considering the line of work they hire us for, we tend to get lucky with the places we end up. This port town is a little oversized and over-crowded for my taste, but at least we can walk down the street with a magical orb, a human and two orcs, and no one so much as considers a second glance. Except the people who take a second glance at me, but when you're over six feet tall, fully bearded, and never feel complete unless you're wearing heels and leather skirts, you expect that people are gonna take a look. They'd quit if they knew how much I like getting looked at.

Our client asked us to meet him in an antique shop that should be nearby. Never been there before since I've never had the urge to go antiquing. It's about an hour after sundown, but it's also the middle of summer in a seaside town, so these people have the good sense to stay inside during the day. The marketplace has recently come to life, lit by glass-cased oil lanterns lining the streets and casting odd shadows, crowded by sound and scent as much as by the people.

A stand manned by a dwarf hawking cinnamon buns that smell incredible turn Dava's head; another stand with an elven woman keeping a close eye on the jewels spread out ahead of her turns Tevin's. All I can do is think about a different town entirely.

A town that is almost a week away from here if we have good winds.

A town that I should have been back to a week ago.

A town that has nothing special except the most important thing in the world.

Max and I rented a cute little apartment in a port town, Baybridge, where he can work and where I can go back to him. The town and the apartment don't necessarily feel like home to me, but my Max... That's home, and I am missing home more and more all the time these days.

It helps that Max always smells amazing, like vanilla and ink and the minty salve that he uses for pain relief. Unlike the stench of magic and the odor of too many people too close together surrounding me now.

"Eli." I turn my head, expecting Dava to be right beside me, but she's gone. Behind me now. Standing with Tevin outside an unmarked shop of some kind, holding the door open, staring at me. She points inside while Tevin gives me a shit-eating grin and says, "You coming or..."

"Fuck you. The hell is this place?" I don't care, and they know I don't care, but it's a good excuse to try and avoid their teasing when I lead them inside. Tevin, of course, takes the opportunity to grab a handful of my ass, so at least I can walk in with a smile on and some pep in my step. I don't want the client to see me scowling like I'd rather be anywhere else. I'd only rather be somewhere very specific.

"Captain Rose!" Oh, I love the sound of that. Now I can smile at the client and not just because I like my boyfriend's hand on my ass. Dawson Welsh, a merchant and collector of all the random crap scattered around this too brightly lit shop, comes through a door behind the counter. He's a human, short and slight, smiling every time we've met whether we were working together or not. He pays well, and he always has interesting jobs, so I don't mind that he talks a lot and asks questions that he then answers. "Welcome! I don't think you've been here before, have you? Well, I'm not here all the time. My cousin runs the shop, you see. You're welcome to take a look around! Anyway, how did the treasure hunt go? I assume it was a success that brings you back to me."

I've learned to wait a couple seconds before responding to him, just in case he's not done yet and will continue. Once I count to two, I feel safe to answer.

"We were very successful, Dawson," I answer, turning back and motioning for Tevin to present our prize. I'm not much into fancy nonsense outside of how much I can charge to find them, so to me, the oval orb doesn't appear to be much. For the client, though, these pieces could mean anything. A priceless antique passed down through generations, something monetarily worthless but emotionally symbolic, a piece from their wife's collection that they never should have gambled. It's not my job to care.

Dawson gasps and takes the piece, holding it up above his head in both hands and staring

11

into the depths of it through the light overhead. There's a glint of something deep inside the orb, catching the light and throwing it weakly. I think he'd have even more to say than usual if he knew that Tevin was just tossing that thing around on the way here. Or that it fell off my desk a half dozen times on the trip here.

"How did you find it? And so quickly! But then, you always do find your treasure, don't you? That must be some secret weapon you have." Dawson gives me a big smile I have to force myself to return. Every single client asks how we do it, and I know there are rumors floating around out there about our 'secret weapon,' our magical talent. None of them knows about Max—not as my hidden partner, at least. It keeps him safe from my competition, other treasure hunters and the much worse types out there. And it lets Max manage his own thriving business. I won't be telling Dawson or anyone else about my secret weapon.

"I'm good at what I do," I answer simply, shrugging. When Dava and Tevin make identical throat-clearing sounds behind me, I laugh and correct, "We are good at what I do."

"That's a little better," Dava grumbles, rolling her eyes when I turn to give her one of my best smiles.

"Well," Dawson chuckles, heading behind the counter again—aiming for the big brass register this time, "however you do it, you always get the job done. Say, are you looking for more work? Of course you are. The nature of any business, isn't it? I have a friend, sort of a friend, who is looking for some specialized work to get done. Would you mind if I passed along your name?"

One. Two.

"I wouldn't mind at all. I'd appreciate it, in fact," I assure him, leaning on the counter. I set one elbow down and turn toward him, casual and relaxed but able to watch him put the orb in the lock box under the register, the key back into his pocket. Now if he tries to stiff us, I can get that key and get the prize back; someone else will pay for it, too. Dawson has never tried anything like that, but I've never been foolish enough to assume he won't.

"Happy to do it—you folks never let me down. This little piece is much more special than it looks. And you know, some of my friends have some pretty interesting jobs they need seeing to." He pauses while counting out the silver and gold from the register, putting it into his palm and closing his fingers around it when he looks up at me briefly. "Are you heading out on another job now?"

I shake my head, meeting his gaze briefly until he goes back to counting. I don't want him to know that I don't completely trust him, and I don't want to give off dangerous vibes. That's also why Dava is nearby, hanging out near the register and examining a couple rings on display, but Tevin knows to stay near the door. People take one look at him and make assumptions that tend to scare them; if only they knew that he's the biggest teddy bear on the seas.

"No job right now," I tell him, surprised that wasn't a question Dawson answered for himself, too. "We're heading off for a little break."

"Well deserved! I'll make sure my friends know the usual info so they know where to find you." He dumps his counted-out coins into a little leather pouch but doesn't pull the strings, turning and sliding it over the counter toward me. "You want to count that? But you never count it, do you? At least not here. I'm sure you count it elsewhere. So, that's everything! Unless you want to take a look around. I did get some new stock in."

I start to turn him down; I'm better at saving my money than spending it. But that's not always a good thing. A remnant of a shitty childhood when I had no money, no home, no nothing. Now, I could spend if I want to, and sometimes, even when I want to, I don't. Maybe today...

"What are the chances you have...turtle stuff? Like figurines or something?" I almost feel silly for the question, especially when Dawson's eyebrows pop up in surprise. I'm sure there aren't a lot of treasure hunters, merchants, or pirates who come in looking for cute animal figurines. "It's for my partner. He loves turtles."

"A partner!" Dawson's whole face lights up. "You know, I've always wondered if folks who live at sea have relationships. I imagine it's not easy, always leaving and always being apart. But I guess most of you must figure it out or else you'd all be lonely folk. Unless you're in relationships at sea, that is. Do you know if that's common?" He laughs to himself while finally coming around the counter. "Not that you take surveys of your fellow seafarers, so I suppose you wouldn't know any better than I would."

"No, I wouldn't." I follow him down an aisle crowded with scarves that brush past my shoulders, a cool rush of satin and silk, but I'm stuck on what he said. Dawson doesn't know much about life at sea outside of what he needs to know to hire treasure hunters, but he nailed one thing. It's not easy, always leaving and always being apart. I should have been back with Max a week ago, but this job took longer than we thought, and now...

"Turtles!" Dawson chirps, motioning to a small shelf where there is an array of beautifully crafted animals from land, sea, and air. Several are turtles—I guess lots of people like them, enough to make this a worthwhile item to stock. "This one"—he picks up one the size of my pinky finger—"is sea glass from the volcanic islands down south, and the shell is turquoise. I think this one is my favorite."

"It's beautiful," I agree, taking it from his hand and imagining in Max's spaces—in his hand, on his desk, in the apartment we share but where I almost never am. The first time I brought Max a gift from a trip, I was barely sixteen and just working on the deck of a merchant ship. Max told me he would think of me every single time he looked at it. Now, the only thing I ever really spend money on is gifts for Max because I want him to think of me every single time he looks at each one. Max likes turquoise, and a volcanic turtle is unique. "I'll take it."

"Wonderful choice. Would you like a gift box? Tell you what! I'll throw that in on the house."

Dawson keeps chatting on the way back to the register and while wrapping and then boxing my gift. I pay him from my own pocket, not the coins that need to be divided among my crew, and I watch his nimble fingers at work, but I barely hear him. My thoughts are a week away from here with a beautiful man who is always happy to see me come home.

I pull my compass out of my pocket. It's a relic, an old piece from when folks used the stars instead of maps, but it means more to me than just about anything in my life. It was a gift from Max, thoughtful in more ways than one . I run my thumb over the wooden case, wondering if he knows where I am right now.

With my turtle gift-wrapped and safely tucked into my pocket, Dawson finally stops answering his own questions and lets us go with promises to be in touch with more work. We step back out onto the street, things even livelier now. Within thirty feet of the shop, a very cute elf propositions both Tevin and Dava, much to the twins' displeasure, a drunk dwarf challenges me to a fight that I turn down politely, and a halfling almost throws up on my shoes. Definitely time to get back to the ship.

"Well, well, well. If it isn't my favorite pretty boy."

I don't know the voice, but there's only one person who calls me that as an insult. As if misgendering me is enough to make me miss the 'pretty' part.

"Scrounging for jobs we've already finished again, Fields?" I ask, turning toward the voice to find the person in question. The captain, I guess, though that's a generous title for this particular dickhead.

He forces a laugh and drags a hand back through his dark hair, probably coating his hand in grease in the process—and letting me know that I hit home. "You'd do well to remember we don't need the jobs to stay afloat, Eli."

"Mommy's money doesn't insult me, Cross. I have places to be."

Nothing bothers rich men more than reminding them that they're unimportant, so I turn on my heel and head off, letting him watch my pretty ass go.

Tevin and Dava enjoy the exchange, laughing and praising me, but I can't manage to find the pleasure in it this time. I love humiliating Cross Fields; it's become a favorite pastime since he decided that our ships have a rivalry. Tonight, it falls flat for me.

"You okay?" Tevin asks, wrapping his big arm around my shoulders and pulling me against him. He gets no resistance from me. "You're sad."

"I'm not sad. Just…homesick," I admit. Of course I do. I'm not ashamed to miss my Max, and Tevin doesn't want me to be.

He nods and kisses my head. "Maybe we should think about spending a few extra days in town this time. We usually stock up and head for another job, but we don't have one at the moment, and you deserve the extra time with Max. Frankly, I deserve the extra time with Max, too."

"You're not allowed to have alone time with him 'til I do," I tease. We both know that's a rule that doesn't need to be laid down; Tevin has been my boyfriend for two years now, but Max has been my partner for forever. Recently, Max and Tevin have started exploring the potential between them, and I love that. But Tevin will give me the time I need. I squeeze his hand over my shoulder in thanks for that. "I just wanna get home."

"Nothing in your way now, Eli."

Finally.

Chapter 3

Max

The tip of a fountain pen scratching parchment
—there is no better sound.

I lose myself in the rhythmic *shhh-shhh-shhh*, that slight resistance under my hand while drawing long lines or words. I freefall happily into the off-rhythm, chaotic *tch-tch-tch* of sketching forms, adding detail, or scribbling notes. I'm paid for what's produced by the magic that flows through me, into my pen, onto the parchment, but I know the truth. The real magic is in that sound.

This stool is doing me no favors, though. I chose a stool as my work seat over a chair so I could move around more often, but it requires a challenging sort of balance from my hips and lower back, and my legs dangle too much for me to stay here for long. Yet again, I have to pause and shift, trying to take some of the pressure off my hip and get it to stop throbbing... without making my feet go numb.

Blaming the chair is probably unfair since it's been proven an impossible task no matter where or how I sit. I'm doomed to move around constantly, searching out a slightly less painful position until it becomes slightly more painful and then seeking another. If only my magic worked to let me just write out how I feel and make it real.

Instead of that, my current project is to help a new client find a lost item. He's an elf who is probably middle-aged, which, for an elf, means he's a few hundred years old, and he works as an accountant in a city that sounds as boring as that job. He traveled for days at least to reach me, and based on the urgency with which he told me about the necklace he lost, I have a feeling he was never supposed to have the necklace in the first place. That, and his willingness to pay me a premium to get this done quickly. But that's none of my business. It's not important, not relevant, for me to do my work.

I know where he last saw it, I know what it looks like, and when this work is done, I'll have a map leading him to where he can find it. I work with a clear mind, losing myself in the sound, letting my magic guide the ink, and the client's necklace will soon no longer be lost. Well, someone's necklace that the client is paying me quite a bit to find.

My new position on the stool only creates the usual dull ache, nothing stabbing or throbbing at the moment, so I'm able to sink back into the sound of the pen and the flow of magic.

I need my body to cooperate. I need to manage my pain really well today, which is something I've always been kind of hit or miss at. If I didn't feel so bad for the desperate elf—I thought he might cry about a hair ribbon he lost on the journey here just to find me—I would have turned down this job or at least delayed the start. I should be resting, preparing, saving up my stamina, and avoiding any new aches, pains, swelling, and stiffness. Easier said than done but much more likely at home than at the desk I rent as my workspace in the local library. Instead of taking it easy, I shift again when the pain escalates once more, mentally scolding my body for misbehaving.

I don't get enough chances to see them that I can squander even one because of pain.

Eli is coming home. Just that thought makes something flutter in my chest, the sensation light and lifting and yet so intense, I have to gasp in a breath. It's like a balloon filling rapidly and then popping, flooding my chest and stomach with...them. With Eli.

It's been months at least since we last saw one another. I choose not to track the exact amount of time they're gone, only making spot checks weekly; I don't start tracking regularly until I know for sure that they're coming home.

When they first bought their ship, hired their crew, and set out to sea for most of the year, Eli would try to surprise me with their visits back home. A sweet effort but a wasted one on someone like me—someone with my magic. I can always find out where they are, how far they are, and when they're headed back in this direction. I have stacks and stacks of maps I've made for the sole purpose of tracking them, just so I can find out when I might see them again.

Never to make sure they're alive, though. I can't allow myself the chance to indulge those fears, not even briefly, not even for a moment. That's the kind of pain I can do nothing to resolve once it sets in.

But Eli is not lost. They were supposed to be back two weeks ago, and now, they're almost here. So close that I can expect to see them tonight. And if I'm in too much pain for a proper reunion, I'm going to be incredibly annoyed. I'm generally very good at being patient with myself, but gods damn it, it has been way too long.

Pushing myself on this project is not going to help. The magic isn't entirely an active one, always present and always ready in my blood and in my pen, but using any sort of magic for any extended period of time is an energy drain. I don't have a lot of physical energy to bargain with in the first place, and more than once, I've lost more than I could afford to by getting myself completely engrossed in work.

That happens if I don't watch myself; I get sucked in and lose hours or days, then realize my legs don't work at all anymore, and I'm totally exhausted for weeks. I have another day before the elf is going to return to collect his answers, the path to his necklace, so for today, I decide I've done enough.

I pop the custom-made shaft from the pen, then carefully cover the tip with the wax that exists for this purpose. It doesn't take much ink or magic to fill and use it properly, but I prefer to conserve as much as possible. It all gets slipped into a leather-bound case that also holds the rest of my pens and a spare shaft that I have to hope I never need since carving the appropriate runes into the narrow, thin wood is exhausting and time-consuming.

My hand drifts reverently over the soft cover of the case. I spotted it at a market almost a decade ago, mentioned one time that I adored it and would love to have it, and went home thinking nothing of it. I knew our budget at the time. But Eli...Eli has never allowed me to want for anything. Even when they had nothing, they found a way—which may or may not have led to a fight or two about the morality of stealing. Eli set their ship-buying plans back by at least a month when they gave me this beautiful gift; I never let it down beyond arm's reach now.

I fold up the almost-finished map with less care than I show my pen. That probably seems backward to anyone who might be watching since the map is the final product, the result of all the work, the way I make my living. I do roll the parchment with care, of course, and I'll make sure that nothing happens to it. But until there is a finished product on the parchment, I don't give it much of a glance. The outcome will be whatever the magic makes of it; the parchment and I are equals, merely conduits.

My father hates when I talk about what our family does that way, as if we're no more special than people who happen to be holding the pen. But once the training to use and focus our magic is complete, that's really all there is to it. I love what I create, I live for what I can do for other people, but it's not the most exciting process.

This job is just like the last dozen I had. Maybe this elf stole the necklace at some point, but the story doesn't change what I do or the outcome. I get the information I need, make the map, return it to the client, and then I wait for my next client. It's not like I get to travel to the end of the map with the client or like I get to go on a treasure hunt for any map I make. Not like Eli can with *Tempest* and their crew. No, I'm merely a conduit for the magic, a piece of parchment in human form. My dad likes to think we're more special than that, but I'm okay with the truth. Mostly.

With the map tucked safely into my portfolio, which then goes into my satchel, and my pen set slipped into my pocket, I shift off the stool and lower myself into the wheelchair parked and waiting directly beside me. Relief sweeps through me right away when my butt and spine connect with the cushion. The relief won't last forever—nowhere is comfortable for too long— but it's enough of a change from the wooden stool that I can ride the ease for a short while.

I move behind the stool, shove it under the desk, and do one last visual sweep to make sure I haven't left anything. I enjoy working in the library, but it means I don't have an office of my own. This is a public space, and anything I leave here may become public property, and not out of any kind of malice. Fortunately, I'm used to not bringing much with me since having a lap-full on a wheelchair is a cumbersome adventure.

The library's front desk is empty on my way out, but I know Elda will just assume I left for the day, and since she doesn't keep tabs on me, we can both live with that. We only ever have an issue if she assumes I left for the day because it's getting so late, and she allows the gas lanterns lighting the entire building to go out. We've played a couple awkward games of 'Max can't move safely in the dark so let's just yell to each other,' and I don't think either of us wants to repeat the experience.

The ward at the entrance of the library pushes the wooden door outward when I approach, an extremely generous gift from a former client who is also a patron of the library. It closes again once I've cleared the threshold onto the street, responding to a matching rune carved into my chair.

It was pure luck that Eli and I were able to find a home so close to the library; I only need to get to the end of the block I'm already in the middle of. When I've lost track of time and worked for twelve hours or if it's very cold or wet out, I might grumble a bit about even this short trip, but today, the setting sun is warm and the breeze is cool. I have enough energy to maneuver my wheels and get myself home.

There's something to be said for adrenaline, too. There is no merit to 'heroic' tales I've heard bards sing of disabled people suddenly leaping from their chair to rescue a loved one from imminent demise; my body can only do so much, and I manage my limits out of necessity. But the path home, up the ramp into the hallway of our building, and then to maneuver the door open and myself inside safely is all a little bit easier thanks to the excitement running through me today.

Eli is coming home.

They never intended to be gone so long on this particular voyage; when they left, they told me to expect them back almost two full months ago. Last month, I got a letter promising that they'd be home two weeks ago. I know better than to take any of their plans as certainty, though. Delays and diversions are the nature of their life and of the sea. It's a glaring example of how different our lives are, mine and Eli's. There's no routine, no schedule, no real ability to even predict what any given day will be like for them.

That's the life Eli has dreamed of since they were a child, the life they told me they'd live someday the very first time we met, back when we were children and Eli didn't have two coins to rub together. They've earned their life, the excitement, and I'm honored to be their safe harbor when they dock.

My excitement, by contrast, is limited to their trips home and the stories they share from a life at sea. Maybe sometimes I'm a little jealous.

It doesn't matter at the moment, though. There's too much to be done to prepare for Eli's arrival tonight. I have to resist the urge to make another map and find out exactly how far they are, how much longer I have to wait. That won't help, and if I get too excited before getting my tasks started, I'll never be able to finish any of them. There's no choice but to dive right in.

When we first purchased this little home, setting out to properly start our lives together, Eli didn't have a ship. It was always a dream, something they were working for, but it hadn't been made a reality yet. We chose a port city to help that along, an active dock necessary for Eli to find work and resources, and we found a space with enough comfort for both of us. It wasn't until Eli purchased their ship and set out to sea for the first time that we realized how many adjustments were needed around our home to make it functional for me while I'm alone. Even if I wasn't in a wheelchair, I'm not tall enough to reach the cabinets above the refrigerator where we used to keep mixing bowls.

It took some trial and error. Nothing can be too low or too high, and while I like my independence, I'm stubborn enough to make poor decisions if I want to get something done, even if it's difficult on my crutches or from my chair. With some help from Eli's crew and some investment in renovations, my home is now a space where I can be independent whether or not I'm alone. Even though I still prefer not to be alone, and maybe I've been noticing the loneliness a little more lately. But some sacrifices are worth making.

I aim for the kitchen first. I got a grocery delivery yesterday, the teenage boy upstairs happy to be paid for running errands like that for me, and I'm happy to pay him enough that he can take his adorable boyfriend on dates around town. Thanks to the delivery, I'm ready to make Eli's favorite dinner and, tomorrow morning, the crew's favorite breakfast. I have more planned surprises, too, including a special scented soap that they love in the shower and fresh, soft sheets on the bed because, in my opinion, nothing is more comfortable to come back home to. I aim all my gifts and plans for what I know they miss most while they're away at sea. And maybe I love knowing that they miss nothing more than me.

Eli has to leave again. I'm constantly aware of that when they come home, and I've mostly made peace with it. I encouraged Eli to purchase their ship in the first place and promised that we would be okay. We've always been okay. But that doesn't mean I don't miss them.

When they come home, I get to show them just how much, and I'm going to make the most of every minute.

Chapter 4
Eli

"We're late. I hate being late."

"You've literally never cared about being late before this moment."

Okay, so he's not wrong. Tevin and I have worked together for a decade; he's not only my first mate on *Tempest* but only the second long-term partner I've ever had. He knows me well enough by now that I know lying in front of him will get me caught. But right now, tonight at least, I'm grumpy about being late, and damn it, I need to say it out loud.

"Shut up," is the only retort I can come up with. I'm a treasure hunter, not a…speechmaker, or whatever the hell those windbags are called.

Tevin laughs at me while I turn away from the railing. The crew preparing *Tempest* for docking is more interesting than watching the dock creep closer slowly—far too slowly because I'm late. We need to bring the ship into dock, anchor and secure her, deal with the dock master and our fees, and prepare for market and restocking tomorrow. Very late tomorrow, if I have anything to say about it.

"You realize that we were supposed to be back awhile ago. You were always going to be late today." I glare up at Tevin, and he chuckles, though he gives me a sympathetic smile. "Max doesn't even know you're coming back tonight, Eli."

"You know that's not true. He always knows when I'm coming back." I huff out a breath, my skin feeling like it somehow doesn't fit my body. I don't fit inside myself whenever I've been away from Max for so long. "And now I'm late. Could you please go help them instead of making me feel worse?"

"Oh, you get off the rest of the night and you get to order me around?" Tevin gasps dramatically and presses a massive hand to his barrel chest.

"The benefits of being your captain. Now go." I nudge him with my shoulder and appreciate that he actually moves forward; we both know I'm not big enough to move him if he doesn't want to be moved. I'm not at all sorry about being appeased at times.

"So much for a democratic ship!" Tevin cries, drawing the attention of the rest of the crew while he throws his arms up and drags himself away from me to join them. Of course, that attention is exactly what Tevin wanted—it's what he always wants. And it is hard not to get attention when you're almost eight feet tall, built like a stone wall on legs, and have tusks. Plus, he's rather handsome.

I can't even be entertained by his antics at the moment, though. I turn back to watch our approach again and think very seriously about jumping into the water and just swimming the rest of the way. Might do it too if I didn't know the sorts of things that sometimes get tossed into the water right off the docks. Don't think Max would appreciate me showing up smelling like a sewer, though. Besides, this skirt is new; I'm not going to risk losing quality leather and a hot look to seawater.

Max would laugh at me for that thought. Gods, I miss his laugh.

We've been at sea so much longer than planned. I could only change those plans because I know Max has his magic to reassure him we haven't been lost to the depths, and even more importantly, because I know how he supports me. Max wants me to stay away if it means *Tempest* is chasing dreams. My dreams. But I know he misses me too, and that doesn't make missing him any easier.

I drag in a deep breath of salty sea air and that unique sour stench that only exists on docks. The life I've forced on both of us is the one I've always dreamed of, so why is it getting so hard? Why have I started to physically ache because I miss him so much? I disrupted us, and now I'm the one complaining about it, too. I'm a dick.

We finally come into dock, and I pull myself out of a very tempting chance to wallow for a while longer to actually help. It doesn't take long now that we're so practiced at it; I don't like to remember what it was like a few short years ago when each of us had far more limited skills. We were once the laughing stock of any dock, and now, we flow almost seamlessly. I almost smile when I think about how much the other crews out here, the actual pirate crews, hate us for being good at what we do—for betting better at it than most of them.

"So, we can come with you tonight, right?"

I turn and give Rosleigh, my crew's halfling chef, as sharp a glare as I can possibly can for that little joke; it's damn hard to glare at someone who's always smiling. "Not funny," I tell her, but she giggles and waves off my ire.

"No, what's not going to be funny is if we get held up because of your nonsense," Jakgrout interjects. The scowling dwarf motions at the crates that need to come off the ship. "How 'bout you just tell me now which ones you fucked with so's we can move that much faster."

"Ah, come on, Jak. You know I never pull the same thing twice," I remind him. He's cranky because I sabotaged a few crates when we last docked. And because those crates held jars of vinegar and pickled vegetables that splattered all over him when the crate bottoms fell out. I have to hold my breath now to keep from laughing at the memory of the master carpenter's expression when he realized what had happened; Tevin snorting from behind me is not helping.

Jak grunts at me and heads off to continue his inventory. I'll be long gone before he realizes that I did, in fact, pull the same thing twice. He'll punch me for it in the morning when we see each other again, but pissing him off is worth it—even if he does pack a mean punch.

A hand falls on my shoulder, and I look up to find Dava. "Go. We can handle the dock master and all the rest. You're late, aren't you?"

"More than you know," I sigh, but I still take another look around. My ship, my crew, my responsibility. I can't just bail. "I should help."

"I don't mean to say that you're not helping because you're too distracted thinking about getting laid tonight...but you're too distracted thinking about getting laid tonight to actually help," she quips. She only really looks like Tevin when she's teasing me. "And since the rest of us aren't getting laid tonight, it's kind of like you're just rubbing it in."

"Wait, who isn't getting laid tonight?" Yen stops beside us, carrying a crate that looks ten times heavier than her lithe elven frame should be able to manage. She gives Dava a pretty pout. "Tell me I'm getting laid tonight."

"Of course you are, darling," Dava purrs at her girlfriend, and Yen brightens again before sauntering off. She's not just managing that huge crate, she's swaying her hips while she goes.

I shake my head at Yen's retreating back but refocus, looking up at Dava again. "You're sure?"

"I'm sure. Mostly because you getting to Max tonight means that we get to come for breakfast in the morning."

I laugh and nod, so grateful my crew knows the deal and doesn't object to it. Everyone on my crew loves Max, and they love being able to get a home-cooked meal with fresh ingredients in a cozy space that isn't on a ship. First few trips home, I had to fight the crew away to get any alone time with Max. I finally put my foot down...and by that, I mean I finally made a deal that the crew voted on and agreed to. I get at least the first night alone with Max, and then they get to come over for breakfast in the morning. For the most part, I keep my pants on while the crew is around in the morning. For the most part, they do, too.

Thinking about Max and reasons to take my pants off would be more than enough to make my pants tight even without such a long separation. It's for the best that I have a skirt on, covering any potential bulge a little better than pants might...except that the skirt might be short enough to give the docks a show. I need to leave soon.

"I'm going," I announce. "You know where I'll be if you need me for anything," I call, heading for the ramp off the ship as Tevin finishes securing it to the dock. "At least pretend to listen to Tevin, never listen to Yen, and do not dare come to the house before the sun is firmly in the sky. Be nice to my ship. Bye!"

I hurry down the ramp and jump off the last couple feet, launching myself into Tevin, who catches me with a laugh. I kiss him firmly on the mouth and give one tusk a playful tap before he sets me on the wooden planks, pats my ass, and sends me on my way. Now, there's only a few blocks' walk between me and my Max.

I walk far faster than I would usually dare. When you're heavily tattooed and pierced while coming from the docks, people tend to assume your career, and a pirate running down the street is a great way to draw the kind of attention I don't want. When you're wearing a skirt and badass eyeliner but also have a beard, people tend to be confused by your gender, and a queer person running down the street is a great way to invite law enforcement to kick my ass. There isn't actually a lot of law enforcement here—one of the reasons Max and I chose this town for our home—but those sorts of lessons are the kind you tend to learn quickly and permanently.

Nothing is going to stop me from getting to Max...except not having the key.

Shit! I stop so suddenly, I almost trip myself and start frantically patting my vest, my skirt, my chest. Why the hell do I like clothes with so many pockets?!

Finally, my fingers graze something cold at the bottom of one of the pockets, and I exhale a wave of relief when I close my hand around the key. Max could easily just let me into the apartment, but even if I know surprising him is actually impossible, I intend to try. I wanna be romantic, damn it.

I conquer the ramp that leads into our building in one leap and then break into a sprint down the hallway to our door. Feels good just to be here at all. And knowing Max is on the other side, only a thin piece of wood away from me now instead of miles of ocean... My hands are already shaking with anticipation and need and a deep well of loneliness that I try to ignore when I have no business being lonely while sailing the world with my best friends.

The key releases the lock, and I slip it right back into my pocket knowing that I absolutely will lose if I don't handle that immediately. Finally, I push the door open and walk into my second home. And, of course, Max didn't just expect me; he intends to make sure I feel welcome.

Even with my eyes open and working just fine, it's all the scents that hit me first. Max always smells like vanilla and mint; it's a salve that he uses to try and ease some of the pain in his joints combined with the natural scent of him. Whole apartment smells like him now. I'll get to smell him on my clothes for a couple days after I leave and crave it until I come back. I soak it in, breathing deeply.

There's more than just that, though. Max has been cooking for hours, judging by the scents. Fresh bread, the warm spice of my favorite stew—a recipe Max learned from his mother who always used to make enough of the dish that I could take some with me after leaving their home—and something with cinnamon. Oh gods, I hope that's his apple pie.

I only open my eyes after indulging, mouth already watering and stomach growling. I once made Max a promise to always come home hungry, and I've never regretted it. But it's not just the meals and the scents I get to enjoy and look forward to.

Max lit candles around the main room, and the lights are low everywhere except the kitchen—which I appreciate since it means he's not moving around in there in the dark and risking injury. I appreciate it too for the romantic glow. It's been so long since I last saw Max, last had my hands on him, last had a chance to kiss him. I came home hungry in more ways than one, and the atmosphere is contributing to my starvation.

I undo my knife belt and set it on the table beside the door to join Max's keys to home and the library and the gloves that he leaves here in case the weather might freeze or dirty his hands. I'm a little jealous he can just put things here, see them, and remember to take them; I'm lucky I remembered the key that was in my pocket. It means I can leave Max here, though, knowing that he won't end up locked out of the apartment or with frostbite on his fingers.

I don't bother to set my belt down quietly, the metal clasp and the hilt of the dagger clanging when they touch down on the wood. I slide my key from my pocket and add that to the pile, trusting Max to remind me of it more than my own brain; I hope this skirt is going to come off at some point tonight, and I don't want the key to fall and get lost in the process. I also want Max to know I'm here and find myself staring at the entrance to the kitchen while unlacing and toeing off my boots, eager for him to appear.

It feels like forever before he finally does. I don't really worry about him when I'm not here, not more than I would worry about anyone I love. Max is more than capable of living his life independently, and he's been dealing with his pain and his symptoms for long enough that he's an expert in managing them. But still, when he comes into view with a smile, looking happy and healthy and so damn gorgeous that it's unfair, relief expands in my chest.

He gives me a once over, too, then cocks his head a little, and his smile grows. "I love that you forgot your bag."

"Damn it! I knew there was something." That's not true—I had no idea I was missing anything.

"So long as you're here, nothing else matters. Someone will bring it in the morning. Now please come all the way in." He says 'please' like I could ever possibly deny him anything.

I finally step out of my boots and nudge them under the table enough that I can be sure they won't become a tripping hazard. And then there's nothing else to keep me from getting to my guy.

Max sets the wheel locks and opens his arms to me while I cut across the room. The second I'm close enough—finally, *finally*—I lean down, take his face in my hands, and kiss him just as hard as I want to. Max reaches up to my shoulders, my neck, his fingers probing with his need. He catches my waist and tugs me down, the request clear, and I trust him enough not to let me sit on his legs if they hurt. I'm so damn glad they don't hurt right now.

I don't break the kiss while straddling him, my legs hanging behind him. Neither of us will dare to stay like this for long or move around enough that we might damage the chair, but both of us take the opportunity to wrap the other up in a tight hug. I only stop kissing him when I need to catch my breath; his mouth is so soft, it might be worth suffocating.

"This is new," Max notes, fingering the edge of my skirt without looking down. His damn brown eyes are reflecting the candlelight all over the room so they look even more incredible than usual.

I push my fingers back through his curly hair, the same shade of brown as his eyes, tugging lightly on the ends and reveling in the peaceful look that sweeps over his expression when my blunt nails graze his scalp. "This is longer," I reply. "I like it."

"I like the skirt."

"You aren't even looking at it yet," I tease.

"That's because dinner is ready, and I don't want to get too distracted before getting you fed."

I look over his head into the kitchen; there's a covered pot on the table, the delicious scent even stronger over here. But my stomach has been just about completely forgotten now that Max is close enough to feel, his hands are back on me, and I still have so much more of him to reacquaint myself with.

"Hate to break this to you...but I am already distracted."

Max smiles into our next kiss, and he moans softly when I sink my teeth into his bottom lip. I adore how easily seduced he is, especially tonight. He beams up at me and says, "I do want you fed, but I don't really care if dinner has to wait or even goes to waste. Welcome home, Eli."

Chapter 5

Max

Between me and Eli, I'm usually the responsible one. I like being the less impulsive, the less reckless, the less emotional partner. I like the way they balance me out, too; Eli brings adventure and fun into my life when it tends to be all schedule and routine.

But tonight, the responsible one between us is horny. We'll eat dinner after I'm done satisfying my more urgent hunger.

Eli slides back off my lap and holds their hands out but waits for me to signal that it's okay to lift me; they respect me too much to question my decisions or pick me up without my permission. We both know that I love it, though.

I wrap my hands around their forearms, extremely aware of the muscles flexing under my hands, and they hold behind my elbows. Eli is strong enough to serve as a steady anchor, holding my weight and letting me pull myself against them and out of the chair. I set my hands on their shoulders, and Eli swoops down to set their hands behind my knees, lift me, and guide my legs around their hips. I trust them to carry me safely, but I don't care to block their vision, so I take the opportunity to kiss their neck and throat. Or at least I'm going to pretend safety is why.

Their skin is always so warm. It's like they've spent so much time in the sun, the light has permanently heated them up to exactly the right temperature. I can't help wanting to feel more of that soft skin, so I shove my hands between us and under the edge of their shirt, groping at the ridges of their abs while sucking at the spot just below their ear that always makes them moan. They don't disappoint, blessing me with that needy sound.

Eli makes it through the apartment and into the bedroom in what feels like a few strides. They set me down on the edge of the bed and straighten up to pull their shirt off, tossing it aside and revealing a gorgeous expanse of muscles, tattoos, and golden skin. I catch their hand before they can loosen their skirt, though.

"Leave it on," I request, tilting my head to look up at them.

Eli shudders all over, but they smile and cup my jaw. "Whatever you want, baby."

I know exactly what I want. I slide my hand up their muscular thighs, somehow also warm despite the chill that's always in the air at night and them only wearing a skirt on the way here. My fingertips find the soft fabric of tight shorts that are doing nothing to contain their erection at this point. When I lean in to nuzzle my cheek against the bulge tenting their skirt, inhaling the scents of the sea and leather and Eli, I keep eye contact and get rewarded with a pained moan.

They watch me closely while I pull their shorts down, shoving them below their knees when my hands no longer reach. My hands have more important things to worry about now.

Eli's sea-green eyes are blazing when I slide my hands up over their thighs again, fingertips teasing the sensitive skin to make their muscles twitch and jump. They hold my gaze firmly when I find their cock under the skirt, stiff and throbbing, a bead of pre-cum leaking at the tip, and run my fingers lightly down along the length. Even when I make a tight fist and stroke them from tip to base, they don't break my gaze or their control over their reactions—and now it feels like a challenge.

But I know exactly what Eli wants. I've spent years learning their body and their responses, both of us navigating changes in how they feel about their body as their gender started to form more completely. I consider myself an expert in exactly two things, and one of them is how to drive Eli wild.

I bite my bottom lip while releasing their cock from my hand to push this lovely new skirt up, getting it out of my way and giving me access. I love that they're keeping it on, though; I've always had a fantasy of ducking under the skirts of one of the ballgowns that Eli will use any excuse to wear and sucking them off while hidden underneath it, surrounded by tulle and silk—and preferably by a lot of pompous rich people who would be appalled if they could see me. This skirt isn't long enough to hide under since Eli isn't one for modesty—thank the gods—but the thought is getting me even hotter.

Eli watches when my tongue sneaks out and flicks the tip of their cock. Their lips part when I kiss the head more fully, pulling it into my mouth and laving that silky soft skin with my tongue, but they still don't break my gaze. But when I flash a grin, showing them my teeth around their shaft, and then dive down onto them, Eli cries out my name, and their head falls back. Success! And a delicious cock in my throat.

We've been apart for too long, and we've both suffered at the distance, I know, so I don't waste time teasing them. Not this time anyway. Teasing can come after the reconnection we both need right now. Reconnection and orgasms.

Eli succumbs happily, their moan sharpening when I grip their ass in both hands to encourage them. I work my lips and tongue around them, alternating between bringing them deep until my nose is buried in the dark curls at the base and mouthing the swollen head. Fluttering my tongue under the crest earns me quick jerks of their hips, and as much as I enjoy that, we both know it's a signal that it won't take them much more of this to go off...and we both know we're not ready for this to be done.

They get some control back when they use a fist in my hair to guide me back off their length, then shift their hands to my shoulders and guide me to lay back on the bed. They take hold of my hips but then eye me, waiting for my nod before using that hold to move me to the edge of the mattress until my hips are almost off. I know why they want me here, and my heart is racing even before they start to work my pants off.

Sometimes, when Eli is gone and I have needs, I take other lovers. But it's rare because of how everyone else who gets naked with me wants to treat me. I've been a fetish, which is by far the worst of it and almost enough to turn me off sex completely. It's nearly as bad, though, when I'm treated like I'm breakable. Some lovers completely ignore my legs, treating them like they aren't there at all; some lovers barely touch me anywhere, afraid that I'll break in their hands. And that's not even considering the complications that come with strangers in my bed navigating my gender. It's rare that I bother to try because I almost never have good experiences...

Except with Eli.

I've been disabled the entire time we've known each other. I was disabled when we were young and just discovering what we liked and how we liked to touch each other, and maybe that's why. Maybe they've just got the experience. I don't actually care to dissect the why. When Eli is home, I get to indulge, I get to enjoy, and I get to know that they love letting me.

Eli isn't cautious on my legs. They massage my thighs and calves with strong hands while undressing me from the waist down, chasing their hands and their fingers with their lips and their tongue. They nip lightly along the inside of my thigh, and when we both realize that I have sensation there today, not numbness or excessive pain, they bite and suck properly. If they leave here again without leaving a mark on me that lasts at least a couple days, we'll both be disappointed. Their dedication to a spot that makes me squirm assures me that's not going to happen.

They nuzzle the crease between my thigh and groin, only careful now when spreading my legs further apart. "Breathe," they remind me when they start guiding my legs up, knees toward my chest. We both know I'll hit a limit, a point where more movement would cause too much pain, and since I don't know exactly when that point will come, my instincts are to tense and hold my breath in anticipation. But Eli knows even better than I do somehow that tensing up brings on more pain. They make sure I can't think well enough to tense by running just the tip of their tongue around my clit, sending a wave of heat surging through my veins.

"There," I warn when a sudden spark that warns of incoming agony lights up in my lower back and hips. It stops instantly when Eli does, and now that they have me where they want me, they stop holding back.

It's a little heady to truly feel how starved Eli has been. I know they don't have to go completely without when we're apart either, and I'm glad for that, but there's a desperation in the way they eat me out that turns me on even more wildly than the pleasure they're delivering.

Eli's tongue delves deep and massages perfectly; they nibble lightly at my lips and the edge of my thighs; they play with my clit masterfully, flicking and swirling and sucking. Every touch is exactly what I want, and the firm grip on my thighs to hold my legs up only turns me on further.

I push at their head lightly, but Eli moans and ignores me, very clearly sending the message that they're happy right where they are. And there's a big part of me that wants to let them stay there all night. The other part of me is more insistent, though.

I nudge their head harder, forcing my throat to work for more than moans and pleas of their name. "Wanna cum with you, E," I manage, panting. "Please."

They moan even more sharply this time, wrapping their lips around my clit and sucking hard until I just about scream. Only then do they relent, carefully maneuvering me up to the pillows. They help me out of my shirt and binder, toss both aside, then grin at me when they crawl up between my legs. I force a scowl even while I want to worship them. "You liked it," they tease, running their nose along mine and guiding my legs around their hips.

I reach between us and catch hold of their shaft, dragging it closer until we can both feel them just grazing where they most want to be. Their mouth pops open a bit, and this time, the cocky grin is mine. "You'll like that," I quip.

"Mmm, I know it," they breathe, speaking against my mouth. Their hips jerk, thrusting roughly into my fist and nudging my clit, drawing a gasp out of me. "Let me inside you, Max, baby."

Oh, I wish I had the patience to make them beg a little more. The need in their voice is incredibly sexy. But it's been so long, and they're going to feel so good, and *gods*, I've missed them.

The second my hand is out of the way, Eli captures my mouth and my body, their tongue and their cock entering me in matching long sweeps that make my mind spin. I cling to them, marveling at the kind of pleasure that only being filled and stretched so perfectly and in such a wonderfully familiar way can bring. There's an absolute freedom in this reconnection, unspeakable joy in the intimate ways that we know and enjoy one another, wave after wave of pleasure that only grows and gets better. We both fall into it, into each other, and I'm soaring in moments.

"Eli!" I cry into the room, my core trembling when they roll their hips to hit the spots where I need them most. I grip their ass in my hands, tugging and encouraging, pleading with my body and my words for more, more, more. Eli's spine arches, pushing them even further inside me, and our combined moans fill the room.

Eli sits back on their haunches, big hands clasping my waist. They loom over me and pick up their pace, hips snapping and cock pounding deep. They smile perfectly at me, the dim light in the room doing nothing to dim the sparkle in their eyes. "Missed you so much, my beautiful Max," they breathe. The words, the affection in their voice, and their expression only make me hotter. "You look amazing, and you feel so good. Will you cum for me, baby?"

"Yes, Eli, please!" I cry out, hands clinging to their biceps. I hold their gaze. "I need you to cum with me. Cum inside me."

They grunt and nod, expression darkening and hips snapping even harder. It's exactly what we both need, and I fight to keep my eyes open and my gaze on theirs for as long as I can possibly manage before I shatter underneath them. I'm vaguely aware of Eli groaning, their thrusts getting more erratic, and then their body stilling completely with their cock buried deep inside me. I'm far more aware of the exceptional pleasure that's swiftly followed by total satisfaction.

Eli collapses onto me, their face landing against my throat and their heavy, rapid breaths gusting across my overcharged skin. They help me lower my legs so we don't risk them getting sore, but I wrap my arms around Eli's shoulders because I have no intentions of going anywhere for a while. Eli shows the same determination to just melt into the mattress when they nuzzle under my jaw and hum happily. That, and they're very much still inside me. Not that I'm complaining.

I drag my fingers slowly up and down their spine, picturing the tattoos that I'm touching in my mind. And picturing how their impressively built back muscles probably looked while they fucked me so soundly. There's a bubble of peace around us that feels impenetrable, Eli's heart beating against my chest and their beard tickling my throat. I'm just thinking that I might fall asleep right here right now, just hold them all night—or until they wake me up for round two—and then the peace is broken by a loud grumbling. One that came from inside me.

Eli is silent for a second, and then a surprised laugh bursts out of them. I can't help joining them, and I roll my eyes at my own body. They prop themself up enough to look down at me and narrow their eyes a little. "You're hungrier than you let on. Why didn't you tell me?"

Before I have to come up with a good excuse or a better retort about priorities, yet another grumble interrupts the moment—and this one comes from Eli. When I narrow my eyes right back at them, Eli laughs and shrugs. "You know I rarely think with the right head when I've missed you," they note. "I can't be blamed."

"Then neither can I! But we can both be fed." I glance down between us and then back up at them. "After you get out of me."

"Only if you promise that I don't have to stay out of you for too long," they counter.

I smile and offer my mouth, which they take in a deep kiss. "That's an easy promise to make, baby," I assure them, then plant a kiss on their nose and a sharp pat on their ass. "Food first. Let's go."

Eli gives a dramatic, whiny groan that makes me laugh. I don't hate that they pout at the idea of getting out of bed with me, but I do need to make sure we both have enough sustenance to make further rounds possible and pleasurable. And even if I spent a good deal of time on the dinner we're going to share tonight, I'm tempted to rush into the kitchen, shovel a few bites down, and drag the sexy person I've missed so much right back into bed. Eli wouldn't complain.

They pull out of me slowly and with another dramatic groan because Eli is nothing if not dramatic. They disappear into the bathroom and return a couple moments later with a warm cloth and my robe, both of which are given to me before they move out of my bedroom and through the living room naked as the day they were born. I have to laugh at the little strut to their step, and before they disappear beyond the bedroom door, they flash me a gorgeous smile.

I take the moment alone to clean myself up with the damp cloth. I then toss the cloth to the floor with our discarded clothes; I'll deal with those later and focus on more important things for now.

As I push myself up to sitting and start pulling the robe on, Eli returns, pushing my empty wheelchair and chewing. I scoff, and they shrug a bit. "It smelled so good, I couldn't help taking a bite. And I tossed it back onto the stove to make sure it's hot enough."

"Well, then you're forgiven for technically starting without me."

"Don't forgive me too quick. Brought you a gift."

I light up at that, sitting straighter. "You did? Why?"

Eli gives me a look that makes me laugh, a clear message of 'you know why.' They bring me back gifts pretty regularly, though I can count the number of times I've seen them buy something for themself on one hand. And they are an excellent gift giver.

"Can I have it now if I make my forgiveness contingent on it?"

"Yes," they laugh, pulling their skirt up off the floor and going into the pocket. I wonder if they forget it was in there until being in the kitchen and something reminding them, but I won't call them out on it. I don't really care when they hand over a tiny package. It's wrapped in soft blue paper with some kind of padding on the inside and weighs more than I expect.

"A turtle!" I chirp when it's revealed in my palm. The shell is a patterned turquoise, hand-carved so the natural dips and curves are revealed instead of polished away. The turtle's head and limbs are shiny, blue and green—sea glass, I realize. I look up at Eli and smile. "I love turtles."

"I know," they answer. "The sea glass and turquoise are from volcanic islands. If you want, you could probably draw it a map home."

I laugh, though I don't discard it as a possibility. "It's beautiful, Eli. Thank you so much—for the turtle and for thinking of me."

"I'm always thinking of you, Maxy." And I know that's true.

I ask for another kiss by offering my mouth, and we're both smiling when they take it. "Would you go get a bottle of wine? I'm good here; I'll meet you in the kitchen."

"Sure."

They head out again, but I call, "Eli!" They look a little surprised at having been stopped but are still smiling when they turn back around. "Are you going to put any clothes on at all?"

"Forgot my bag, remember?" They shrug again, grinning even bigger. "Besides...you deserve a little show, baby."

When they wiggle their hips—and everything else that wiggles with the movement—I reach back for a pillow and launch it at them. Eli ducks around it and skirts out of the room, and I laugh at the continued wiggle in their walk. Thank the gods Eli is home.

Chapter 6
Eli

On the ship, I'm usually the first person up. I've never needed all that much sleep in the first place—a side effect of growing up in an environment where I was never safe—and I have enough anxiety to make sure I never sleep again if I don't keep a handle on it. Being on the ship, out at sea, means that there is always something to do, something to worry about. I love my ship, but I don't sleep well.

But that's absolutely not the case when I get home. I'll happily forsake a lot of sleep for more time with Max, and I don't want to feel like I waste a minute, but when I do sleep, I sleep hard. Haven't woken up after sunrise since the last time I was with Max! It's a little disorienting when I'm so not used to it. Disorienting but really, *really* nice.

I'm safe here. I don't have a hundred things

to worry about here, even if things still need to be done for the ship and the crew before we head out again. My ship and our work are a priority, *Tempest* will always be a priority, but when I'm with Max, nothing else has ever mattered quite so much as he does.

I watch Max sleeping beside me, a picture of peace. He feels safe with me here, too, and that makes me feel better than anything else I've achieved. It also makes me a little sad now, though, because I am leaving. Soon. I always leave. It's never been this hard.

Before I can let my anxiety and loneliness ruin or at least challenge that peace, I indulge in the opportunity to just watch him.

We were just kids when we met more than decade ago. Back then, neither of us was using the names or pronouns that actually belong to us; neither of really knew who we were then. But I walked into that library, tiny for the size of that city, looking for a dry, warm place, and the second I spotted a kid my age with a head of curly dark hair buried in one of the biggest books I'd ever seen, I was drawn to him.

I approached him, my clothes ratty and dirty—I choose not to think about how I must have smelled—and asked what he was reading. He instantly smiled at me, and I knew then that Max was special. No one smiled at kids like me, kids who clearly didn't have homes or adults to protect us; adults ignored me, other kids ran from me, police and shop owners assumed I was a criminal. That was the reality I'd always known. Max has always been different.

"I can feel you staring at me," he announces, startling me a little. I had no idea he wasn't still sound asleep. He hasn't opened his eyes at all. A really good guess, or can he feel me somehow? I know his magic doesn't afford him any kind of power like this… He cracks open one brown eye. "You're still doing it."

"Sorry," I laugh, then tug the blanket up higher and snuggle in closer so we're in a little cocoon underneath it. Max's eyes are closed again, but he reaches for me and nuzzles his face against my chest when I gather him close. "I don't get enough chances to look at you, so I have to take them whenever I can."

"You have a portrait of me in the captain's quarters on your ship," he mumbles against my skin.

I trail my fingers over his spine and resist the urge to shrug because I don't want to risk disturbing or moving him at all. "Not the same."

"You're cute." He kisses my sternum. "I like having you here, too. Even if you snore."

"I do not!" I protest, and when he laughs, and I drop a hand to pinch his ass. He yelps and his body twitches, but it has the intended effect of bringing him closer to me. I wrap both arms around him and roll, bringing him up onto my chest where he smiles down at me. I force a scowl. "I do not snore, thank you. And even if I do, you're a blanket hog. Serves you right to suffer a little."

"I am a blanket hog," he laughs, already reaching for the blankets and pulling them up again. I catch the edge to help, bringing them back up over his shoulders. Max sets his forearms on my chest and beams at me, seeming very comfortable up there; I'd be happy if he never went away.

Instead of letting sadness ruin this morning, I lift my head to capture his mouth. Max smiles wider when I tease his lips with my tongue and moans in a soft little way that makes my dick jump. I slide both hands down his back this time and use them to grab his ass. He wiggles against me suggestively, and the smile is mine this time.

"You know they're going to be here soon," he warns me, then drops a kiss on my nose to soften the blow of stopping us. "They never manage to stay away for long."

"I know," I groan, pressing my head back into the pillow and glaring up at the ceiling. He chuckles at me, and I'm sure he's calling me dramatic in his head. I don't complain because he's not wrong; I am dramatic—especially about having to share Max's attention and affection. "Door's is locked. Let's just not answer them. We can stay in bed all day," I offer with a wink.

"Dava has a key, and I'd prefer that they didn't all walk in on us. As one. While demanding breakfast."

"You love that they want your cooking and to be here with you," I tease, then brush a stray curl off his forehead, tugging a little. "I love that they want to be around you, too. But I want you to myself most of all."

Max rewards me for that with a kiss, even though he already knew it to be true, and even if we have this conversation every time I come home. I'm not about to complain, sinking into the kiss, the way he tastes, the feel of his body on top of mine. He'll hold strong and keep me from escalating this morning because he truly does love when the crew is here and he gets to cook for them, and I don't want to steal that from him or the crew, but I'm taking advantage of the moments he'll give me. I'm taking advantage of his incredibly soft mouth for now, too, and I'll find more ways to do that as soon as we're alone again.

And, of course, the moment is shattered by a knock on the door. I knew it was coming, but that doesn't mean I have to be happy about it.

"Later," Max promises, then drops one more kiss on my lips before motioning for me to let him down. I could just release him from my arms and let him roll, but I tip him to the mattress a little more gently than he would move himself. I don't care to try and baby him, and he'd probably eviscerate me for it, but I like taking the opportunities that I can to show him a little kindness. "You can borrow a pair of shorts to go answer the door if you want. I'm going to get dressed quickly and then be out."

"Should just go out there naked and make them regret interrupting us." I slide out of bed and go to his dresser, taking the shorts and a pair of socks because the wooden floor is a little chilly. Both the shorts and the socks are too small for me, but it's better than freezing. "Want me to get anything out for you while I'm over here?"

"The door," he deadpans, then laughs when I narrow my eyes at him. "No, thank you, E. I promise I'll put you to work in the kitchen."

"I promise I'll try not to make you regret that."

His laugh follows me out of the room—the only way I like walking away from him at all.

The crew is knocking again by the time I cut across the room. Judging by exactly where on the door those knocks are coming from, it's Rosleigh impatiently demanding entrance. My

C. Knight

crew's resident cook and nurse isn't usually the one who finds waiting a challenge, but Ros loves my Max and doesn't want to be kept from him for a moment longer. I wish that thought didn't make me open the door with a smile when I want to pretend I'm annoyed.

"I got them to wait as long as they could," Dava says immediately, the only one who ever feels for my needs.

"I know. I should be grateful it lasted this long. You might as well come in," I say with a forced sigh, stepping aside and motioning them inside with a wide flourish. Ros rushes in first, but I warn, "He's still getting dressed. He'll be out in a second."

"Speaking of getting dressed..." Yen presses my bag into my chest. The bag I packed, intended to bring with me last night, and then left on the deck instead to my chest. She smirks at me and notes, "I knew you were gonna leave it. I believe I even told you that you were gonna leave it."

"And yet you didn't help me remember it," I tease. "But thank you anyway."

She laughs and walks in with Dava, their fingers entwined between them. Jak appears next, and I barely have my mouth open before he punches me in the gut, connecting solidly and knocking the breath out of me for a second. "You know why," he grumbles, marching in. He loves me, and he knows it.

"Morning, sweetheart." Tevin has to duck to come under the doorframe safely, and then instead of straightening up, he swoops down and kisses me. I lean into him, relishing the cool press of his lips, the sharp edge of his tusk teasing my upper lip. When he pulls back, he beams at me and tugs my sloppy ponytail. "You look like you had a great night. Told you the skirt would be a hit."

"It was the access the skirt provided that was the hit," I note with a wink. "Everything go okay with the dock master?"

"I can't answer that question before breakfast," he informs me, moving out of the doorway so I can shut it behind him.

I hear the bedroom door open a second later, and then I'm completely forgotten by my entire crew. I don't mind in the slightest.

Ros, of course, squeals and dashes across the room to Max. She practically climbs into his lap for a huge hug, and Max doesn't resist, obviously just as happy to have his best friend here. Yen kisses his forehead, and Dava leans down to hug him. Even Jakgrout greets him, almost smiling though he'd never do such a thing in front of all of us. h

"You have to quit getting taller," Max tells Tevin with a faux frown. Of course, he's blushing the moment the orc looks at him. I roll my eyes even though I can't help smiling about it; I have to work to make my partner blush like that, but my boyfriend only has to look at him—it's unfair! It's especially unfair since I know it's probably only true because the two of them have never gone beyond flirting and blushing no matter how much they both want to. Unfair because it turns me on unreasonably.

"You have to quit getting cuter," Tevin replies, and I swear, even Max's ears turn red.

I make a gagging sound, finally drawing attention back to me, and I'm fine with them all laughing at me. Max rolls his eyes, but I can tell he appreciates the chance to gather himself. He really likes Tevin, but he's not a fan of being thrown off so totally in front of other people; Tevin just hasn't spent enough time with him to know that yet. I'd love for them to really get to know one another...and if we didn't have to leave Max behind here, that could change.

I follow Max into the kitchen to feed my crew. Much as I wanted them to stay away a little while ago so I could stay in bed, I like the distraction I have now from the dark hole in my mind that wants to constantly remind me this is short-lived, temporary, that I'll be lonely without Max again soon. Feeding this crew is always a dramatic affair, and that's especially true here when they show up so hungry.

My appetite has been only for Max since I got here, but now that I'm getting a good look—and smell—of this food, my stomach is eagerly reminding me of all the energy I spent last night and this morning. Max went all out. Decadent double chocolate pancakes, fluffy scrambled eggs, bacon and sausage, hashed potatoes that he fries up with pepper and onions, golden brown biscuits, and my favorite: his mom's unbelievable four-berry jam. I didn't even know four kinds of berries existed until the first time she fed me that stuff, and then I wanted to bathe in it. I still do.

"Don't worry," Max murmurs, appearing at my side at the counter. He winks. "There's extra jam hidden just for you."

"You really do love me!" I lean down and kiss the top of his head, then scoop up one large platter in each hand. "Hope you hid some of that whipped cream too, baby. We can have dessert."

"Excuse me! I don't think breakfast should wait while you're disgusting." Yen hip-checks me out of the way and snags the huge pile of pancakes. "Make them keep it in their pants until we've been fed, Maxy. You love us more."

"You're lucky I love you at all," I growl at her back, though I do follow her to the table. Everyone is standing around it for the moment, creating a little extra room for Max's wheelchair to be able to move around which disappears once the chairs are pulled out. I flash a smile around, grateful they remembered. Doesn't really surprise me. I've got a good crew here—proven more by the way they care for my partner than anything else.

Max hands out the remaining platters for all of us to set on the table. Jak takes care of the three big carafes of coffee waiting on the stove without so much as being asked. He won't help me without begging, but when it's Max…

Maybe they care for my partner too much more than me.

When Max comes to the table and transfers himself onto the chair at the head, on the opposite end from me, everyone else practically throws themselves into chairs. I swear the whole room rocks with the force of it. Can't focus too hard on that, though—time to eat, and I know better than to wait.

There are a few minutes of near-silence, no words shared, only happy moans around full mouths. Plates are piled high, mugs are filled, and Max is smiling. Works for me.

"Hey, how long do you think you'll be able to

stay this time?" Max asks, and for a second, all I can do is blink at him.

This is not a conversation we have—we've regularly agreed not to have this conversation, actually. This conversation makes us sad, makes us fearful, brings a weight down over us instead of allowing us to spend our time together happily. He's not supposed to ask that question, and I'm not supposed to bring it up until the night before.

"I asked for a good reason, E, I promise," he says, catching my expression. "The solstice is in two days, and it's been a few years since you were home for it. The festival starts tonight."

That gets me smiling. Max and I aren't religious in any way, never have been, but shortly after getting our apartment and moving here, we learned that we accidentally moved to a town with a strong religious presence—and that's ended up being a good thing. The people here worship a few nature gods, so they celebrate natural events like solstices and eclipses with huge festivals. People come from all over to see these celebrations and join in on the fun. I've only been able to go to one in the four years we've had this apartment, and it was excellent.

"I don't need to ask what you're talking about to know I want to be here," Yen announces, giving me a hard look. "We can take the time off."

"Talk to me about the food at this festival," Rosleigh says, leaning eagerly toward Max, smile stretching across her whole face.

I think it's been decided for me, and I'm not even upset about it. We're staying, and I'm gonna get as much time with Max as possible.

Chapter 7

Max

"It would be easier to believe you're reading that instead of staring at me if you were actually turning pages." I turn my head toward Eli to find their sea-green eyes already on me, as expected, the only part of their face visible above a book they're absolutely not reading.

Eli chuckles and closes the book without bothering to save the page in any way. Proof, as far as I'm concerned. "You caught me. But I'm not sorry. I don't get enough time to look at you these days."

"Well, then I consider it an honor to be gawked at."

I wish it was an option to take off whenever Eli is around, whenever *Tempest* docks. I'd love nothing more than to spend every one of these precious few minutes in Eli's arms, listening to their stories, enjoying my partner's body and their obsession with mine. Unfortunately for both of us, Eli can't always predict when they'll be home, which means I can't always ensure that I don't have a client waiting on a map. Right now, I have a client waiting on a map.

The crew is still working on the ship today, getting *Tempest* restocked for when they leave and making the kinds of repairs that apparently can't be made at sea. I assume that's things that could cause a big hole in the side or something, but I have no idea. Eli trusts their crew, and they have a few extra days thanks to the upcoming solstice festival, so I get to have Eli here at work with me.

"I warned you this would be boring," I note. I didn't think Eli would enjoy sitting in the library all day; it'd be a dream come true for me to get a whole day in the perfect place to read and read and read, but Eli and I are not alike in many small ways—including this one.

"I'm not bored," they protest. "And if I get bored, I'm a grown-up. I can go take care of myself."

"You have a knack for making everything sound dirty, you know that?"

Eli flashes me an incredibly familiar grin, my favorite one. It's the grin they gave me the first time we met when a rail-thin, dirty, gorgeous kid walked up to me in a different library in a different city and asked what I was reading. One look at that face, that grin, those eyes—bright as they are now despite everything they were obviously going through at the time—and I knew I wanted this person part of my life forever.

Now, we spend more time apart than ever... but I'm still just as happy to have them.

"Hey, does that sweet old lady still make those meat pies for the festival? The ones that were hot enough to make your eyes burn?"

I laugh and nod. "Mrs. Grimley, and yes, she still makes them. They've gotten even spicier, actually. Last year, someone had to go to the healer because of them. And then a dozen more people had to go because they didn't believe the first person."

"I'm gonna eat a dozen of 'em," they inform me. "Or at least convince Jak to try one."

"When he ends up putting the filling in your underwear, I do not want to hear about it," I warn them, pointing my pen like a weapon but unable to keep from laughing at the thought. Jak and Eli would both have much, much emptier lives if they didn't have one another to tease and torture.

"Pardon me," an unfamiliar voice calls, and I follow it to look up at an equally unfamiliar face. "I don't mean to interrupt a tender moment, but I'm looking for quite a famous map maker…and the treasure hunter he spends his time with."

Eli is tense in an instant, their feet sliding off my desk and landing back on the floor with a thump. I don't have to ask why they have that reaction. Eli and I have separate careers, and considering what they do on *Tempest* and the company that attracts, that's by design. I help Eli with work all the time, of course; they come back for maps to items that they've heard about, that there are rumors about, or that they're being paid to find. And my work is going well with people coming from all over for similar maps to their own treasure. Once, we had a situation where a client commissioned me for a map and then paid Eli to go find the item on the map without ever knowing our connection.

This person knows about our connection, and this person is not supposed to know. It raises concerns and questions, neither of which we're going to be able to ignore. But unlike Eli, I can swallow that down for the moment and smile up at someone who has done nothing wrong. Yet. And who might be a potential client for one or both of us. For a successful treasure hunter and self-proclaimed grown-up, Eli does business with their heart instead of their head pretty often.

"Hi! I'm Max." I hold out a hand over the desk in front of me; more than one person has looked at me like I'm rude not to stand up at this point in the greeting process, but this one smiles even bigger and accepts the handshake. Very soft hands—not someone who does physical labor then.

We both look at Eli, but my gorgeous ship captain doesn't say a word, only staring up at the stranger—and I know they're struggling to stay in the chair instead of standing and likely intimidating the slim person in front of us. I quickly jump in and offer, "And this is Captain Rose. He and him for me, they and them for the captain."

There was a time when Eli gave careful, necessary consideration to who they told their pronouns to, who they hid it from, who they allowed to misgender them without correction. In those times, Eli was smaller and less strong-looking. They had a less fierce beard, too, and the beard goes a long way toward that intimidation factor. The sexy factor, too. Now, Eli expects to be gendered correctly, and the people who choose to argue it or get it wrong after being told have to face the consequences.

Fortunately for all of us, this stranger smiles and nods. "A pleasure to make your acquaintance—a pleasure long-awaited, I assure you. I am Magnus Wellerby." He says his name like it's a grand title, like he's making an announcement that should impress people. I have to bite the inside of my lip to fight off a smile that will definitely form if I look at Eli right now; there's no way Eli isn't going to make a face in response to that name. "I am here as a representative of the Western Merchant's Union. We have come under contract to find a set of very hard-to-find, very special, very *lucrative* items. I have been assured that the two of you are what I need."

Magnus reaches into the breast pocket of his jacket and extends a small cream-colored rectangle of paper to me. I accept it and find my father's wax seal and signature on the back, instantly familiar to me as a mark of his business. This man went to my dad with his proposal and was then sent on to me. If my father couldn't help him, Magnus wasn't exaggerating about what he's looking for.

I turn the card to flash the proof at Eli, and they give me a little nod but doesn't stop frowning. We know now that this man came here from my father to find a map, but that doesn't explain how some random merchant would know about Eli. About my connection to Eli. My father wouldn't divulge that information. We work together privately; we keep our work separate in front of the world. If Magnus knows that we have a partnership, professional or personal, then other people could know, too.

But at the moment, I find it hard to focus on that, and I can see by the shift in Eli's seated stance that they're interested too. Hard-to-find, special, and lucrative—Magnus knows how to speak the language of people like us.

"Okay, Magnus." I set down my father's card and fold my hands in front of me on the desk. "What can I help you find?"

"He means what can we help you find," Eli notes, and they flash me a wink that manages to loosen the knot in my chest at the idea of being caught by a stranger in a secret we've kept for more than a decade. We both know that Eli's anxiety is sky-high; even if I couldn't read it in the missing glint in their eye, the tightness at the corner of their mouth, the rigid way their hands are holding the arms of the chair they're in, I just know them. Eli's anxiety is almost always sky-high, but they're trying to make me feel better, and I'm going to let them.

"I knew I would like you two," Magnus laughs, smiling at us like we're old friends. "Now...let me show you something very exciting."

Magnus lifts the bag hanging from his shoulder and sets it down on my desk. He doesn't put it down on anything, but I instinctively pull the leather case guarding my quill-tip pens out of the way. He can bend or break other things on the desk, but not these.

"Tell me, friends. Have you two ever heard of the elements of the gods?"

My gaze snaps to Eli as they lean forward in their seat, intrigued but frowning even deeper now. Magnus asked that question knowing the answer. Everyone has heard of the elements of the gods. Every child who ever had a bedtime story told to them or talked to other kids on the playground. Every reader who ever explored books created by an artist's imaginings or an explorer's discoveries. The pieces in question are an ancient legend, one that many have chased after but none have ever discovered.

Those legends say that millennia ago, the old gods went to war with the new gods, each side fighting for the right to be worshipped by the people and creatures populating the world. The battles, of course, were devastating to the gods and to the world, and some of the gods were even killed. When the gods' lives were ended, their essence—elemental and immortal, by the nature of gods—was trapped in small orbs that plummeted to the land and were lost forever. If you believe the stories, then somewhere out in the world are treasures that contain the pure, untapped, untouched pieces of actual gods and their powers.

"I've had people send me after legends before," Eli notes, leaning back in their chair to feign relaxation. "I've been successful in finding what they wanted more than once"—I bite my tongue instead of adding a 'we' there—"but whenever I have to prove a legend is only that, I find people get a little testy about it. They don't like to hear they paid money to make me chase something that was never real. I'm not interested in the Western Merchant's Union getting pissed at me. And I'm especially not interested in them getting pissed at *us*."

Magnus puts his hands up, palms facing us. A gesture intended to show us that he means no harm. He doesn't know Eli all that well if he thinks we're going to believe him just because of that or any fancy words. I almost feel bad for the uphill battle this guy is fighting. Almost. We'll see what he has to say before I decide if I totally feel bad. "I assure you, my friends, that there is no reason to be concerned. The Union has sent me because we have proof."

Grinning from ear to ear now, Magnus starts pulling parchment out of that bag, multiple rolls and even a journal of some kind, and sets it on the desk in front of me. "This will contain everything you to need to make you believe as we do that the elements are very much real. Keep them tonight. Examine them. Talk to your crew. Tomorrow, I will return for your decision. And if you agree..." Somehow, that smile grows even bigger. "I will provide you with everything you need to start your journey."

Chapter 8

Eli

"**I don't trust anyone wearing a tie. In fact, I** have a rule against trusting anyone in a tie." I slap my hand on the table, trying not to think about what makes the wood sticky under my palm. "New rule: no one in a tie is ever allowed on *Tempest*."

"Magnus Fancypants doesn't want to come on *Tempest*," Max laughs, rubbing my shoulder to try and soothe me. I rub his leg under the table in a more direct message of how I want to be soothed, and Max winks. A promise I intend to cash in on later.

"What have we learned about the Lord Fancypants?" Tevin asks, eyes on our resident spy. Only spy in the world who will brag about her skills and profession, but Yenvyl is good enough to get away with that.

She gives a smug grin now, throwing down

the shot in her hand and wiping her lips with the back of her hand before answering. "He's staying in the Tower, that rich person's hotel on the beach. Apparently, he's got one of those whole floor suites. He's been here for three days ordering shit like caviar and champagne."

"Shit that tastes like fish ass and sour bubbles but costs as much as a house," Jak grumbles, pulling a face that crinkles his eyes and makes his mustache and beard cover his mouth completely.

"I could buy *Tempest* all over again before I could afford three days of a suite and that stuff." I make a face and add, "You know, I'd rather buy *Tempest* all over again."

"Caviar is delicious—you're all just heathens," Rosleigh informs us. Of course, the halfling chef is also smiling about popping a piece of dry bread in her mouth because food is her happy place. Wish mine was that easily found. At least he's right next to me for now, and I lean over to plant a kiss on his curls.

"Okay, okay," Dava calls, trying to regain control of the conversation. I let her lead these things for a reason; I'm far too easily distracted for the leadership these people have heaped upon me...but I'm also too stubborn to give it up now. "We can assume our new friend Magnus is a representative of the Western Merchant's Union, as he said. And Max, that stamp from your dad is legitimate?"

Max picks up the card from the table where we dumped all the evidence we have upon arrival; he stared at it for a while earlier and does the same for a moment now before nodding. "It definitely looks legit to me. That's my dad's signature, and I don't know why else he'd sign this. It's a signal we've shared before."

"I'm prone to distrusting parents as a rule, but not Max's dad," I note. "If he sent someone to Max, he believes the work is legitimate."

"But my dad does not believe in legends and myths," Max counters, almost laughing at the thought, "so he probably didn't know exactly what Magnus was coming to hire us for."

"Still, it's a sign this is someone we should believe, yes?" Dava asks, looking at me and Max for a nod from each of us. I'm more than okay with his approval being sought, all things considered. "Okay. So are we willing to look at his proof of the elements?"

"I'm always willing to let someone talk out their ass if they find it necessary," Yenvyl answers around a mouthful of food.

"It could be legit!" Ros argues.

"It could be more nonsense—the likes of which only humans can cough up and spew at the rest of us," Jak counters with a pointed glare at me and Max—the only humans at the table. I blow him a kiss for it, and that gets me flipped off in return.

"Let's see what's here," I announce, reaching for the parchment folder we were given—and I've been dying to say that since a stranger first dropped his little bomb in the library. I'm a treasure hunter, after all. My entire life, I dreamed of traveling the world and searching for things no one else could find. It was pure kismet when I met and fell for a boy who was learning to make maps to treasures like that, and it was years of work to get myself out onto the seas. Now, if there's any possibility the elements of the gods are real, I can't pass up a chance to learn more. I can't pass up a chance to be the captain who finds them.

Everyone takes some of the papers to make the work a little easier, whether or not they think the pieces are real. Max drops one of his, and Tevin ducks under the table to retrieve it. I watch them have an adorable little moment when Tevin hands them over, fingers brushing and cheeks blushing and the whole flirty deal. I hide my smile so neither of them feels pressured by me, but whenever I see them together, I can't help getting excited about it. Someday.

I want to know what's on all this proof...but I skim more than read. I'm excellent at pretending I know how to do something I'm only marginally capable of. Max was the first person to figure out I didn't know how to read, and it took him a couple years. He taught me, which ended up being more fun than I expected. I don't dislike reading now, but I still prefer not to do it in front of other people.

"Hang on...you have my second page," Max says, leaning over to check out my parchment. He slips all three out of my fingers and gives me a map in exchange.

"Thank you," I whisper, and without looking away from the pages he's now reading, he reaches under the table and squeezes my leg.

I look around the table instead of at the map. My crew is made up of my best friends, the best people I know. Some were always part of *Tempest*, others came along later, but it wouldn't be right without any of them. And they all deserve this.

They deserve a chance at adventure. A chance at a truly incredible payday, at name recognition if we pull off a treasure hunt like this.

"We should do this," I announce, setting the unread map down on the table. "What do we have to lose?"

"Other jobs while we're focused on this one," Dava answers, ever pragmatic. She then picks up the contract that Magnus slipped in with his proof, the official offer. "But if we pull it off, we'll make more in this one job than we have on all of them in the last year."

"Wow," Tevin notes, faking a wide-eyed stare at his twin. "If Dava is dreaming, you know it's big."

It earns him a chunk of cheese to the face while Jak says, "We could buy more ships. A fleet. A better captain."

"You could buy my love," I tease, then duck the cheese that comes for me this time. Max laughs, and it draws my attention back to him. To the biggest obstacle in the way of me signing that contract and getting my ship back out on the waves.

"There is some evidence here," Max notes, oblivious to the turmoil building inside me. "Magnus is offering a piece I should be able to use to make an initial map, get things started, as a deposit. He wouldn't just hand something over if he didn't think it was useful."

"Between your magic and the captain's, we'll find something out there," Yenvyl quips, grinning when I roll my eyes at her. I have no magic, never have, but my crew and other friends like to argue otherwise. It started as a way for other captains to calm their egos when

I swooped in and found a treasure before they could, pieces they'd declared impossible. Max's magical maps make a huge difference, but I have a knack for the sea and for treasure hunting. It's good instincts, practice, and necessity—no magic.

Still, if the thought is enough to scare off others who might challenge us, and especially if it means we can charge a little more to anyone who believes I'm using magic, I won't discourage it with more than an eye roll.

"Hey." Tevin reaches around Max's shoulders to tap mine. "Why do you look so unsure? You're the one who said we should do it."

"About ten seconds ago," Ros chimes in.

"I..." Hesitation sweeps through me and away again. What's the point in lying to the people I spend every moment of my life with? "It'll be a lot of time out at sea. There are eight elements—so say the legends and the contract. We'll probably need each one as the anchor to make a map to the next one. That's a lot of time going out, and even if it's more stops at home... It's a lot of leaving."

Suddenly, I'm staring at way too many sympathetic faces. The table is flooded with pity, and I'd rather drown than face it.

"I have an idea, but I don't know how you're gonna take it," Max says, and I'm surprised that he shrinks away a little when I look at him. He's nervous—since when is he nervous to tell me anything? "I could come with you."

I wince, not from the suggestion but from the reaction around the table. A cheer goes up among my crew, instant excitement, the whole group eager for that plan. Even Jak. Not that he'd ever cheer, but he thumps his canteen against the wooden tabletop a few times, adding to the cacaphony of support my partner just stirred up for himself. For his plan to come to sea with us, his plan to come on *Tempest*.

And I'm an utter asshole for not feeling the same enthusiasm.

I'm the dickhead who can't think of anything but Max's disability, his constant pain, his limitations. I'm the wank rag who immediately forgets everything I know about how capable and strong this man is only to fear everything that life at sea, life on a ship, even temporarily, could do to him. I know all those things about myself, and yet...

Max deflates from the excitement when he looks at me again, and a sharp pain lances through my chest when he looks away. He's hurt. I hurt him. I should have at least pretended to be excited but... I'd rather be the one to hurt him than let real harm come to him out there.

"Isn't there a festival on?" Tevin asks, standing up with a screech of his chair against the wooden floor. "We're supposed to be out there celebrating something or other—"

"The solstice," Dava notes.

"Yeah, that's what I said," he agrees. "Let's put the work away for the night and remember how to enjoy ourselves."

Tevin meets my gaze over Max's head while they all start gathering up the evidence we were given, and the message is clear. He's giving me an out, a way to fix this at least for the rest of the night. A way to try and make things right, to make Max happy again.

I lean down and kiss Max's cheek, smoothly releasing the break on one wheel so I can spin him toward me. He startles a bit and reaches out to me but grins at the maneuver; I've always liked to take advantage of how easily I can move him and that I'm the only person allowed to touch his chair without getting his permission first. I kiss his lips this time, lingering. "We'll figure it out, but please know I'm aware I suck."

"Well, so long as you're aware," he laughs, rolling those dark brown eyes at me. He reaches up to hold the back of my neck. "You don't suck. And we will figure it out. But you have to promise me a dance."

"Maxy, I'll promise you the world—and I'll deliver it, too."

Chapter 9

Max

There is something delightful about watching polished, polite, reasonable people get drunk and make fools of themselves. And that, of course, is the purpose of this festival. Tradition, sure. The solstice, maybe. An excuse to let go and forget yourself? Definitely.

I'm not drunk, and I haven't made a fool of myself...but even I'm feeling the urge to let go more than usual.

The town mayor and his wife have been on stage and singing at the top of their lungs for hours, Elda the near-ancient librarian is dancing in a rather shocking way with an even more ancient dwarf who runs a carpentry business, teenagers of all sorts have stopped pretending that they aren't drinking, and the townsfolk have completely welcomed *Tempest*'s crew into their musical, drunken festivity. So why shouldn't I forget myself a little, too?

I asked for a break from the dancing in the crowd for a little space, a chance to breathe. I also asked so I could get a chance to watch Eli and Tevin, to think about Eli and Tevin...to think about them with me.

Tevin has flirted with me since the day we met, and he flirted even more after he started officially dating Eli—I think he appreciates knowing I gave Eli the confidence to go for that. He's never hidden his attraction to me, and I've never been able to hide any of my emotions in any given scenario. Eli knows how both of us feel, and Eli knows that I've been thinking about being in bed with both of them. They won't pressure me about it, but I know how much Eli likes that idea.

Eli finishes dance with an elven woman who runs the docking manifests in this town, an important connection for sure, and they turn right into Tevin's arms. Eli is tall for a human and built like a pirate, all hard muscles and cut lines. They're brazen about it too, wearing an almost indecently short skirt both for the gender euphoria and to show off more of that muscle. The lacy top that they have on tonight does the job, too. Tevin is even taller and even more muscular; orcs don't have to try hard, from what I understand, and Tevin looks like he could move a ship off dry-dock all by himself. Together...wow.

They obviously know one another's bodies, the way they each move, and watching them dance—even to an upbeat song—makes it clear to everyone who can see them that there's a connection. Warmth grows inside me at the smile on Eli's face, their comfort with Tevin. I love seeing them happy, seeing them loved. I love how sexy they are, too; a lot of my fantasies revolve around Tevin helping me make Eli feel amazing.

Of course, the rest of those fantasies center on all the things I imagine the two of them could do to me...

But I've never had the courage to go for it. Timing has been a small part of it. If Eli is only home for a day or two, we want to keep each other all to ourselves, and we aren't ashamed of that. They'll be here a couple more days this time, though. I didn't drink much, but something about the extra time and the fun of the festival is making me feel a little more courageous. And a little more horny.

As the song ends, Eli turns and finds me immediately, spotting me with no effort despite the other people and the distance. Their gorgeous smile erupts on their face, cradled by the beard they're so proud of, and they say something to Tevin before aiming right for me. "Hey, there, hot stuff," they call on approach. "Come here often?"

"Did you drink way more than I realized?" I laugh even as I reach for them. I catch them by the belt and pull them closer, Eli landing with their hands on the arms of my chair. "Don't bend over any further or you're going to give this crowd a view."

"They should be so lucky." Eli swoops down to close the distance between us and kiss me. It's an inappropriate kiss for a public setting, and I'd normally slow them down, but tonight, I lean into it and reach up to hold the back of their neck. "Come dance with me, Maxy."

"Only if you kiss me again first."

They grin against my mouth. "Easy ask, baby."

Eli continues to kiss me, teasing my tongue with theirs and nipping at my bottom lip while wrapping their arms around me and slowly guiding me up out of the chair. I keep a stabilizing grip on their shoulders and then their biceps once they straighten up in front of me, wobbly more from the heat flooding my veins than from having to find my feet. I half expect them to start moving me toward the crowd, toward everyone else dancing, but instead, Eli just wraps their arms completely around me and starts to sway me to the slower tune now playing.

"You're the very best crutch I own," I inform them, leaning against them enough that I can safely reach up and drape my arms over their shoulder. My fingers find their ponytail, their blonde hair always so soft, and I play with the ends while we dance.

"I'm thrilled to have a purpose. Are you having fun?"

"Of course. It's been a great night. And..." I have to swallow to prepare to continue, and I have to look right into Eli's green eyes. I need the strength that I can find there, the knowledge that this is someone who will never judge me. "I was thinking that maybe we could keep up the great night. Maybe make it even better."

They make a thoughtful, playful, sexy sound, sliding one hand around my hip to cup my butt. "I'm dying to know what you have in mind."

In response, I tilt my head enough to look past them toward the dance area. Toward Tevin. Eli looks back to follow my gaze and then grins at me, this smile one of their more danger-ous—and so also one of their sexiest.

"Really?" they ask, cocking a brow at me. It's not entirely suspicious and definitely not a chal-lenge; I can't blame them for being surprised.

"Don't be so surprised," I tease. "You know I've thought about it for a while. Maybe now I just want to stop thinking and start doing. Too easy—let it go."

"I'm also too easy, so it's my responsibility," they quip, and I don't bother trying to temper the laugh that escapes from deep in my bel-ly. Eli leans down and tugs my earlobe with their teeth, making sure that my attention is grounded and on them. They run a hand back through my hair, tugging lightly at the ends, and it brings a smile to my face...and a not-in-significant amount of heat to my core. "You don't need to say yes," they tell me softly. "And even if you do say yes now, you can change your mind or decide what you do and don't want in the moment. You know that, right? No one will be disappointed."

"I know." And I do. Mostly. But it's still a new experience, and I'm not as bold about tack-ling those as my partner. Although I did offer and even suggest that I should join their ship and go off on a treasure hunt earlier today. Maybe I'm letting go even more than I real-ized. Maybe this is an exciting new trend in my life. Or maybe—

"Don't overthink it. In fact..." They lean down and kiss me hard; they taste like the sea and the whiskey they've been drinking tonight, and I want to drown in it. "Only think about what you want. Go on instinct, pleasure, not logic."

"I'm not good at that, and I think you know it."
Their response is to kiss me again. Gods,
they're a wonderful kisser, and they know exactly how to take my mouth—and what to do
with theirs—to drive me wild. When they pull
back just a second later, I'm already breathing hard, and I lean in to try and chase the
kiss. They only brush their mouth over mine,
though, and murmur, "Tell me, Maxy. Do you
want me?"

"Yes. Gods, yes." That's so easy. Too easy.
Too obvious. I want them more than I should.

"I want you, too. I can't get enough of you."
They nip my bottom lip, and I'm about to stop
caring who else is around us—or that everyone
else is around us. "Do you want Tevin?"

"Yes." I don't realize the answer is there
until it's out of my mouth, and when Eli smiles
into their next kiss, I know that was the inten-
tion. Shut off my brain and get the honest,
non-logical, unfiltered answer from me.

"Let's go home, Maxy."

I'm not sure what happens next or how. It's
all a blur. One minute, I'm saying yes to going
home. The next, I'm being pulled back out of
my wheelchair and guided by Eli's strong arms
into our bed. And Tevin is here, too. He came
home with us, came to bed with us, and my
heart is thundering.

Eli slips their hands under my shirt, warm
and calloused hands skimming my spine and
gripping my waist, then sliding as far into my
pants as they can from this angle. They apparently decide almost immediately that the
angle doesn't allow for enough, so they throw
themself backward on the bed, taking me with

them, and shove their hands down to grab my ass in both hands. I giggle into the kiss, loving this mood they're in. This is exactly the mood I need them in for the rest of the night to go the way we both want it to...the way I've fantastized about.

Tevin tosses himself down onto the mattress hard enough to make it bounce—and to make me bounce up off Eli. I brace myself to land on them again, but strong arms catch me, and in the blink of an eye, I end up in Tevin's lap.

Eli sits up and leans in to kiss Tevin, perfectly confident. They're a really adorable couple, and it's always made me happy to see them together, but Eli has never turned from kissing Tevin to kissing me like this, and it makes my heart race in a way I'm definitely thinking I could very much get used to.

It's never hard to enjoy Eli's kiss, that perfectly soft tongue and the incredible familiarity there. I'm still floating on their kiss when they very gently guide my face by the chin to Tevin, who takes my mouth. His mouth is cooler than Eli's but no less pleasant, especially when he lets out a needy little noise.

I *really* like thinking that I can make Tevin needy.

I'm vaguely aware of movement, arms that definitely belong to Eli wrapping around me, and my head is spinning when they kiss me again. I end up laying on the bed again, this time between the two of them, and I don't actually remember shoving my hand under Eli's skirt and taking hold of them, but that is definitely Eli's dick throbbing in my hand. I manage to focus enough to watch Eli and Tevin kissing above me, both their hands working open the buttons on my shirt and the clasps on my binder, exploring my overheated skin underneath it.

I'm absolutely rapt, feeling Eli thrust into my hand and listening to them moan and watching their tongue slip into Tevin's mouth. A smile explodes onto my face when Tevin's hand covers mine, huge and calloused and squeezing our joined grip tight around Eli. Eli has to break the kiss, drop their head to their chest, and moan deeply. The throb between my legs and the cool air moving over my bare chest with warm bodies on either side of me assures me that I'm not going to end up disappointed in any way tonight.

But even if this was just about Eli and their pleasure, I would love this. I'd do anything to bask in the lust and need I can see on Eli's expression right now. Doing things that I'm going to enjoy too is not a big ask.

Eli's eyes meet mine, and they smile too. "You look very happy, Maxy. I love putting that look on your face."

"I was just thinking the same about you," I admit, and I lift my head to kiss them. Against their lips, I murmur, "But I'd really like for you to put something inside me instead of on me."

Tevin barks out a laugh. "That's an excellent line. Can I borrow that?"

"Only if you do your job and get inside things, too," Eli quips, flashing a big grin at him and waggling their eyebrows with a suggestion that absolutely no one needs to guess at.

"Please tell me that this entire night isn't going to turn into the two of you trading innuendo and puns," I groan dramatically.

They both laugh at me, and Tevin leans down to nip my throat. The tusks make that feel almost dangerous and much more exciting. "No, I promise you more than that," Eli assures me, also leaning down. They nudge my nose with theirs, then nip my bottom lip before joining Tevin in laving attention over my neck, my throat, my shoulders, my collarbone…

I get lost all over again, hands and mouths and teeth traveling my body while they trade kisses with me and one another. I'm not ashamed to be just about begging before long, especially since the two of them are just as needy based on the sounds and the intensity of their touches. I almost protest when Tevin sits up and slides off the bed, until he starts stripping. Eli chuckles in my ear, tugging the lobe with their teeth, and we both pause to enjoy the unveiling in front of us.

Tevin gets naked as quickly as I'd like him to in a moment like this, but my heart stalls when he's fully revealed. He's as big all over as I expected him to be, but I wasn't totally prepared for it. I've slept with a couple orcs before, so I was ready for the dark gray color of his cock, the shape that tapers toward the tip and doesn't have any significant crest. I was not ready for the size, though. That is more than a little intimidating.

I'm impressed with Eli for having handled all that in all the ways that I might have imagined they have. Maybe a little jealous, too. Though I don't think I'm ready to handle that size with more than just my eyes. And my hands. Maybe my mouth.

"Hey, come here, baby." Eli doesn't need to do more than ask when I want them this badly; I practically throw myself at them, and Eli moans deeply before rolling on top of me. They yank my pants off, and my legs fall open for them. When they duck down to take my nipple between their teeth, I cry out from the rush of pleasure, and I get a view of Tevin coming back onto the bed behind Eli, pulling off their skirt, running those huge hands over their ass and back.

Tevin catches my gaze and grins at me. He reaches up to take a handful of Eli's hair and then starts pulling Eli further down my body. "I think Max would like you to make your way to right...here," he murmurs, guiding Eli's head between my legs. Gods, that's hot. And when Tevin then takes my thighs and pulls my legs apart, spreading me for Eli with Eli guiding the pace and distance, I shudder from the intense throb of my clit before they ever touch me.

I don't need to wait long for that touch, though. Eli dives in like they've been starved, tongue delving into me and lips sucking hard. We're already both so hot, so turned on, and Tevin's needy moans with his hand working behind Eli assures me that we're not the only ones—and I don't want to be. I want everything both of them have to offer, anything I can get. And I want so, so much more of Eli's incredible tongue.

I let myself come apart for them, giving myself over to the waves of pleasure they deliver and unworried about how I sound. Neither of them cares. They want me just like I want them, and Eli scrambling up my body to kiss my mouth while pressing their cock between my legs is almost hot enough all on its own to send me back over the edge. I really almost lose it when

Eli throws their head back, body shuddering and voice breaking around Tevin's name as the orc presses that huge cock deep inside his boyfriend, his captain, my partner, my best friend, the love of my life, our Eli.

Eli rides Tevin's next thrust into me, taking me while being taken, and all three of us cry out. The noises grow rapidly more lewd, more needy, more demanding. I lose track of who I'm kissing, who I'm touching, who is touching me and where. Eli takes me perfectly, and Tevin takes them hard and in tandem so it feels like all of us have become one. One mass of lusty, sweaty, hot fantasy coming to life. And I'm thrown into a new depth of pleasure I hadn't known possible when we come apart together.

Eli's whole body rocks and stiffens, and they cry out some garbled version of both our names. Watching their orgasm, feeling them erupt inside me, gives me no choice but to follow them, and distantly, over my own cries, I hear Tevin roar and feel the echoes of his rough, stagnated thrusts into Eli through my body.

I regain my senses with Tevin at my side, slipping one huge but surprisingly comfortable bicep under my head, and Eli on my chest. We're all breathing hard, all clinging to one another, our skin sticking…and I've never been more comfortable. I feel familiar lips pressed to my jaw and less familiar ones on my head before falling asleep with Eli still buried inside me and Tevin holding both of us close.

Sometimes, fantasy can't match reality, but if this is any hint of the kind of adventure I could expect if I really do start sailing on *Tempest*, I don't think I'll ever want to leave the ship.

Chapter 10
Eli

Last night, I think we could've had a dragon land on the street outside, and none of us would've even noticed the chaos; we were too caught up in one another, in the pleasure. I never thought Max would get off so much on watching me with Tevin, and then watching him get so excited only made things better for me, which then rippled into Tevin and...gods.

The sex, the three of us, used to be the whole dream. But Max flipped that on its head yesterday with one sentence. One suggestion.

Max has never talked about joining *Tempest* before. I never would've imagined it was on his mind, even in his imagination. He has a successful business, he loves our home and our town, and... Well, he's disabled. Max is capable of much more than most people give him credit for, but he's realistic too—about his limitations, his pain. Living on a ship is hard on the body even when that body always works in the best possible ways. For Max... I never would have dreamed that was something Max considered a possibility.

Now that it's out in the universe, though, now that I've heard him say it, my mind is swimming with the potential. I wouldn't have to leave him, wouldn't have to say goodbye, wouldn't have to miss him so much that it hurts every damn day. I could share my life with him, show him my passion and my world out at sea; I've told him stories, of course, but it's not the same. Max is the most important piece of my life, and he's been kept away from so much of that life, and this...

This could be everything.

I could have treasure and Max all at once.

As if my first mate hears the call of a treasure hunt in my mind echoing his own, knowing I'll need him to make that happen with our crew, Tevin blinks his eyes open slowly. There's a moment of confusion since he's never slept in this room, and he and I very rarely fall asleep in the same bed even when we're on the ship. When it passes, golden eyes meet mine, and he smiles softly.

I press a finger to my mouth in warning about our volume and then greet him softly. "Morning."

"Morning, Cap," he replies with a cheeky grin. It never takes him long after waking up to become himself—I'd have him no other way. I'm only sad I think I'd have to wake Max or squish his face to lean over him and greet Tevin with a kiss, but the smile is enough to satisfy me for now.

I startle when Max mutters, "Morning." I hadn't realized he woke up too, probably because even now his eyes are closed, and he hasn't moved. I watch his hand flex around Tevin's fingers, though, and then he smiles just a bit, like he's remembering exactly what happened last night and what's going on around him. I'm thrilled it puts a smile on his face.

I hug him a little closer, giving him the option to hide his body if he wants to, but the way he nuzzles into me, keeping hold of Tevin's hand so he pulls both their arms around me, tells me he's confident now too, just like he was last night. Maybe not immediately, but he got there faster than I expected, and his comfort is all that matters.

Which is why I shouldn't be thinking about Max coming onto the ship. Shouldn't be wondering if it's possible, shouldn't be eager to ask Max about it as soon as I can today.

Does he really want to? Should we really be thinking about this?

Max's fingers tap my bare chest, and when I look down at him, his deep brown eyes are worried. "You okay?"

"Of course, Maxy," I answer, and it's mostly honest. "I'm just trying to figure out a way to throw my oversleeping first mate out of bed without sounding rude. He has work to do."

"I quit," Tevin announces, rolling to his back and pulling the blankets up over his face. Which exposes his feet, of course—and mine.

Max laughs and snuggles into me even more, wrapping his arms around me. I can tell by the tight sound of the laugh that he's still worried about me, that he didn't believe my little lie about my mood. I'm not surprised; he knows me better than anyone and reads me like a book. Still, he looks back at Tevin and asks, "Can I make you breakfast before you go hand in your resignation or get to work? Whichever you prefer."

"No, thank you," he laughs. "I'll snag some coffee if you're offering, though."

"Always."

"Does that mean I have to get out of bed now, too?" I groan. I might be eager to get Max alone, to find out if the vision of our future I've always had is changing, but that doesn't mean I'm eager to stop being naked with them.

"Yes," Max answers simply. He slides one hand down my back and lands a sharp pinch on my bare ass, making me yelp and jump. "Oh, look, you're already halfway there!"

I growl playfully but let Max shove me out of bed. He keeps the blanket tight at his chest and gives me a pointed look I do not need explained. Being naked in front of other people, no matter how well we know that other person, is different in the morning than it was last night. Max needs privacy.

I give him a nod and talk to Tevin about the crew's plans for the day while he redresses and I pull on shorts. And toss clothes to Max.

"He's okay, right?" Tevin asks when we're alone in the kitchen, the coffee pot doing its job on the stovetop enthusiastically. He glances back toward the bedroom. "I don't know if I should have left last night. If staying made him uncomfortable—"

"Oh, hey, no," I assure him, leaning into his side. "He wanted to get dressed alone, but I know he's glad you didn't leave last night. We both are." I tilt my head back to offer my mouth, and Tevin is smiling when he kisses me softly, slowly. "I'm sure you didn't get much sleep, though, sharing a bed, so if you need to hit the ship for a nap today, do it. I'll make that an order from your captain if needed."

"I'll keep that in mind. Thanks, babe. We'll see you on the docks later?"

"You will." I smack his ass when he has coffee in hand and is headed for the door. And then I lock the door behind him so I can be sure there's real privacy ahead for me and Max. I need it today—and not just because I'm hoping I can get him naked again.

Back in the bedroom, Max has maneuvered into his wheelchair and is pulling on a shirt. No binder. I love that he's comfortable enough around me to forgo that thing. I think his ribs are probably happy about it, too. We met before Max realized everything true about his gender, and I helped him pick out his first binder; we've been through a lot together. I'm not sure if that should be pushing me toward bringing him on *Tempest* or away from it.

"You are deep in the overthinking hole this morning, E," Max says, laughing a little but concern thick in his eyes. "What's going on?"

"You mentioned coming onto *Tempest,* and I don't really know how to deal with that."

Max blinks at me, used to me being blunt and honest but probably not ready for that one. He may not even remember saying it if he was buzzed and not serious. It wouldn't be the first time I stressed myself out endlessly over nothing at all.

His face softens immediately, and he motions for me to sit on the bed while taking my hand. "I didn't think about it, but I should have known just dropping that would stress you out. I'm sorry, Eli."

"My broken ass brain and its passion for making me freak out is not your fault," I quip, relieved when he laughs. "Can we talk about this for real, though? I'm dying to know what you're thinking."

"I'm…not sure," he admits, pulling his hand back into his lap. It's not a slight; Max curls in on himself when he's unsure or uncomfortable. "I was thinking about how much work is ahead of you all if you're gonna go after the elements. Some of those last spotted locations, if they're valid at all, are weeks and weeks apart! And…" He looks up at me, eyes soft and wide. "I'm gonna miss you. We'll be apart even more."

"We're already apart a lot, and that's been getting harder."

He cocks his head at me, curls flopping onto his forehead adorably. "Harder?"

"Come here." I help him get back out of the chair and into bed—the bed we bought together and consider ours but I only spend a few nights a month in. On this job, it'll be even fewer nights. "I miss you when I'm not here. You know that. But I don't see a good way to change it either. It would be dangerous as hell for you to move onto the ship, Max. Besides, it would be selfish! You have a thriving business, a whole life here. I can't take that away just because I'm lonely without you."

"It's not selfish—it's pretty adorable," he teases, definitely just intended to make me laugh, and I don't bother trying to hold it back. I kiss him out of gratitude and just because I want to. When I pull back, Max is smiling, but he looks down at the light blue blanket between us instead of right at me. "Besides, I..."

"What?" I press. "Is something wrong, Max?"

I can't help the protective tone. I thought Max was happy here—safe here. If that's not true, I need to deal with it. I can't imagine it's his business, considering Max has a reputation for being at the top of his field; people come to him from all over the world. So it has to be personal, and I—

"Eli, you're spiraling again. Everything is fine," he assures me, pressing a hand to my still-bare chest. I cover it with mine and nod, inclined to believe him but still anxious until I know what's going on and if I can do something, anything, to make it better. Max huffs out a big breath, and the words come tumbling out with it. "I make maps to these incredible places for people to go on amazing adventures. You're about to leave and go after something legendary, the kind of thing people write about in books. I make the maps, and then I stay here. I never get to see the adventures or these places for myself, and I..."

"You're bored," I realize, almost relieved. Would be if I didn't feel bad for him. "I get it. You know how I felt when I was prepping ships for other people but couldn't get one myself." He nods, playing with something nonexistent on the blanket. "It's okay to be bored, Max."

"It's ridiculous," he snaps softly. "I know how hard it is for disabled people to find work and homes; I can work for myself doing something that I love, and I'm complaining about it."

"And beating yourself up for being even a little unhappy," I add, running a hand back through his hair. I tug the curls to tilt his head up toward me, and he smirks while rolling those beautiful eyes at me. "You're not doing anything wrong or hurting anyone by wanting more. But I hate that you feel that way."

"I hate that you've been feeling lonely," he counters. "I feel like I'm neglecting you even though I know that's silly because…"

"Because it's not like you can be on the ship."

We stare at each other, my mind thrashing in the storm of my thoughts, and I can imagine he's dealing with the same. We've always said that—Max can't be on the ship. We've designed our lives around that reality because I need to be at sea and Max can't. We've both made dozens of sacrifices because that's always been true. It's not like he can be on the ship. Now…

"Is it really impossible?" he asks, leaning forward the way he does when he's trying to get me to agree to something. "I know that it won't be easy but—"

"Maxy, it's not just that it wouldn't be easy," I argue. "We could alter the ship to make it work for you, and you know I would. But what are you supposed to do in a storm? Do I tie you to the hull so you can't get thrown around, or do we just let the breaks off the chair and let you fly around with the waves?"

Max barks out a laugh, surprising me. I didn't mean it as a joke, but when I picture Max shouting 'wee' while careening across *Tempest's* deck, I have to laugh too. "If it helps, I promise to only try that once."

"Okay, that is not funny. But...are you serious about this? You really want to?"

"I'm not being childish, Eli," he assures me. "I don't think this is going to be some magical, perfect journey. I know it'll be hard at times, and I've smelled you guys when you come off a long trip, so I know it'll be gross at times. I know I'll have to work hard to stay safe." He squeezes my hands. "If you tell me no, I won't be angry, and I'll let it go. I know it's not an easy choice, and I'll trust you. You're *Tempest's* captain."

Gods, I want to tell him no. I want to keep him here, keep him safe. This is the first and best friend I've ever had, the first person who ever made me feel valuable, seen, loved. I'd do anything for Max...

And at the end of all the concerns, at the bottom of the anxiety black hole, that love is why I say, "Okay. We'll give it a try—but we're just trying. No permanent promises, okay?"

"I get it," he assures me, putting his hands up with palms facing me. "We'll just try and see if it works...and we'll make *Tempest* a legend in the meantime."

"Oh, this is sounding better and better."

Max launches himself at me with a fantastic little squeal, throwing his arms around my neck and holding me close. I know I might have just made a huge mistake and put the love of my life at risk, but if it makes him this happy, I might be willing to do it again every single day.

Chapter 11

Max

This whole thing is extremely weird.

People come to me. That's how my business works. Someone has an object or another person that they need found, and they need a map or at least a location to pull that off, so they come to me. I meet them in the library, and before then, I rented out a couple other places. Even as a child, watching my father and my aunts and uncles and my grandmother operate their own cartography businesses, people came to them. That's how I understood this to work. I never realized how much that's a comfort factor until right now.

Eli is taking me to the client. Over the last couple of days while I was focused on wrapping up my current projects and working with Jak on options to make *Tempest* more wheelchair accessible, and while I've been enjoying the solstice festival, of course, Eli and Yen were getting word to our new client and setting up a plan to meet with him. I didn't know that we wouldn't be doing that in the library until today, but I trust Eli to make the right choice. Even if I do not like being away from my home turf.

"It's better this way," Eli assures me again, somehow reading my stress and the source of it. We separate to go around a puddle, and their hand comes down briefly on my shoulder when we rejoin. "Magnus is making a deposit with your anchor piece and promised more proof. Something big. If we ask him to come to us, he's taking on the risk of traveling around the city with all that. If we go to him, we prove we aren't worried about risk."

"Making clients like this comfortable is part of the job pretty often," Dava chimes in. She's coming because she's more pragmatic to Eli's emotional, and they like having her around to balance them out. I like having her around, too. I'm not sure about Yen and Tevin being here, though, since I know that's exclusively for the muscle and the weapons—just in case. I don't operate in a 'just in case' field.

It's more stressful, all of this, because I can't let on just how much I'm feeling and how much I'm worried about. Eli has almost wavered on their agreement to let me temporarily join *Tempest* at least once a day since we made that agreement—and I didn't know how badly I wanted to join until then. If they change their mind now, I'll be crushed, and since I told Eli it was okay if they said no… It's all a mess. I need to hold it together long enough to join, and I can't let Eli know how badly I want that.

Magnus meets us at the door to the nicest hotel in the city, a place where each night costs more than our monthly rent. I don't doubt he chose this place for a reason—both his own comfort and to show off for us. "Good morning! I'm so glad you agreed to discuss this little adventure with me. Please, join me for breakfast. I took the liberty of ordering a selection."

We follow him through the unnecessarily fancy lobby and into a dining room area. He already has a table with more than enough chairs and at least twice the amount of food we could eat. There are people in this city who won't eat this much all month, and Magnus is fine wasting it. If all this is intended to impress, he's chosen some strange paths thus far.

"Please, sit. Enjoy."

Magnus sits first, and Eli pulls a chair aside for me to be able to access the table. I notice that the others don't approach until Eli nods for them; I know that they're the captain, but I don't really see this dynamic between them very often. At home, they're all just good friends, and Eli isn't the type who needs to throw power around. It's interesting to see it now, Eli obviously in charge. It's sexy, too.

"Have you had a chance to enjoy the solstice festival?" Eli asks, grabbing the carafe of coffee and signaling to the others on the crew that they're allowed to eat. Eli fills a cup for me first; I won't be taking any sort of leadership on the ship, not even close, but they're still taking care of me and being sweet. Their small talk with Magnus is surprising, though, and not just because Eli hates small talk.

"I have had to travel a bit while staying here, but I've had a chance to partake, yes. It's delightful. People here are quite kind." He smiles at me while breaking apart a croissant so fresh, steam billows up from the newly exposed center. "I'm not surprised, based on what I've heard about you, Max. I don't think you've had a single unhappy client in what has been an impressive career so far."

"I do my very best for everyone," I answer, trying not to be unnerved. I knew he asked around about me since he knew where to find me and my father, but I still don't like to think about it. It's unnerving—he unnerves me.

"And you succeed. Especially when paired with such an impressive captain and crew."

Eli tenses beside me, reacting to the obvious attempt at flattering us. They have even less tolerance for brown-nosing than they do for chatter and small talk.

"We brought the evidence you provided in case you want it back," Dava announces, jumping in just as she's needed—before Eli can say something that they might regret out of anger and an inclination for impulsivity.

"And we want to see the final piece of evidence you promised," Eli adds, settling a bit. "What you showed us so far was solid, but you can understand our skepticism."

"I wouldn't have much faith in you if you weren't skeptical," Magnus says. His face twists a bit and he adds, "That is why I chose to come to you as well, actually. Another crew couldn't quite gain all of my trust, and acquiring the elements is very important to me. I want this done, Captain Rose."

"And you came to the best to do it...which is why I'm surprised to hear you say you hired someone else first," Eli presses, leaning forward a little. I pop a piece of muffin—an incredibly delicious blueberry muffin—into my mouth to keep out of this part of the conversation. It's weird to have other people controlling the whole discussion too, but I kind of like being able to listen. And watch Eli at work.

Magnus nods, growing serious for the first time. "I went to another crew first, and I gave them all the information that you were given so far. I...then began to doubt their abilities. That is when your name—and yours," he adds, looking pointedly at me, "came across my desk. This is important enough to me that I would like to hire you *as well* as the original crew contracted. Whomever retrieves what I need will walk away with the entire bounty I am promising. Well worth the effort."

"This is all or nothing then?" Yen asks, and I can tell by her tone that she's excited by that, not put off.

"I'm afraid so," Magnus answers, not bothering to do anything about his smile. "And before you ask, no, I won't be sharing the name of the other ship hired. They do not know you were brought onto this job, so that seems only fair."

I watch Eli, unsure how they're going to react to all this. Now, it's not just a job but a race. Now, it's not just about getting what we can but bringing back every single element of the gods—which we still don't completely know are real—in order to get paid.

Now, it's really not an option to leave me on the shore.

I kind of like being a secret weapon. Especially a very necessary one.

"We need to see the rest of your proof before we go any further," Eli says, leaning back in their seat casually. They don't look disinterested, just calm. I know Eli well enough to know that they're almost never calm. "You're offering a lot, but with the time that I'll be spending on this and resources I'll need to apply if we're in a race...I'm not going to waste my time or put my crew at any risk."

Oh, now I'm a secret weapon *and* a resource. This pirate thing is kind of fun.

"I can prove to you that the elements of the gods are real beyond a doubt," Magnus announces, turning to reach into the bag hanging on the back of his chair. "More than the accounts that I provided, more than the legends. You see, Captain Rose..." He produces a chunk of what looks like glass and stone, a sapphire in a deep shade of blue glittering in the sunlight. I wouldn't look at it twice except Eli tenses beside me, and Tevin shifts enough for me to notice. "You have already found one."

I blink, staring at the chunk of rock. "That's... an element of the gods?"

The stones are legendary and not just for their source or the myths that tell us they disappeared. It's said that the elements of the gods were gifts to the world, the dead gods final offering, a way to access magic which—prior to their existence—had never been an option for humans. Once the elements were in our world, the power spread, and some people were even born with magic. The story is a little harder to believe as someone who has a non-elemental magic generations of my family has been born with...and because they're rocks.

"Indeed." Magnus sure sounds confident, but he needs to in order to do his job. Well, to get Eli and *Tempest* to do his job for him. "You recognize it, I'm sure, Captain?"

Eli nods and explains for my benefit, "We were hired to acquire this for a client a few months ago. We weren't told what it was. Frankly, we were way underpaid."

"To be fair, the client that I hired and who then brought you on as a third party did not know what he was sending you after," Magnus says with a slight shrug of one shoulder. I choose not to ask questions about the client or the job because 'acquire' is the word that Eli uses when they stole something but don't want to admit that to me. It's a white lie that I appreciate very much.

And something I won't be able to hide from if I join *Tempest*...

"You understand I need proof," Eli says, and it's definitely not a question.

Magnus slides the candle on the table in front of him and then holds the blue orb directly over the flame. I nearly jump when the flames leap, reacting to whatever is inside there—not like they've been ignited or antagonized but like they are drawn to it. And in his hand, the element starts to change and shift, the crystals I can now see inside the glass expanding. In the light, I can see flames dancing inside it, too, but when Magnus pulls the element out of the flame, he wraps his bare palm around the glass that should be scalding only to have no reaction. That is definitely not an average sapphire orb.

He hands it to Eli who accepts it, looks it over, and then holds it out for me while asking Magnus about specifics on the contract—dates and prices. I'm captivated by the stone and eager to take it, not just because I know why Eli wants me to take a moment with the thing.

My magic can find just about anything, and I don't need a direct connection; I've been able to find heirlooms based on pieces that are part of a set but haven't been together for decades. I do need an anchor, though, something related to whatever or whoever I'm looking for. I gifted Eli with a compass that they always carry with them, and it allows me to track them no matter where they're going in the world simply because the compass is theirs. If we're going to be able to start looking for the other elements, this orb is going to be my anchor.

A familiar sensation blooms in my gut the second I have hands on the element. Part of that, I think, is my magic recognizing what exactly I'm holding since the sensation isn't usually this strong. But the usual feeling, the one that calls me to create a map, is still there. This is an anchor. While the other ship can only use the myths, accounts, and historical records of questionable authority to chase down the elements of the gods, I can use this. I can give *Tempest* a real edge.

I nudge Eli with my elbow while placing the element back on the table, my blood all itchy now with the need to create, to seek, to find. Soon enough, I will.

Eli sits up straight beside me, their jaw set and their green eyes glimmering with the promise of an adventure. Looking every bit the ship captain and treasure hunter that they've built themself to be, they hold a hand across the table to Magnus. "On behalf of *Tempest* and her crew…you have a deal."

Chapter 12
Eli

If I get through the day without taking off my boot and whacking a dockhand upside the head with it, it'll be a miracle.

We pay our fees, we load our own gear, we always give a correct inventory. We've found more than our fair share of treasure, and we've put all the profits back into the ship. *Tempest* stands tall, proud, and beautiful. The siren figurehead, the cobalt blue paint and flag, the dark brown wood—all of it right out of my dreams. But none of it matters.

There are only a couple ways to gain respect on the docks. Dockhands have notoriously little patience for anyone and anything that isn't making their day easier, and ships generally don't make their day easier. Neither do rowdy ass pirate crews, stuck-up brats who begged their daddies to buy them a ship, and jackasses who can't count their inventory or try to haggle their fees. They're going to assume every new or up-and-coming ship is one of those no matter how the ship looks or the flag it's flying...unless the captain knows the ways.

I grew up on the streets. My first orphanage was right on the docks, a grungy little place that slumped into the next building over instead of standing on its own. I can still remember the smell of old fish keeping me up at night. But I watched the ships come in and out of harbor, and I knew even as a kid what I wanted to do with my life.

Lots of people watch ships. They're a sight to behold, and I stand taller when I spot crowds checking out my ship these days. But what you learn as a street urchin is who to watch, and before I even knew how to count, I understood what worked for currency on the sea and at a port.

Two things make life easier when trying to find a dock to call home without getting robbed and while getting back out onto the waves without delay. And oh shit, can these people create a delay. I'm not in a rush, but I'm also not a fool. Gold is necessary first and foremost. Money makes the world go round—forget what the fairytales say about love or any other nonsense. Gold. Everyone needs it, and the more someone has, the easier things get.

Only one other thing makes any difference at all for ships, for pirate crews and adventurers. It makes so much of a difference, in fact, that no matter how much gold we have, without this, we can't get anywhere:

Reputation.

We need the dockhands to recognize our flag. We need them to know the name of our ship. We need stories to have been told and sung in taverns all over. Whether that reputation is for good or evil doesn't matter one bit; the crews known for slaughtering other ships are just as well respected as the ones with the biggest treasure-hunting successes tucked into their coffers. We just have to be known.

I need to be known. I need *Tempest* and my crew to be recognized, respected. And yeah, I need that for myself, too. I'm done being a dirty, hungry kid with their nose pressed up against the window of one orphanage or another, watching everything happen in the world around me, never getting to make anything happen myself.

This treasure hunt is going to make sure that's never me again. We've put a dent in things with the impossible treasures we've recovered so far, but the elements of the gods are a different level of legend entirely. Discovering something like the elements is special in a world and in a life like mine when nothing else ever actually has been.

Nothing except Max. And it was thinking about that little kid watching the world go around without them that really made me agree to bring Max along on this adventure. When he told me how it feels to create maps for other people to take on their own treasure hunts, leaving him behind, I know how that feels. I've been in that position, and all I needed was a chance to get away. It was Max who gave me that chance, and now, I get to give it back to him.

Well, not exactly 'now.' First, we have to get the hell out of port in a reasonable amount of time.

"And this one is…"

"Same thing it was five minutes ago," I snap. Deep brown eyes nearby turn to look at me, and shame washes over me. There's a version of me Max has never really had to deal with, and I'm not eager to introduce him. I force in a breath to calm down, though I know I can't afford to get too soft. I pull out the inventory sheet yet again and show the dockhand even though he has a copy right in front of him; Dava makes four these days since we've gotten so used to bullshit. The kind that comes with no reputation. "Look… these crates are marked right here. Supplies for repairs—lumbar, hardware, tools."

He grunts at me and doesn't actually look at the sheet with me; he already knew the answer anyway. "And your crew is gonna load all this?"

"All of it," I agree, flashing a smile I hope doesn't look like a grimace. I'm not a kiss-ass, but I can charm when I have to. "We know you're all busy, and we aren't asking you to load. Just sign off on the inventory and fees, and we'll get all this out of your way."

"Hmm. And when are you leaving?" His eyes, a very boring brown unlike Max's, flash down to look at all of me. I have no interest in finding out exactly what people are thinking when they look at me—pants tighter than most men would dare and a beard more impressive than most of them could manage—but I'm good at learning when people like what they see. I'm not ashamed of taking advantage of that if I have to.

I'm also not ashamed to use lies to take advantage.

"Two days. Plenty of time."

"Mmhmm." I get one more look, a messy signature, and then he's walking away. Done.

"Get moving," I shout to the rest of the crew, tucking the approved inventory into my pocket. "We're ready to start loading. Dava and Ros, head out to the markets. You have lists?"

"Got 'em," Ros calls. "Maxy, do you wanna come with us?"

"I...don't know." I turn toward Max, hands resting on the first crate that will come back onto the ship with me. He's smiling at me, but there's a tension to it. "Any orders for me, Captain?"

"No, baby," I laugh, "you'll have enough work to do soon. Whatever you want to do today works for me."

"Oh. Okay, then, sure. I'll come with you," he tells Ros and Dava, smiling at them. He looks a little anxious, but I think that's probably because he might find the dock markets a little tough to navigate with the crowds. Dava and Rosleigh will look after him. And I'll kick some ass if he needs me. These people might not know *Tempest* yet, but they will damn well make a path for my boyfriend if he needs them to.

Ah, fuck. He's blocked already, unable to find a path with his chair off the end of the docks unless—

Well, damn. I need twenty minutes and a great ass to get a signature, but two men just *ran* across the docks to move a few hundred-pound bags of sugar for another ship and get them out of his way. I don't even get a chance to take a step toward helping him, and now, these strangers are falling all over each other to help my partner.

Apparently, we don't need a better reputation; we need more cute curly-haired guys with adorable smiles.

"You doin' any work today?" I nearly startle at Jak's voice from inches behind me and only manage to control it by clenching just about every part of my body. He'd never let me live it down if he thought he scared me, but it's really unfair such a heavy-footed dwarf who stomps all over my ship night and day can move so quietly when he wants to. I turn to face him and find the scowl I was expecting; I probably wouldn't recognize him without it.

"I am working!" I protest. "I got our inventory and docking approvals."

He scoffs and waves me off, stomping right back off. "Paperwork. You call that work?"

"I'll stick my boot up your ass and call that work," I shout after him, loud as I can since Jak hates getting extra attention. I'm rewarded with a scowl while he lifts a dried goods box that is almost as big as him. He could lift me if he wanted to, and we all know it. But I can make him blush, and that's a true superpower. "Jakgrout, how dare you threaten to spank your captain. Just because I like that kind of thing—"

"Fuck's sake!" he practically screams, storming off as fast as his legs will carry him—though he still manages to stomp on the way.

I laugh at his retreating form and roll my eyes. He'll get me back for that later, I'm sure, but now that he's gone, I can admit he's right that we need to get to work.

Most people don't realize what life at sea is actually like. Whether or not folks want to call us an adventuring ship or a pirate ship, it's the same for all of us, and we're misunderstood. There are lots of fairy tales out there about a pirate's life, the drinking and the gunfights, the songs and the alcohol, the sex and the treasure. Those things happen, sure. Well, not the sex for all of us, but the point stands that those stories miss the one thing that makes up the majority of a pirate's life.

Carrying shit. Lifting, moving, and organizing boxes, crates, and sacks. Big ones. It's how we spend the rest of the day, climbing up and down the ramp and ladders onto the ship, up and down the new ramp below deck, on and off the docks with the hundreds of pounds in supplies and materials we need to bring with us. Since Max is coming this time and I won't have an excuse to come back here soon, we're getting more than usual...so we're lifting, moving, and carrying more than usual.

I don't mind the physical labor, really. My first job on the docks and on a ship was doing this kind of thing, so I'm used to it. Even like it sometimes. Well, unless it's raining or too hot, and then only people who hate themselves like it. Besides, Max and Tevin both like my body, and I don't have to worry about my biceps when I'm lifting a few hundred pounds a day to make the ship function. Nothing wrong with admitting I like showing off the shape I'm in for the people I adore.

Max is my concern today, though. He gets back from the market with Dava and Ros, and though they're all laughing, it's still tight. And it stays tight…until Tevin plops a too-big box onto Max's legs.

"Hey, I can take that one," I interject, though I have to put down a too-big box of my own to make that work. But in response, Max heaves out a sigh, and Tevin narrows his eyes at me. Oh, I missed something important. "What?"

"I can help, Eli," Max tells me, wrapping his arms around the box and adjusting it a little, then taking hold of his wheels. "I want to help. You asked me to come onto the ship, so for now, I'm part of the crew. I don't want to be a useless part."

"Maxy, you are not useless!" The idea is absurd. "We wouldn't be doing this without you. At least not as well."

That gets him to smirk, but he's still shaking his head at me. I definitely did miss something. How come I can never figure out what that is on my own?

"Yeah, but you gave orders to everyone else," he notes, shrugging a little. "I was just sent to the market to keep myself busy, and then I've been standing around. Sitting." He giggles at his own joke, and I can't help but laugh with him.

Tevin nudges my shoulder and gives me a pointed look when I meet his gaze. "Every member of the crew helps. You know that."

Fuck. They're both right. I told Max he could join the crew, that he gets to make his own choices for his safety, for the risks that he faces—I've told him that since we were kids. Always meant it, too. But here I am, expecting Max to… What? Stick to the rails and out of the way, watching all of us, doing nothing until he makes a map? That's unfair. I'm being unfair.

"Okay," I sigh, "but we need a compromise." I lift the box off Max's lap and push it back into Tevin's arms. He starts to argue almost immediately, which makes me adore him even more because he's doing it to protect Max, but I point toward the stairs below deck. "Tevin, go. Please." Captain voice...even with the please.

"Just be nice," he mutters at me on his way past.

I want to make a joke, but Max looks completely dejected, so I need to make this right fast.

I lean down, my hands on his thighs, and wait for him to look up at me. "You're right. You should be able to help, and there's a lot that you can do. But squishing your legs and being in more pain for it later is not one of them. I happen to like your legs...and I can't take advantage of you being on board if you're too sore to enjoy it."

That gets him smiling, even though he's trying to hide it. I deserve that. But it makes me desperate to earn a real smile.

"Dava fucking *hates* dealing with the records—making sure everything we bought ends up on the ship and we don't get arrested because we didn't claim something or grabbed the wrong things. But I would hate getting fined or arrested, so those records are important." I hold up a hand when he starts to talk. "I know it sounds like I'm giving you busy work so you don't drag heavy shit around all day, and I kind of am. But if you tell me no and say you want to drag heavy shit around instead...I'll respect that."

Max considers it for a moment, studying me. I was honest, so I don't hide anything. "Does

Dava really hate it, or are you trying to get me to agree because you know I want to help her?"

"I do know you want to help her, but she really does hate it." I motion toward the starboard rail, facing the docks, where Dava has a graphite pencil between her teeth and is running both hands back through her inky-black hair. She's staring down at a stack of parchment like it's just offended her personally. "You'd help me out, keep us all out of trouble, and get the bonus of Dava's undying love."

"The bonus is not being so sore that you can't take advantage of me later," he informs me, finally smiling for real when I look back down at him. "Okay. It's a fair compromise. Thank you. I just want to help, E. I want to be as useful as every other member of the crew."

"I'm confused by that because you're so much more useful, but I'll try to understand. You need busy work too. Got it." I cock my head and lean a little closer, giving him a specific sort of grin that often gets me my way even though he knows what I'm doing. "Have I earned a kiss along with your forgiveness?"

"We both know you can always have a kiss." Max tilts his head, an offer I'm never going to refuse, and I take a long moment to luxuriate in the way the sea and the sun taste on his lips. He's only been out here for a few hours; within the next few weeks, I'm going to be desperate to devour him.

Chapter 13

Max

"Max..."

I have to bite the inside of my cheek to keep from grinning at Eli. I don't piss them off on purpose, but sometimes when I've frustrated them without trying, I find it more amusing than I should.

At the moment, running their hands back through their hair and glaring at a wall of the ship, I can't help but be a little amused. It helps that the position is flexing their biceps and pulling their shirt up enough to reveal a couple inches of muscle, dark hair, and soft skin. Now I'm amused and horny, and I don't think I can be blamed for either.

"You told me to bring what I needed, Eli. I brought exactly what I need and nothing more," I inform them. And then I have to bite my cheek much harder to keep from laughing at the look they give me.

"You do not *need* books, Max. Especially not books that need to be on shelves." They motion at the wall, though it's more of a flailing of their limbs than anything else. I asked Jak to put a few shelves up for me in Eli's quarters, which I get the dubious honor of sharing now, and Jak found some beautiful wood at the docks to do it. "How do you think the books are going to stay up there when the ship is tossed around by waves? We're going to be picking these up every day!"

"Well, if we're getting tossed around, you'll also be picking me up so. Feel free to prioritize."

That does the trick of breaking Eli's tension. They throw their head back to release a husky, musical laugh.

I close the distance between us, trusting my crutches to hold me up; it didn't take me more than a day on the ship in the docks to discover that I'm more comfortable moving around the often-narrow and all-wood spaces of the ship with the crutches than my wheelchair. I think we've all come to the conclusion that we'll cross the bridge of how to handle a storm safely when we get there, and I'm comfortable with it for the moment. I like the option to stand and walk more often, which is more difficult at home sometimes.

I also like the option to step up in front of Eli and move directly into their arms. Eli takes my weight when I wrap my arms around their back and look up at them, the crutches hanging from the safety straps around my wrists. "Thank you for making space for me," I offer, maybe batting my eyelashes at them more than I need to. They wear more leather on the ship than on land, and I love the way it smells on them; I'm going to be constantly turned on around here. "Even if you don't think all my things are necessary."

"This is what I get for falling in love with a nerd," they reply, rolling their eyes dramatically.

"True...but now you also get the nerd in bed whenever you'd like," I note, and their grin grows.

I choose not to add 'for now' to the end of that; I don't even want to think it. I've only been on the ship for three days, and we're setting out to sea this afternoon; I have no business already worrying myself—or worse, worrying Eli—about whether I can stay and how long we have together. Or what comes next.

Fortunately, Eli is effectively distracted from any concerns by my reminder of bed, even though we've only been out of bed for a couple hours. I can't say it's not tempting to stay there all day.

"Whenever I'd like, hmm? I want to test that theory," they inform me, then take one slow step backward so I can safely follow their steps without getting dragged or forcing my legs to do things they just aren't capable of. I don't mind the option to lean this heavily against Eli, to feel so much of their hard body under their clothes.

But since we have only been out of bed for a couple hours, the ship needs to get underway today, and there is a lot to be done, it's probably for the best that Eli's new plans are interrupted by a knock at the door. When there's no separation between the knock and the door opening, I know that it'll be Tevin without looking.

"I knew you'd be down here fooling around instead of working," Tevin laughs, shaking his head playfully at Eli. He looks to me and asks, "Are they still giving you trouble about the books?"

"They are! That's why they're all still in boxes." I put on a pout without giving it much thought, but when Tevin's gaze immediately drops to my mouth, there's a distinct clenching deep inside my stomach. And the way Eli squeezes me tells me that they notice it—they always seem to notice it when I have any spark of attraction to their boyfriend.

Or maybe more than a spark.

"Alright, well, Rosleigh and Dava need their captain to finalize inventory," Tevin announces, coming fully into the room now. "You go deal with that, and Max and I will get the bookshelves organized without all your complaining."

Eli grumbles playfully but smiles when they look down at me. "You good with that?"

"Of course. You have work to do." My smile comes with no effort when I add, "And I'll get to see you around the ship."

Their whole face lights up at that, at the idea of seeing me around *Tempest*, at us being together full-time and truly living together again. It's a heady thing to make someone like Eli so happy at the thought of being around me.

Even if it's only temporary. Even if I'm only here for the elements—that's the deal we agreed on. Temporary change, and then we both get back to our lives.

"Yes, you will," they breathe, then lean down

and kiss my lips. They're a tiny bit more serious when they add, "You know where I am if you need me. Or you at least know how to send someone to find me."

I get one more kiss, and then they shift away from me while holding my hips and waiting until I'm securely rested on the crutches again. I nod to assure them that I'm stable and steady. My legs need more rest at night to get used to all this walking, but my balance isn't suffering as much as I'd feared it would on the ship. Not yet anyway.

"Be nice to my partner," Eli tells Tevin, who rolls his eyes and makes Eli laugh. They kiss softly, briefly, and I like that it makes me smile. I've always liked Tevin with Eli; he's good to my partner, and I don't have to worry about Eli being alone or lonely or unsafe when I'm not around. Tevin really cares about Eli, and that's really all that matters to me.

Though when we're alone and Tevin turns to me, ready to help with my books and smiling that incredibly handsome smile of his at me, I realize that Tevin has gone out of his way to be good to me, too. They're a shameless flirt and have always somehow made me feel good about myself with just a glance—especially one as loaded as the one they're giving me now. Which might be because this is the first time we've ever been alone in a room with a bed.

Okay, so there might be more than one way that living on a ship is going to throw me off balance. I think I like this way.

"Point me to the books, sweetheart," he says, and when I motion toward the crates, he gets on it right away. I join him, Tevin holding each very heavy box up in one hand while each of us take the books and arrange them on the shelves. He laughs but doesn't complain when I regularly rearrange what he's already added to a shelf. "Eli told me that you love to read, but I didn't realize you have a library."

"I wish I had a library," I laugh. "Although this is only a small fraction of all my books."

"How did you decide which ones get to travel with you?" he asks. I almost assume that the question is just asked to be polite, maybe to tease me in that wonderfully flirtatious way he has, but he's watching me. He actually wants the answer. I can't totally explain why but the fact that Eli's incredibly strong first-mate, the man they couldn't run the ship without, wants to know something as silly as how I chose books to bring with me makes my heart flutter a little. I really hope I'm not blushing while I answer.

"Um...some are old favorites, the books I like to read over and over and over again. Others are my research books, tomes on my magic and on cartography, just in case I need them. Some I haven't read yet and really want to."

"Ah. And...this one?" Tevin turns around the book in his hand to show me the cover, a painted illustration of a half-naked, sweaty orc with an elf—also half-naked—draped across their chest. The image makes it clear what the book is about even without ever cracking it open. "Is this one an old favorite or...something you still want to discover?"

Now I am definitely blushing, and I have absolutely no hope of rescuing myself from that. "That..." I swallow around a dry throat. "That's a book I would not have brought if I'd known you were going to see it," I confess, pulling the book from his big hand and shoving it onto a shelf. It's not in the right place, but I don't dare pull it back off to reorganize right now.

It can't possibly be lost on either of us that the orc on the cover is at least somewhat similar in appearance to Tevin. Even if that weren't true, it's now out in the open that I have interest in reading sexy stories that involve orcs, and that came out in the open while I'm in a bedroom alone with the sexiest orc I have ever met. It doesn't help my situation at the moment that Eli has been kind enough to share some stories about Tevin's body and what he's like in bed, and gods, I'm never going to stop blushing again.

Tevin chuckles, the sound dark and doing things to me that it has no business doing, but he's kind enough to let it go and let me catch my breath. For now at least.

We get my bookshelves filled and in order, and just that small thing makes me feel like I'm much more welcome, more at home here. It feels like this space is partially mine, not just that I'm occupying part of Eli's quarters and their ship. Tevin helps me arrange the desk that I'll use for making the maps right under a window, too, even though that requires moving the couch. Eli already told me to try whatever I want in the space, and I think this is going to work.

My legs are feeling all the standing at this point, so I sit on the couch. "Do you have to get right back to work?"

"If being first mate doesn't get me permission to slack off, what is it good for?" he quips, plopping down beside me. Even sitting, he's massive, at least a foot taller than me; Eli is taller than me, of course, but Tevin towers over them, too…and maybe that turns me on more than a little. "Eli said you're gonna get the maps started tomorrow?"

"Should be, yeah. I'm itching for it after getting my hands on the first element; it tends to be hard to focus on anything else for a little while after the magic first really starts to flow." I shrug. "We figured it would be better to wait 'til we're already on the move. Eli is very excited for me to start, though."

"We all are," Tevin admits, tusks further revealed when his smile is this big. "This job could change a lot for the whole crew if it goes well. *Tempest* will have a real name, a real reputation. That means everything out here. Which means we're excited for you to be here too."

"I know." My own smile, for the first time since he came in here, is forced.

I saw the contract that Magnus offered, and I know what a difference that kind of money will make for the ship and the crew. I also know that, for Eli, the prestige that comes with hunting down rare and legendary items is even more important than the money as a reward. After growing up a forgotten kid, it's not all that surprising that they want people to know who they are. More than anything else they've done, maybe more than anything they could ever do, this is going to get Eli and *Tempest* known for their adventuring.

And they need me to do it. That's quite a bit more pressure than I'm used to with a job. It's not the task itself; I can find the elements we're after, even if they're getting moved or the other crew that was hired for the job finds them first...unless I can't manage to live on the ship. Then I'll fail at this job, and I'll make Eli fail at their dreams. I'll make Eli believe that bringing me onto the ship was a mistake, and I'll never get a chance like this again. None of that is an option.

This needs to work.

Chapter 14

Eli

As incredible as Max's skills obviously are, as proven as his talents might be...I was a little nervous setting out with this first map. Even Max agreed it appeared to lead us right into open water, and to say a location like that could make finding an object difficult is a massive understatement. I should have had more faith.

Takes a few days and a good deal of research on other maps, but we finally figure it out. We're not going to open water; we're going to an underwater cave system at the base of a mountain range....which does happen to be in the middle of the sea.

Max still seems just as anxious about what that means, how it means we'll need to search, but this time, he's alone in that worry. The rest of us are more familiar with this part of treasure hunting. I've done dives before, and I'm as comfy in the sea as I am on it.

The one very new thing for me on this hunt is creating much more anxiety than I was prepared for, though. I'm not adjusting to Max being on the ship as well as I want to be—as well as everyone else has adjusted, and worse, as well as Max has adjusted. He likes it here; he trusts me and wants to spend time with me. It's not like I wanted him to be miserable here, but his happiness makes it harder because all I can think about are all the ways he could get hurt.

More of them come to mind every day, and they're getting both scarier and more ridiculous. I woke up in the middle of the night panting and covered in sweat from a dream that an eagle had come and scooped him off the damn deck. Max is happy here, and it's making me feel like shit about wanting him off the ship, and I hate myself.

I can't tell Max. Can't hurt his feelings like that. Max assured me he could handle life on the ship, I agreed to let him give it a try, and we've barely scraped the surface of that. He's been on the ship for more than a week and hasn't been hurt once. He doesn't know what else we could face, though. He doesn't know how dangerous it can get out here. And if I tell him I'd really prefer he just go back home, that I'd rather suffer through the loneliness without him and potentially lose this job...

Fuck, I can't even convince myself of that. None of it is true. I want to find the elements of the gods, I want to be *that* captain, and I want Max with me when I do it.

And much, much more selfishly...I don't want to lose him. Not as my cartographer or anything else.

"We can't have you taking a bunch of trips up and down, so here." Tevin drops a bag on the table in front of me with a loud enough thunk to make me frown up at him—and we both know the noise isn't my problem. "It's not as heavy as it sounds, I promise," he adds, grinning. I mostly believe that Tevin would prefer to have me alive and at least wouldn't drown me if he was going to get rid of me. Easier ways.

"Alright." I pull it open and peek inside. "What do I got?"

"A couple tools in case you need some elbow grease down there, extra rope, another knife." Mention of another knife makes me check my belt, my dagger securely where it belongs. I make sure my compass is secure, too. I'm not going anywhere without that. "The bag expands since we don't know what you're grabbing."

"I'll know it when I see it," I say, confident enough in that. My upbringing helps with that part of the job. Rich people, folks who never had to worry about having enough gold, are shit at treasure hunting because they don't know value at a glance. Me? I can find a brown diamond in a pile of dragon shit if I need to. Granted, I'm hoping this dive will be much more pleasant than that.

I stand and follow Tevin out of the kitchen, aiming for the deck where we should be arriving at our destination any moment. Tevin takes the bag from my hand though I'm more than capable of carrying it myself; he knows it makes me feel precious in a good way when he takes care of tiny things. He squeezes my hand with his free arm, and I lean against his side, taking a bit of his strength for myself.

"You're gonna keep an eye on Max for me while I'm down there, right?" I press him, aware that we've talked this over half a dozen times in the last day but needing to hear it again.

Tevin gives me a heatless scowl. "You wouldn't be so tortured about Max's safety if you talked to Max about it."

"Don't be logical with me," I snap playfully. "It's not his burden to bear."

Tevin sighs the way he always has when he's trying not to be annoyed with me about something—usually something I'm being stubborn about, which means he sighs like that a lot. "How many times has Max told you that you and your busy ass brain are not a burden? How many times have me and the whole crew said it?"

"Shut up."

Tevin laughs at me, and I can't blame him for it. I know when I'm being stubborn...and I know that stopping or changing is easier said than done.

"Any eyes on that other ship again?" I ask, slowing down a little so we don't have to bring this up in front of the whole crew. I saw sails a couple hours ago; there's not much out here, not a lot to draw a ship in this direction, so it's odd, but I don't want to panic. And I'm somewhat prone to intense, stomach-cramping anxiety if not panic.

"They disappeared. It was probably no one."

He's probably right. But it could've been someone following us. Could've been that other ship Magnus hired, whoever the hell they are. It could have been authorities after us, especially if they caught wind we're going after something so valuable.

No. It was probably no one. I have to keep my heart and my breaths calm under the water, so it was probably, definitely, certainly no one.

"Good timing, Cap," Yen calls from the helm when we emerge onto the deck. "We're dropping anchor."

"Beautiful. Thanks, Yen." I cut to the rail for a look at where we are, the mountains looming over us. The moon isn't quite full, but it's more than bright enough to provide light, and we're going to be able to avoid the shadows of the mountain range for a while. The water is a beautiful pale green, and we're far enough out that it's calm, more like sea glass than water. I'm instantly eager to jump in.

I turn back to the crew, all of them staring down at the water, too. I can guess at what's on some of their minds.

"Everyone ready?" They all turn to me, and not a single one of them looks ready. Too late now. "Jak and Tevin, help me with the rope?"

"Rope?" Max asks, coming over. He's chosen to use his crutches on the deck tonight; they look much more painful to me than just using the wheelchair, but I can see why he'd want to stretch his legs every once in a while. Calm seas are a great opportunity for that.

"Yeah, they're gonna use a harness, basically," Dava explains while Tevin kneels in front of me and lets me step into the harness he and

Jak came up with. It's not going to be the most comfortable thing I've ever had up against my balls, especially if I come to the end of the rope, but I feel more secure as soon as it's pulled up around my hips. "The rope secures them to the ship so they can find their way back, and if something goes wrong, they can alert us by tugging."

"Something could go wrong," Max echoes on a soft breath, like he's only now letting that become reality in his mind. Even in the moonlight, I can see his skin start to pale, and much as I don't want him to worry...something inside me warms.

I'm distracted a bit when Jax yanks the rope behind me, tightening and securing it but squeezing my personal jewels in a very unpleasant way. "Easy!" I growl at him. "I'll take you down there with me like a cannonball, make my dive faster."

"You should learn when to watch your big mouth," Jak informs me, tugging the rope again and very effectively making his point. The embarrassing squeak that escapes me has the bonus of making the crew laugh, easing a little of the tension that's been building dramatically. I love me some drama, but not like this.

Even if it's kind of nice to know people would worry about me. Not a future many orphans get to so much as dream of.

"I'll make sure there's warm grog waiting when you get back," Ros promises, and she beams when I wink at her gratefully.

Yen marches right up to me and takes hold of my belt, yanking me toward her. She pulls me to one side to see where my knife always sits and then tugs me to the other side where I am suddenly ashamed there is no knife. "You have no idea what's down there." Yen pulls one of her blades loose from where they've been at home on her hips since the day we met; the only time I've ever seen them loosed is when she fully intends to insert them into another person. This time, it gets slipped into my belt, and she narrows eyes as dark as the night sky, even darker than Max's and a few shades darker than her skin, at me. "You'd better have an idea of what happens up here if you lose my knife."

"Promise I'll take care of it," I assure her, then drop a kiss on her forehead. She wipes her skin off with all the disgust I'd expect, but she fails to hide her smile entirely.

"Alright." I take a breath, inhaling the salty tang of the sea, bringing it even further into my veins than it always has been. It's the one thing that's always been able to soothe me, no matter what and no matter where. If I can smell the ocean, even if I can't see it, something inside me settles. "Tevin, you have control of the deck while I'm gone. Dava, you have control of the Tevin."

"I'm on it," she laughs. When she approaches me, she takes the opportunity to tighten the rope a bit and then does the same to the braid my hair is pulled back into. I get a once over, and I hear her take in a breath, like she's inhaling me. Like she needs the comfort.

"I'll be right back," I tell her.

"You'd damn well better be." I'm the one blushing this time when she leans down to cover the couple inches between us and kisses my cheek. "Be careful and quick, Eli."

Tevin doesn't leave me hanging or without a blush for more than a second, wrapping his arm around my waist and tugging my back up against his barrel chest. He kisses the other cheek, the twins always opposites even if they aren't trying, except without knowing it, Tevin whispers the exact same thing in my ear that his sister just did. And then he makes it even better by adding, "Love you, E."

"Love you too, Tev. Now get off me. You're making me look like a sap in front of this big, brash pirate crew." Tevin laughs, and I spin around to kiss the smile before it fades, before I have to jump overboard.

"Okay, everyone to work. We don't all need to stand here and watch," Dava calls. It confuses me for a second since I thought they would stand here and watch me dive in at least— they usually do. But then I remember how smart that woman is. She's creating space for me and Max. Even Tevin and Jak, who are going to stand here and watch the rope while I'm under, can do that from a dozen feet away.

"Hey, you. Come here." I sidle up to Max, delighting in his soft laugh, and wrap my arms around him. "Lean on me."

"Love to," he murmurs. He presses himself against me—gods, he feels good—and I happily take on enough of his weight so he can wrap his arms around my neck. It leaves the crutches dangling at my back from his wrists, but they aren't bothering me at all. Not that I think much of anything could keep me from a chance to kiss him.

Max lets out a soft moan that makes me hot all over and then breaks the kiss far too soon. "Are you trying to distract me from wondering why it's a good idea that you dive down there? It sounds a little suicidal to me, but no one is saying bye so…"

"They aren't saying bye 'cause they know I'll be back. You'll have to trust me on this, Maxy. I'll be back. I always come back, don't I?"

He studies me, deep brown eyes flicking back and forth between mine. Instead of answering, he kisses me again and murmurs against my lips, "Always come back, Eli. Okay?"

"I promise," I whisper, holding him tighter. Almost too tight. If anything happens to him, it'll break me. I know exactly what he feels right now and how it'll feel. And I know it scares the crap out of me. "I really think I need a dunk in this cold water now."

"Yeah?" Max laughs, hugging me tighter; I've never been so glad working on ships my whole life made me build enough muscle to hold his weight easily. "If you make it back safely, Captain…I'll warm you up more than any grog ever could."

"Oh, that's an excellent incentive." I kiss him again, re-memorizing the feel of his mouth against mine, the way he tastes, the vanilla and mint scent of him, the way his lithe and lean body feels in my arms. I know I'll be back, but just in case…I want Max to be in my mind, in all my senses. And I want him in my bed when I get back.

I let Max control the pace of getting his legs steady under him again, and once he's solid, I have to force myself to step back. I only risk one more look at him, taking in Max in the moonlight, and then I'm over the side. I let the sea take me, certain that at least in this, I can do the right thing.

Chapter 15

Max

The ocean out here is nothing like I'm used to. Near the docks, the water is too dark to see more than a few inches down even during the day. There's always a slightly fishy smell to it, and it's is never completely calm with all the movement, either from ships in port or from people walking on the docks just above the sea. I've been to beaches, and there, the waves are a constant disruption to the surface, but the smell is better—more salt than fish.

Out here... Now, I understand why Eli has always been so enamored with the sea.

The ship is anchored above the deep caves that I led the crew to. Around us, there is no thrashing or even rolling; it's a steady, soothing lull. Like the water doesn't have anywhere that it needs to be and is content just existing. The scent is salty and tangy, and even after adjusting to it, a slight breeze can always sweep it up again. The weather even has a smell out here. Magic still doesn't, but I'm not going to be the one who tells Eli that.

The most incredible thing about the ocean here, though, is the color. I've seen paintings where people colored the water in greens and blues, but I don't think I ever really believed it until seeing it for myself. The water tonight, under the nearly full moon hanging directly above us, is an incredible green, a color I've never seen in nature before. And even in just the light of the moon, I can see far deeper into the water than I ever knew was possible. Far enough to watch Eli swim...and I'm not sure that's a good thing.

They dive under the surface almost as soon as they're in the water, and they swim with confidence I can read on them even from here. Like they're comfortable down there somehow. I know how to swim in theory, but without truly effective use of my legs, it's a challenge. I'm a big fan of floating, getting all the weight of the world off my joints and limbs, but swimming? Diving underwater with the intent the get even further under? That seems kind of wild to me. And watching the love of my life do that wild thing isn't exactly a comfortable experience.

When Eli gets deep enough to disappear from view, I have to turn away. That's enough of that. I'll look back when I can see their face above water again.

"Can't leave it too loose, else they could lose it." Jak and Tevin have control of the rope wrapped around Eli. A harness and a guide, they said.

"You know Eli," Tevin counters. "If it's not tight enough that they're aware of it, they might get anxious about it falling off and get distracted down there."

Jak scoffs at that. "The only time that dickhead doesn't panic is in a crisis."

I'm impressed at how well Jakgrout knows his captain, especially considering their intentionally antagonist relationship. He's absolutely right. Eli is the most anxious person I know; they can work themself up into a panic over something that has not happened and might never happen. But in a real crisis, in any sort of event where most other people are panicking, Eli is the one I want in change. They slip into a totally calm, controlled mode that they can never achieve at any other time. It's truly impressive. It's also more than a little heartbreaking to know why; most of Eli's life and all of their formative years were spent in constant chaos, so that's a standard, almost stable, existence for them.

I should try and let that soothe me about where they are right now.

Tevin, at least, laughs. "You're not wrong," he agrees, then looks up enough to see me watching them. "All good, Maxy?"

"I'm good," I answer, making my way over on legs that are more tired now. The adrenaline of waiting for the dive has worn off, and I'll need to shift into my chair soon. "So, you two will stay and take care of the rope the whole time? That's your job on dives like this?"

I only ask to learn more about the ship, the crew, the procedure. In the near future, with the other elements we need to collect, I'd like to be given a job more significant than waiting while things like this are happening. I'll need to show Eli I understand expectations and limits to be able to convince them of that, though. But Tevin and Jak exchange a glance, almost wary.

"It's a little different this time," Tevin answers. We haven't spent all that much time together yet, but we're getting closer all the time. We're close enough by now that I know when they're hedging around saying something. Tevin is hiding something from me.

"Jak?" I press, going for the one of them who is much more blunt and more likely to tattle on Eli. I just *know* Eli is involved in whatever is happening.

He huffs out a breath and says, "Eli ain't worn a harness on most'a these dives before, and we ain't watched the rope the whole time. 'Specially not both of us. They wanted new procedures tonight."

"Oh. Because of the element? Or...where we are?" Neither of the answers me, and I have to resist the urge to huff like a child. "Tell me it's because of the element!"

"We all know it's not, Max," Tevin says softly, giving me a sympathetic look.

"Is this supposed to make me feel better?" I ask, lifting one hand briefly from my crutches to motion toward the rope. "It's like a show or something?"

"Supposed to make their chances of coming back even better than usual," Jak answers gruffly. "Making sure they ain't gonna risk leaving you without 'em."

Well...damn them, that's actually kind of sweet. "Wait, but what if they'd died in the ocean while I wasn't on the ship? It was okay to take extra risks then? Why is that logical?"

Tevin laughs. "You were expecting logic from Eli?"

I hate that I can't help laughing, too, but I still roll my eyes and hang on to being annoyed about this. I intend to do so until I can give Eli a piece of my mind about it. "You two had better plan to put that ridiculous rope diaper on them for every dive from now until eternity," I inform them, turning away and aiming for my chair. I'm gonna sit right here and wait for that butthead treasure hunter to get back up here and explain themself.

And then I'll thank them for being extra careful. And for coming back to me.

Maybe I'll let go of being annoyed about their recklessness when I'm not around so long as they come back to me.

Chapter 16
Eli

For as long as I live, I will never admit to trying to hide from a fucking shark.

One of nature's most perfect predators, a beast much more capable of surviving and thriving down here than I am, and I tried to hide from it behind a rock from it. It doesn't work, of course. The shark absolutely sees me, and of course, it comes over to explore me. I've seen sharks before, I've even swam with them before, and I know them to be curious creatures. Apex predators, of course, but curious in the same way cats and dogs are.

For a second, I almost start swimming back to the surface instead of dealing with this, instead of risking anything further. Can't remember the last time I even thought about bailing on a treasure hunt. Not just for being treasure-obsessed and for all the death wishes that come with that but for being too stubborn to back down and too traumatized to risk a loss of gold. But here I am, thinking about it pretty damn seriously.

It's Max. Max is on board, on the ship whose shadow is no longer able to reach me at this depth, though the moonlight is still effective enough. Max's presence nearby, not just at home and waiting but *right there*, makes me think about risk. About whether a risk is worth it. New feeling for me, and it's not one I like.

Too stubborn to know better, I swallow that down and push myself back to work. Max brought me here, for fuck's sake. I'm down here now, waiting for a shark to decide I'm uninteresting and inedible, because this is where Max's magic led us. This is where I'm going to find another element of the god, a legend in real life. Max would be disappointed if I went back up there. Probably insulted, too.

Carefully and slowly, not daring to make any rapid movements, I release my knife from my belt and keep it in-hand. Yen will become an apex predator if I lose her knife in the side of a shark or because the fucking thing ate it, so I'm not touching that blade unless it's a last possible resort. I start swimming slowly backward, moving my arms and legs in slow, fluid motion instead of rapid kicks, keeping my eye on the shark at all times.

The caves are very close now, but I can't waste much more time. I'm good at holding my breath, but I'm not magical. The second the shark turns away and shows disinterest, I send up a thanks to gods I don't much care for and haul ass into the caves where Max said I need to be.

The light doesn't reach more than a few inches into the entrance, which means I'm exploring by feel mostly. I swat at a fish that comes too close to my face, both of us hampered by the dark, and start dragging my fingers through the sand. If I have to really dig, I'll need to retreat for multiple breaths. The more times I have to go up and down, the more likely the crew is to suggest a break. If Max suggests it, I won't argue—I'm stubborn, but I'm not that strong.

"Fuck!" escapes me before my rational brain can register that letting the air out is so foolish, but I don't think I can be blamed when something just smacked me in the face. A fin or tail. The cave is full of fish, constantly brushing my face, my arms, my body, my legs. I've done a lot of cave diving and never found them in the dark like this…meaning something drew them here. And magic can definitely create that kind of draw.

I don't have much more air, much more time. Knowing that soothes me—pressure I can handle. I feel around in the fish instead of the sand, letting them lead me to a wall. It's warmer here. I'm close, so close, the feel of a treasure at hand sending heat surging through my veins like nothing else. It's here, and I'm about to have my hands on it, and gods, this is what I live for.

The second my fingers wrap around an oval-shaped piece of something much heavier than it should be for the size, a familiar spark ignites inside me. The same spark I've felt every time I've recovered a piece of treasure since the first time when I was just a kid playing on the shore. And nothing has ever been more valuable than the treasures I'm after now.

I use the weirdly textured wall for a boost, turning to kick off it and toward the moonlight that marks my escape. The shark gets a quick bid for my attention and probably needs more since I'll be swimming up and they attack from below, but the scream for air coming from my lungs is a much more immediate concern. It'd be intensely embarassing to drown down here with the treasure in my hand; at least dying by shark is a badass story.

It better not eat the element, too. My crew has a job to finish.

My legs start to ache by the time I can see the ship waiting for me, *Tempest* a haven from these depths. It's cold down here, and my muscles need air, and I need to get up there quickly. I avoid tugging on the rope for fear it'll change my direction, keep me under here even a second longer. My brain and body are demanding a breath, willing to risk the sure death that would come with taking that breath underwater.

It's right there—the surface, the ship, Max, the future. I shut my eyes and scrunch up my face, keeping my mouth from opening on its own, on poorly reasoned instinct.

I explode out of the water, still kicking, grasping for a solid surface on the waves, gasping for air. The cold smacks me in the face like it has the teeth of that shark, but I force my eyes open again to find them. *Tempest* and her crew and Max, all of them at the edge, watching me and calling for me. Calling for the element.

Freezing fucking cold and still unable to stop gasping, I hold the orb up over my head. Victorious over the sea once more.

Chapter 17

Max

"It's been too long."

Whatever relief I might feel at someone else confirming my fears instantly fades at Tevin's words. It's been too long. Eli has been under too long.

"Can they...can they come back up if they need to?" I ask, realizing the question might be foolish even as I say it. Instead of making someone answer me that, yes, Eli could change direction if needed, I ask, "They'd tug on the rope if they needed help, wouldn't they?"

"That's the idea," Yen notes, leaning well over the ship rail to look down into the water. We can't see as far down as Eli went, but all of us are staring at the glassy green surface and the way the moonlight moves underneath it. "Whether they would tug it is a different story."

"Stubborn dickhole," Jak mutters, and it

almost makes me laugh.

"It's cold; they're gonna move slower when it's cold," Dava reminds us. It's intended to be comforting—I know that just because it's Dava who said it—but I'm not really sure it comforts me. No one else looks comforted either, Dava included.

"There's a warm drink waiting in their quarters," Ros says. She was in the kitchen until about a minute ago, her arrival on the deck a signal that we all should have expected Eli back already. "And whiskey. Whiskey's good for warming."

I rock my chair back and forth a little, the only thing I can do in the chair that has the same mental effect as pacing around a room. Tevin is tapping his left foot loudly, and though I don't think either of them is aware of it, Dava is standing six feet away and tapping her right in the same rhythm but softer. Yen is now leaning so far over the railing that I think she might fall in, the entire upper half of her body dangling over water. Ros has one hand on my leg, not bothered by my movement, and she's biting the nails on her other hand; tomorrow, she'll complain about the state of her nails like she doesn't know she did the damage herself. Jak keeps muttering silently to himself, mouth just moving a little, and every few seconds, he slams a fist down on the wooden rail. I'm pretty sure he's cursing Eli out in his mind.

I'm sitting between all of them, centered with the opening for the ladder that Eli will climb back up. Jak and Tevin are on my right with the others on my left. The tension is thicker than any fog I've ever experienced, barely anyone taking a breath or blinking. If Eli were here, they'd know what to do, what to say. Eli—

Eli bursts out of the water, coming up in a rush and with a gasp that's so loud, we can hear it from the deck and over the loud splash. They hold something up in the air in one hand, a triumphant look on their face, but I barely notice the thing, and no one else so much as reacts to it. Of course Eli thinks we're all standing here waiting for the rock in their hand; they have no idea what they really mean to the people who love them.

Those people are jumping into action right now. I shift back a little and guide a frozen Rosleigh with me. The other four know what they're doing to get Eli out of the water as quickly as possible, and much as I want them back in my arms as soon as possible, I'm not about to get in the way.

Eli's lips are blue, and I can see how hard they're shaking the second they start to emerge onto the deck. Dava has a towel waiting that she wraps firmly around their shoulders, and Tevin is rubbing their arms vigorously, but Eli stands there with teeth chattering and legs practically wobbling, just staring at me. And the element of the gods is still in their fist, waiting to be acknowledged. They need to hear it.

I force a smile, shoving down my fear and my worry—neither of them relieved by Eli returning to the ship in this condition. "I told you it'd be down there," I tease.

"I told you I'd get it," they quip right back. Gods, even their voice sounds cold. That's enough.

"Okay, bed—now," I announce, turning my chair and pointing toward the door below deck. Jak is given the element and Eli is herded inside, the rest of the crew waving away whatever concerns their captain attempts as an excuse not to take the rest of the night off and warming up. Tevin steers them toward the door and down the ramp, looking back to make sure I'm good on the way down and into the captain's quarters. "Tevin, will you get them some dry clothes out? And are there extra blankets on the ship?"

"On it. I'll have Yen heat up some water bottles." Tevin kisses Eli's cheek and then hurries out of the room, shutting the door behind him though we both know Eli wouldn't think to check.

"I'm fine," Eli protests before I can say a word, which is a good sign that they are not. They look around, shaking even harder now, and admit, "Don't know where to sit, though."

"Don't sit yet, E. Let's get you out of all these clothes. Come here." I don't make them move even though I said it and then change my mind, pointing to the wooden chest that holds my clothes. "Sit there."

With Eli sitting, I have much better access to them, and Eli doesn't resist when I start peeling absolutely frigid, soaking wet clothes off them. For the first time, I want to curse them for wearing such tight clothes, though they didn't dress casually for jumping into the ocean at least. Instead of that, I get Eli to tell me about their dive so I can make sure they're at least breathing now.

"I think fish are attracted to the elements," they inform me, and before I can ask questions, they babble on, likely just talking to keep themself warm and awake. Tevin walks back in as I start working their shorts off from where they're clinging to their legs and they say, "It was in one of the caves, like you said. Followed the fish—that helped. Shark didn't help much."

Shark? I look over at Tevin, tucking those hot water bottles under the blankets on the bed; he looks like he wishes he hadn't heard that detail either.

"We're gonna talk about the shark in the morning," I tell Eli, grateful that they didn't wear anything like shoes down there now that I can work their shorts and briefs off without extra effort or bending. I'm generally okay with who I am and how I am, especially now that I've transitioned and started medications to help with that, but right now, I wish I had the kind of body that would let me stand up, scoop Eli into my arms, and carry them to bed. It's what they'd do for me.

I don't have to do that right now, though. I don't have to be the one who does that, and the realization makes me feel light. I turn to Tevin and ask, "Can you please help them into bed?"

"My pleasure," he rumbles, grinning at me, and I swear his expression is grateful. That seems ridiculous all things considered. If anything, I'm grateful to have another piece of this partnership, especially one who balances me out in moments like this.

In moments, Eli is in bed, almost completely tucked under the blankets, sandwiched between me and Tevin. They moan and pull both of us closer with ice cold, trembling hands, Tevin at their back and with arms long enough to hold both of us. Eli tucks their head under my chin, and I don't even mind that their hair is wet. Tevin and I just lay there with them, running our warmer hands all over them, staying as close as possible. They finally start to feel normal to the touch—not their usual temperature but like a person instead of an icicle on legs—before they fall asleep, breathing slowly and deeply.

Breathing. Safe on *Tempest*, successful from a treasure hunt, sound asleep and warm. There's nothing more I could ask for.

"I really like having you on board, Maxy," Tevin says very softly, smiling at me over Eli's mess of blonde hair; it's going to give them hell in the morning. The golden flecks in Tevin's eyes are glittering in the low light from the gas lamps on the wall above us. "Eli would have fought me so hard on all that."

I laugh quietly, not daring to wake them, and note, "But I couldn't have carried them into bed. We were both needed."

"We're a good team. All three of us."

"A good partnership," I agree, and Tevin's smile spreads from ear to ear. I lean forward a little, offering my mouth, and he kisses me softly. I then kiss Eli's hair and their forehead, hug them closer, and snuggle into sleep with both of them.

I have so much more than I'd ever dare to ask for.

Chapter 18

Max

Once I get going on a map, everything just... flows. It's all a completely natural, open, easy movement between the magic inside me and the runes that charge my pen, down through my hand and into the ink, all of it linked into the creation of the image I need.

When I was little and first started to master this, I didn't get a mental image. Until I was looking at an almost finished map, I had no idea where I was sending my client, no clue where the missing item really was. Now, I get a mental image as soon as I get my hands on the item I'm using an anchor. A picture of where to find it, the path from the anchor to the missing piece. And once that mental image forms, I find it almost impossible to think about anything else.

That's probably why Eli has to come all the way around their own desk, kneel beside me,

C. Knight

and then touch my knee to actually get my attention. Even then, it startles the hell out of me—so much that the pen falls right out of my hand, and I let out an extremely embarrassing yelp.

"I tried my hardest not to scare you!" Eli says, wincing as they grab my pen from where it rolled away. They hand it over quickly, knowing I'll want to make sure I didn't hurt it. Fortunately, I didn't hurt it. Or myself. "I swear, I said your name at least a dozen times before I touched you."

"No, no, I'm not angry—of course I'm not," I assure them, catching their hand and squeezing it. My heart is still racing a bit from being startled, so I pull their palm to my mouth and kiss it, their touch settling both of us. "We both know I can get a little...obsessive."

"Absorbed," they correct gently, smiling at me from where they're still kneeling beside me. They're being kind because we both know the truth. At times, I have forgotten to eat or sleep or move or use the bathroom for *hours* while working on maps. Sometimes, I get sucked way too far in, and I can't think about anything *but* making the map. It's really nice to have someone around who checks, who asks where I am. When Eli isn't home, I don't have that.

When Eli isn't home, I don't have anyone.

"Do I want to know how long I've been in here?" I ask, daring a look toward the window. At least it's still light out, the sun shining through the window over the bed.

"Did you come here right after breakfast?" I nod, and they echo it while shifting to sit on the edge of my desk. Their desk. Our desk? "Then

152

about four hours. Not even close to your record, baby."

"That's a good thing," I laugh.

Eli picks up the little volcanic stone turtle that they gifted me recently; it has made a home on the edge of my desk, living beside my ink well and always in my line of sight. They smile at it now and look almost surprised, like they didn't think I'd cherish such a thoughtful gift enough to bring it. Turtles belong at sea.

"Well, you're taking a break now. In fact..." The way they grin tells me that I'm in trouble. "You are under order from your captain to go take a break. Get out of this room, move around the ship, talk to people, eat and drink."

I narrow my eyes at them, though I can't manage to muster up any real heat, and I'm certain they can tell I'm fighting off a smile. "You're really going to enjoy taking advantage of the whole 'captain of the ship' thing with me, aren't you?"

"Oh, you have no idea, Maxy." They lean down and plant a kiss on my head before brushing the curls back from my forehead and getting to their feet. They motion to me. "Do you want to stay in the chair for a while or grab your crutches?"

The ship underwent a lot of work to make sure I can move around comfortably, and I'm still in awe of how quickly Jak was able to do things like change every door from opening into the wall to opening into the room. I can move around pretty easily with either method, and I know Eli isn't going to judge me one way or the other, but an opportunity to stretch a little sounds nice.

"I'll use the crutches, I think. But I can't get up to the deck on them."

"Then I'll put your chair right by the ramp for you; just leave the crutches in the hall to deal with later." I open my mouth to argue about leaving something in the way, but Eli immediately adds, "They aren't going to be in the way; everyone else on the ship is more than capable of picking the crutches up and moving them, and they'd be happy to do that for you. Plus, you need sunshine. Travel on a ship does weird things with time, and I don't want you to suddenly realize you haven't had any direct sunlight in days."

"Ros mentioned that, too. I'll remember." I give them a smile—which is much easier than trying to scowl at them. "Thank you for looking out for me, Captain."

"Anything for you." I get a kiss on the mouth this time, and then I take a moment to check out their shapely ass when they turn and head for the crutches that are resting against the wall. I follow them and happily accept the help standing up—especially because once I'm standing, I can feel exactly how long I've been sitting still and hunched over the map.

"It's almost done, by the way," I tell them. "The map. I'll be done tonight."

"You're incredible. Now get out."

Eli's quarters—the captain's quarters, a status they worked so hard to achieve—are near the back of the ship. I'm sure there's a technical term for its location, but that's not for me to worry about. It's near the back of the ship at the end of a hallway. The other doors in the hall lead to the kitchen and a few rooms for storage—food, tools, extra equipment. There's one that has weapons inside which I choose to ignore; I've chosen to ignore the weapons that they all carry, too. Eli is kind enough not to make me watch them with a pistol.

I aim for the kitchen first, knowing that I'll find a little ball of sunshine inside. Most of the doors on the ship open and close with a doorknob, and they stay open once pushed. But the kitchen door swings, which makes getting through it more challenging; Eli and the crew have taken to propping the door open so I can get in and out safely. The open door also means I can hear Rosleigh humming from down the hall.

Eli and I met Ros when we were living temporarily in a little village further north. The area was a bit too determined to keep to its natural roots for me to get around safely, or else Rosleigh's presence alone might have been enough to convince me to settle down there. She's a halfling, a chef, and the happiest person I have ever met—the happiest person anyone will ever meet, I'm willing to bet. Nothing gets to her or gets her down.

She's amazing in the kitchen, especially when she doesn't have much to work with, so I wasn't surprised when Eli asked her to join their crew or that she accepted. It soothed me, really, to know before they ever left that Eli would have at least one person around who I knew and who would make them smile.

I step into the kitchen as Ros is turning from the stove; it's one of the biggest appliances like it I have ever seen, and Eli warned me just once that I didn't want the answer about how they got a hold of the equipment their ship chef swore she couldn't function without. Considering the quality of the meals I've had so far, the quality of food I can be sure my partner is eating even when they aren't home, I'm not going to ask and risk upsetting myself over something that is a net positive.

"Maxy!" she chirps when she spots me. She then immediately disappears from view as she steps down off the stool she uses to reach into the oven safely. She reappears at the counter a moment later, using a different stool to set down the small pot she's carrying. "I was hoping to see you today. I don't want you in there working non-stop, okay?"

"Promise," I assure her, coming to the opposite side of the island counter. For the moment, I lean against it instead of sitting, resting my weight on my crutches to carefully stretch my legs a bit. Though a lot of me got stretched wonderfully this morning.

I'm blushing and trying to hide thoughts of the fun I had celebrating last night's dive with Eli and Tevin in the pre-dawn hours when Ros says, "Oh, I thought I might have to bribe you. Which is why there are some treats under there." She turns and points toward a tray resting on the counter in front of me, which I lean over to snag and pull closer.

"I don't need to be bribed, but I do always need treats." Especially treats that smell this wonderful. I spot chocolate, various fruits, and caramel all baked into round and square shapes of various sizes and colors. I don't ask questions before popping one into my mouth, and even then, I still don't have questions about the food.

"Did Eli tell you I'd work too much? They complain about that sometimes."

"I wouldn't call it complaining so much as caring," she counters, looking over her shoulder now to grin at me. When I roll my eyes, she laughs; the sound is like a bell tinkling, and I adore it. "They told us that you take your craft very seriously and tend to get lost in it. They can get pretty busy, so they asked us to help make sure you came up for air at times."

"Oh. Well, I guess I can't complain about that." I wouldn't even if I could. I know I'm lucky to have someone like them, even if Eli would argue that they're the lucky one.

"Eli works pretty hard too, huh?" The question doesn't come from a place of doubt; I know without having been a ship before that the captain has a lot of responsibility. I also know Eli, so I know they don't like to be idle, and they can't stand feeling like they aren't contributing. I hear stories about their time on the ship, but I don't get to be part of Eli's daily life anymore. I have a chance now to see it and to learn more about it, and I'm eager.

"They do," Ros answers with a nod, bobbing her head repeatedly even after the nodding could be done; she's now moving to a song in her head, I'm sure. "There's always something to be done on a ship, and Eli likes to take on most of it themself—when they aren't spending time with you or Tevin, or if they aren't making Jakgrout angry, of course. Somehow, Eli always finds time in the day for trouble."

I laugh and note, "Eli has been like that since we were kids. They can't sit still, and they can't stay out of trouble."

"That's our captain," she giggles. She turns all the way around to face me now, smile stretching from ear to ear. "They're a good person and a good captain. Not like some of the others out here. But you knew that about them. You should know they're much happier with you here, though."

My face falls a little, even though I try to school my expression. "Eli hasn't been happy?"

"Oh! No, that's not what I meant!" She shakes her head so vigorously that her pigtails start flying. "No, no! They love being out here—happier on the water than at port—but they're happiest when you're around. They miss you is all. I'm sorry I misspoke."

"No, you didn't," I assure her, waving it off and snagging another treat; I refuse to count how many I've already eaten. "I worry about them, that's all. It's nice to be here and get to see them, see that they're okay for myself. I'm not sure it'll be nice if something dangerous pops up but..."

I shrug, and Ros offers me a sympathetic smile before mirroring that shrug. It's a simple gesture from a really good friend who knows me well and knows that I don't love not being able to plan. We also both know that Eli is going to be more anxious than I am. They've battled intense anxiety for as long as I've known them; somehow, they can spend hours and even days worrying about things that have not happened and may never happen. I wish I could protect them from their own brain, and I don't know if being here will make it worse or better. I have to hope it's better, though.

Ros hops down from that stool and moves to another in front of a long cabinet, searching through it for who knows what. I'd like to know what. "Ros, would you mind if I help sometimes? You know I love cooking, and I don't want to invade your space but—"

"I would love that!" she cheers, whirling around so fast I'm surprised she doesn't face plant right off that stool. She then frowns so quickly after just beaming at me that it's almost comical. "Are you sure you can use this kitchen? I know you have yours at home all laid out. Oh, but we can move things here!"

I wave it off. "There's no need to move things around. We'll figure it out as we go. Me and you have always worked well together, Ros."

"We have." The smile is back, much to my relief and delight. Someone so kind and happy never deserves a frown. "We'll make it work, yes. Dinner tonight?"

"I will let you know. Just let me...make sure I'm not too sore by then." I flash a smile just in case that scares her and add, "And let me make sure that your captain isn't in need of my attention by then."

Ros laughs and gives me a huge dramatic wink. I get steady on my feet again and let her get back to work, aiming further down the hallway this time when I leave the kitchen again. Halfway down the hall is a stairwell that leads down. My understanding is that there is one large, open space down there, and it's the crew quarters. The only person with their own space is Eli, which seems like a great deal of prestige. I don't think the others are used to anything else, though, and as far as I've seen, none of them are complaining.

I think about going down there and seeing who is around, making conversation and getting to know the whole crew in their natural environment instead of when they're in my apartment, but if I go all the way down there to find no one in their quarters, I'll have wasted the energy and need to get back up. Maybe if I make my way around further and miss someone, then I can head down there and find them.

I'm not the least bit disappointed about walking away when I hear Tevin's laugh coming from the far end of the hall where the other 'office' on the ship is. Eli calls it that to avoid fights between Jak, Tevin, and Dava who all claim they need the entire space for different reasons related to their role on the ship. Now, it's an office that smells like sawdust and has a workbench covered in Jakgrout's tools, ledgers and books and sheets that allow Dava to coordinate and manage the ship's inventory and expenses, and a desk shoved into a corner for the dozens of things Tevin seems to have his hands in. It's a crowded space anyway but especially with the orc twins inside.

They both beam at me when I appear in the doorway. "Oh, good, you came out on your own and we don't have to drag you out," Tevin teases.

I roll my eyes. Eli told everyone that I'm a workaholic, apparently. No one is mentioning that I'm not on the chore schedule that the rest of the crew has to stick to, the list that keeps them busier than I'm going to be. And with that thought, I ask, "Am I interrupting anything?"

"Just my brother being a tool," Dava answers, and that's an answer I should have expected. "How's the map magic coming?"

"Really well. I'll only need a couple more hours to finish it, so I'm planning to get it into Eli's hands before dinner tonight."

Tevin nods happily. "Perfect. It's a good thing Eli pulled their head out of their ass and asked you to join the crew finally. Like I told them to months ago."

"It wasn't months," Dava counters, scoffing at him. "And it's not Eli's fault that they suspected part of the reason you told them to bring Max on is because you have a crush on him."

"Well, that was part of it." Tevin winks, and my cheeks heat up instantly. I was holding onto at least a tiny bit of hope that now that we've seen each other naked, I wouldn't blush so much and so easily; I now think that I'll be red-faced around him forever. But it might be worth it for more nights and mornings like we've been having...

And of course, that thought only makes me blush harder.

"Your partner is at the helm if you were looking for them." Dava gives me a soft smile, far less teasing than the kind of grin her brother usually gives me. They look quite a bit alike, but that's about all they have in common. "I'm sure they'll be happy to see you if you make your way up there."

"I think I will do that. Thank you. See you both later?"

"Of course," Dava agrees, and Tevin gives me another blush-worthy smile. That's unfair.

I head down the hall, taking my time so I

161

don't risk falling. Eli is not going to handle me getting injured on the ship very well, but walking on a moving ship which is on a moving sea takes some getting used to—especially when using crutches. And I guess I don't want to get hurt for my own benefit too. Mostly Eli, though.

"Hey, you." I pause while passing a room I'd thought was empty. On second glance, I realize that there is a figure sitting in the dim candlelight at the far end. Yen, of course. She would hang around in dark, silent spaces. Adds to the legend she's creating. One that she seems to deserve.

"Hi." I step inside, examining the room that looks like it exists to hold more weapons. I don't want anything to do with the bags marked as gunpowder, though since Yen has a lantern lit in here, I can assume they aren't too volatile. Or at least I can hope. "Why are you hiding in here?"

"I'm not hiding," she laughs. "I like to get out of the sun when I can. And I like to sharpen my knives alone." She shrugs a bit, and I notice then that she's running a menacing-looking blade along a strap of what looks like leather to me. But what the hell do I know about sharpening a knife with a hook on the edge that I just *know* has some horrifying purpose.

"Oh, I'm sorry. I can leave you be," I offer, starting to turn, but Yen shakes her head and kicks at the barrel sitting across from her, making it rock a little.

"You're good company. Sit."

It feels like quite the compliment from Yen, to be welcomed into her peace and her space. She's a very kind person, and no matter how dangerous she is, I have no doubt that if I asked her for any favor in the world, she'd find a way to do it for me just because she wants to be good to the people that she cares about. I've seen her laugh, and I've seen how easily she can make other people laugh. But Yen feels… different to me. Untouchable, maybe. I can't say that it's because of how she acts or treats me, more just that I feel like she deserves that status.

"How are you settling in, Maxy?" she asks. I grin at the nickname that seems to have infiltrated the entire crew; I don't mind.

"Good, I think. Ros was pretty sure I'd throw up at least a few times, and that hasn't happened. I think Eli was sure I'd fall a few times, and that hasn't happened either. Feels like I'm winning so far."

"Congratulations," she laughs. "The bar is low when you first get on a ship. It was a big adjustment for me. Don't tell anyone about this"— she punctuates that with a look that makes me damn sure I'd better never tell anyone even though she's smiling—"but I did throw up at first. A lot."

"I forgot that you weren't on ships before joining Eli," I admit, setting back against the wall so I can take any weight off my feet. Yen could probably catch me before I hit the floor if the barrel rolls or gives, but I feel pretty steady. "They've always been on or near ships, like they were drawn to them. I forget that it's not the same for everyone."

Yen shrugs a little. She hasn't lost her rhythm, and the light *shoosh* of the blade skimming down the leather is soothing; I see what she means about being alone to sharpen her

163

knives. "It wasn't the ship that drew me in. If I could have joined the crew for adventure on land, I'd have been just as interested." She flashes me a smile that makes her eyes catch the flame between us. "It's all about the treasure for me. Cap loves the adventure, and I love the reward."

"And there is nothing wrong with that," I laugh. I didn't grow up wanting, and even when Eli and I were finding our own way, we never really suffered. My parents were there as a safety net too had we needed it. But I saw enough, heard enough, watched Eli go through enough to know that financial security is nothing to turn your nose up at. Every piece of gold, every reward and every ounce of treasure, goes toward making *Tempest*'s crew and captain—and me, by extension—financially secure and stable.

I know Eli inside and out. I know them better than anyone. I know that if given the choice between an extremely exciting adventure in new parts of the world or a fairly standard but better-paying adventure with a huge reward, Eli would be inclined to follow the excitement. Maybe having someone like Yen around to pull them toward the reward is not such a bad thing. So long as Eli still gets their adventure eventually.

I spend a couple more minutes with Yen, never daring to ask what the hook on that knife is for. We talk about adjusting to the ship, and she promises to show me her hometown someday. Neither of us dares to mention that I'd have to stay on the ship a while for that to be feasible. I don't take up too much of her time, though. I want Yen to get the peace she was seeking in here, and I want to see our captain.

As promised, my wheelchair is waiting in the hall for me to transfer into. I have to get some leverage by backing down the hall a bit before tackling the ramp, but I don't mind at all. This is a much easier, faster way to access Eli in the middle of the day, and on a whim is far better than the way I've needed to access them for the last few years. Eli is right there, close by and available for at least a hello, whenever I want. I think that's something about being on the ship that I could very easily get used to.

I find Eli by sound more than sight, arriving on the deck and hearing their distinctive voice humming. They're humming a song that they've sung and whistled to around our house since we moved in when a neighbor happened to be singing it; sometimes, I think they've had it stuck in their head for all these years since. Apparently, it doesn't even leave them alone at sea.

"You whistle at home but hum on the ship?" I ask, moving to where I can see them leaning on the small rail that sits behind the wheel.

Their head flies up, and they beam at me. "Look at you, roaming the deck! You look damn good in the sun at sea, you know that?"

"Yes," I answer, though I also roll my eyes dramatically. They laugh, roll up the papers they were looking at and tuck them into their pocket, then hop the railing to come down to me. As much I appreciate that their need to hug and kiss me even makes the few stairs seem too long, I wince a little and look back up at the wheel. "Shouldn't someone be steering?"

"There's a lock to keep us in the right direction. And we are in the middle of the sea." They kiss my forehead and help me up out of the seat to sit on a barrel full of gods know what. "And there's no whistling on a ship. Especially not on deck."

"Wait, really? Why?"

"It challenges the wind." When I give them a doubtful look, they laugh. "No, really. Old pirate legend."

"Oh, but you're an adventurer, not a pirate," I tease.

"True. But I'm also no fool, and if not whistling might do anything to keep the wind on our side, I'm not going to whistle."

"An excellent point, Captain." I sneak a hand around behind them to squeeze their butt, but I end up squeezing the papers instead. "What were you working on?"

The second the question is out, I falter a little. Eli has always been very open with me about their business and their life, but I've never been around it all before, and I don't have the right to—

"Just tweaking the ship charter a bit," they answer, pulling those papers out and unrolling them to show me as if it's perfectly natural. And I guess it is. I didn't need to worry, and I try not to smile about that. "I need to make some adjustments with this newest job, especially if it goes the way I'm hoping."

"And a ship charter is..."

"Basically the rules and agreement for living on the ship. Everything from how we split up any treasure we find to everyone's role to the disciplinary stuff I hate." I laugh at their grimace but

I know they're serious, too. Eli loves being a ship captain but they never wanted to be anyone's boss. I think that's why I like this crew so much; they work with my partner, not for them. "Anyway, anyone who becomes a member of the crew has to sign it. It's *how* someone becomes an official member of the crew."

"Oh. Cool."

And then we both tense because we both know what was just said…and what wasn't.

I haven't signed the ship charter. I haven't been asked to. I shouldn't be asked to. There's a job and an apartment waiting for me back on land and a life that's been functional, comfortable. More than most people get.

I haven't signed the charter because I'm not an official member of the crew; I'm only here temporarily, and none of us knows if that's going to change.

When I look up at Eli, I know that neither of us knows if we actually want it to change.

Chapter 19

Eli

"Is this really the painting?" Tevin makes a face at the page in his hand. It was borrowed from a book Max owns...though Max didn't know I was going to tear the page out until it was too late. I wince at the memory of his pain and at the painting.

"That's it. Bigger, obviously."

I grin when Tevin gives me a dry look for clarifying we're nabbing a painting bigger than a book page.

"It's awful," Dava agrees, snagging the page from her brother's hand and slipping it into the pocket on her vest. Gods, I hope she doesn't sweat and ruin the page completely. Max'll probably kill me.

The twins are joining me tonight. Yen is a slippery little thing, fast and nimble. But a painting in a frame is heavy, and I need someone who can run while carrying it so me and Tevin can provide protection. Dava might run a lot heavier and louder than Yen, but it'll get the job done.

And it still leaves Max on the ship with protection. I don't want to think about what happens if I ever need to take Yen, Dava, and Tevin with me.

"I still find it incredibly disturbing that some rich person has had an element of the gods in storage for decades," Dava notes. "Where could they even have found it?"

"Someone found something shiny, had no idea what they really had, sold it to some fool with more gold than sense." Tevin scoffs and shakes his head. "Hate people like that."

"I'd like to become people like that," I announce, and I laugh when the two of them look at me. "Seriously. My goal is to cover the whole interior of *Tempest* in horrendous paintings of terrifyingly ugly people I've never met and don't know anything about."

"Suddenly, I hope we get caught," Dava quips, and we all have to control the volume of our laughter.

We're nearing our target but not quite in whisper range yet. These warehouses are only sporadically guarded in cities like this one that can't afford a lot of security for things like this. So someone paid a likely horrifying amount to buy a painting whose frame holds a legendary, magical, god-crafted gem only to then pay to have it stored in a warehouse...in a city with crumbling buildings and muddy paths instead of brick or stone underfoot. And the painting they stole is gross, some random pale human

man who looks like he sucked on a lemon and got smacked by a fish. Bad taste and poor decision-making.

"Max says it's the second warehouse, which means it's the second one," I remind them, now dropping to a whisper. "Tevin, you're on lookout. I'll break in, then me and you will find it, Dava. We meet Tevin and keep moving, taking the lower level of the docks."

"Oh, that's why you didn't wear your heels!" Tevin gives me a once over and shakes his head a little, failing to hide a smile; we both know he likes what he sees. "And here, Jak thought you were being sensible. Should have known you just didn't want to get your better shoes wet."

"Shoes over sensibility any day. Now let's get to work."

Dava and I tuck into the edge of an alley and watch, waiting for our signal. Tevin makes for an excellent lookout because if there are guards around, they're going show themselves to someone of his size and build. Just in case. They don't need to know Tevin wouldn't willingly hurt a fly.

When Tevin is in a position he feels gives him a view of every angle we need, he lights a cigarette. He won't smoke it—hates the things—but it's a natural enough effect. And the spark of light from the match makes for a great signal without being obvious.

Dava and I get on the move, walking directly and quickly but without hurry. We look like two people out in a dark part of the city who want to get out of that part of the city. The guards don't need to know that if there is any part of a city where two seafaring adventurers belong, it's right here. Shadows, scum, stolen treasure, us.

The lock on the warehouse is a big one, heavy. That doesn't mean it's a tougher lock to crack than any regular or cheap one, though; it only makes the people who paid for it feel that way. In my pocket—custom sewn into this skirt because I refuse to exist without pockets and don't know why tailors are so sexist—I find my kit easily. I don't pull the whole thing out and risk fumbling, making noise; I've taught myself to find the right pieces without looking.

With the right tools, this intimidating-looking lock cracks open like I just shoved a sword into a bag of flour. Makes my heart happy to know people paid a premium for this only to have an orphan with little more than their name and their ship bring everything to ruin so easily. I'm only here for a painting, but if I wanted to...

I shake off those thoughts and focus on helping Dava push the heavy door open quietly, just enough for us to get through. I know what I could do to this place, to the people whose things are stored here, if I want to. But I want to be better than that. I'm not a pirate, not a thief. I'm going to make my name for my adventuring, for the treasures I recover, not for the blood I spill in my wake. I grew up on the streets, but I'm better than those streets. Or I've become better anyway.

I've never once felt bad about stealing from the rich. Don't much think I'd feel bad about setting them on fire, actually. But Max would be disappointed in me. That threat is more effective at holding me back than anything else—my own good sense often included.

Searching through a warehouse for one painting isn't the easiest task, especially since the process with these places tends to be that the owners just put their things where they can find space. Fortunately, with Max's abilities and some research into the contents of this warehouse, purchased from a city guard smart enough to screw loyalty for coin, we know to expect a golden frame with roses in the corner. Big, obnoxious roses that stick out from behind a pile of very plane frames.

"Gods, this thing is gaudy," I groan, shaking my head. I guess I understand some skill went into creating it, but why would anyone value a painting of a really ugly man only made uglier by the gray tones used for the paint? Is this supposed to be a villain? I wouldn't want to cross him on the streets. "You good to grab it? Don't forget we have the straps if you need 'em."

"Please," she scoffs, then smiles at me. "I'll tell you if I need 'em."

"Good," I laugh. "I could carry the painting home, but I cannot carry you *and* the painting."

"Eli, I respect you as a person and a captain, I love you like family, but if you ever try to carry me"—she hefts the painting up into her arms easily, a bit longer than wide but not awkward to hold—"I will keelhaul you."

"I wouldn't lift you like a princess; I'd throw you over my shoulder!" I nudge her with my elbow, though not hard enough to risk making her drop our prize. "You're a proper gods damned sailor, and I'd treat you like it."

"Better, but my tits'll probably hang down to the ground if you turn me over your shoulder."

She adjusts the fifty-some-pound frame with little effort.

"Is that a complaint or a brag?" I double-check our path out so I can be sure she won't have to dodge or step over anything.

"You just try not to step on 'em, okay?"

I laugh and nod, slipping a dagger into the hand she can't see. Just in case. "You got it. Ready?"

One more adjustment, and then she nods. We're off with our treasure.

The second we're through the warehouse doors, I look for Tevin. Exactly where we left him. Which means things are going exactly as planned.

"I think we should hang this beauty up on the ship before we return it." Talking is normal, and we need to appear normal—especially as Tevin rejoins us. Now we look like three very muscular, tall people walking in a dark area late at night with a very large item. Normal is the goal.

Normal has never been my forte. Let's hope whatever gods give a shit about this like Tevin and Dava a whole lot more than they've ever liked me.

We get to the creaky, creepy set of wooden stairs that winds below the stone seawall and down to the lower docks. Tides are low enough that we can walk instead of swim, but we're still splashing along. Impossible to stay quiet, but chances are, anyone who hears will assume we're just vagrants searching for something to eat in what washes up.

We have to climb back up to street level to get to the ship, but once *Tempest* is in view, everything feels lighter. Home. And now, there's no caveat to that. No 'home except it doesn't have Max.' No 'home when I can't be with Max.' Max is here, so *Tempest* is a complete, full home.

And Max is waiting on deck again. I love seeing his curls highlighted by moonlight.

Tevin relieves his sister of the painting as we reach the dock and the ramp onboard, and she shakes out her arms but is otherwise unaffected by the walk. I can't breathe until Tevin disappears through the door below deck, where we can secure the treasure we so badly need. The treasure Max led us to. And then I can breathe much, much better when Max is in my arms.

His chair is on the deck, which I like, but Max is standing when we arrive, leaning on the ship rail. "Everything go okay?"

"Perfectly," I answer. I'd probably answer that way even if we did have a problem. Max doesn't need to worry about those things, doesn't need to worry about me.

I slide up behind him, wrapping my arms around his waist and leaning down to rest my chin on his shoulders. I press in close not just because I want to hold him tight but because it lets him lean back against me, get some pressure off his legs. He squeezes my hand in silent thanks for that.

"Company," Jak warns, calling from where he stands at the helm, guiding us out of the port while Dava, Yen, and Tevin handle the sails.

I first look toward land. Worst case scenario would be guards with guns that would force us to return fire; I don't want to do that in front of

Max. Also bad would be anyone asking questions, wanting to see inventory. Mostly, we could just keep going and force that person to swim or give up. But I see nothing there, no one on the docks.

That means our company is at sea. Yellow sails and a red flag—absolutely atrocious color scheme but it makes identification easy.

"*Sunbeam*," I mutter, explaining for Max and grumbling for myself. "Captain is some rich prick who decided he wanted to give treasure hunting a try. Mommy bought the ship and the crew. Probably threw around money to get him here, too."

"Does that mean he's on the hunt too?" Max asks. "Gods, that yellow is awful."

"It does, and I love you," I laugh.

"It's nighttime. I shouldn't be able to see that it's yellow in the dark!"

I kiss his cheek. "They're not gonna wanna see us at all…"

Cross Fields, ridiculous name, is one of the worst types of rich people. He believes his money should get him anything he wants. He fully expects to find whatever treasure is out in the world not by hard work and connections forged through trust but because he can pay for leads, for ships, for people. I've enjoyed beating him to treasure more than once since he doesn't need the money, but it's the entitlement that really does me in.

"Do you think they're after the elements, too?" Max asks. "Magnus did say he hired someone else."

"Can't know for sure. It's not impossible." I can't help a little laugh. "Oh, I hope so. I want to win this for all of us, and it'd be sweet to beat anyone else...but that guy?" I shake my head as our sails open and the wind carries us swiftly away, leaving Captain Fields to berate his crew behind us. I can't see him on the deck, but I can hear him being a dick. "I want to beat him more than anyone."

Max turns around carefully in my arms and grins up at me. "You will. Thanks to your secret weapon."

"And your crew," Tevin chimes in, throwing himself against the rail beside us, watching *Sunbeam* disappear.

"You can both have the credit so long as we keep going. We need to stay ahead of whoever else is out here if we're going to keep this from getting bloody." I drop a kiss on Max's lips and make sure he's secure against the rail before I turn back to face my ship, my crew. "I'm not about to waste our advantage. Get us on the wind."

Chapter 20

Max

I've been on the ship for almost four weeks now—twenty-six days. It's been a completely new lifestyle, a huge transition in every way. I'm aware mentally and logically that I live on a ship. But this, today, is the first time I really feel like a sailor. Definitely not a pirate. Still not quite a treasure hunter. But a cartographer employed on a ship, so 'sailor' feels right. At least it does now.

Today, we're coming in to dock. We have a scheduled meeting with Magnus, a planned check-in for our progress; fortunately, Eli and the whole crew agree that having two elements already is an excellent start—one that Magnus should be pleased with. Eli also has every intent of pressing Magnus about the other team hired because he wants final confirmation from a source that it's *Sunbeam*. For whatever reason, Eli is extra pissed that it might be *Sunbeam*. I don't know all the history yet, and it's weird to me that my life partner and best friend has a separate life from me, but at the moment, I'm not bothered. At the moment, I'm a sailor.

People are noticing. The crew is working on... whatever they work on to make the ship dock properly, and there are lots of others around the docks, and they see us. They're watching us. They see me on this ship, part of this crew. A sailor.

"Rosleigh, wait, shit!" I hear Eli shout from behind me. In the second it takes me to turn around, they're laughing, and so is the halfling who doesn't appear to be in any danger. I wonder at how she's managing to control the size of the rope in her hands. "You're gonna go flying overboard one day, you know that."

"I can swim," she replies, and my laughter at the retort brings our captain's green gaze to me. I love that their smile grows when they see me.

"You need a hand?" I call to them. "If you need some muscle, that is."

"I'll let you know. For now, just sit over there and be gorgeous, would you?"

I mock salute, my cheeks heating up when Eli's response is a dramatic bow. They might be the ship's captain and a treasure hunter after one of the most legendary treasures anyone can name, but they're also still the same big goofball I knew as a child. They're still the easiest person I've ever had to try and get along with. And gods, they look amazing pulling on that big ass rope to control the sails. Part of me feels like I should be above those thoughts, but despite being in my late 20s, I'm still just a boy in love. A horny boy in love.

Dava is at the wheel, and she calls out a bunch of directions and instructions, back and forth with Eli, and I shift up in my chair enough to watch the ship come up to the dock smoothly. There's some bumping, but I always imagined it would be more jarring than this. Louder, too. And I've been trying not to think about the one time I had the misfortune of watching an out-of-control ship crash into and through the docks, severely injuring everyone on board and way too many people on the docks. It turns out, *Tempest* doesn't get out of control, and this whole process is pretty great.

And I really, really enjoy the way people are noticing the ship. She isn't mine, not the same way that she is Eli's, but pride swells in my chest about *Tempest*. The ship is beautiful, a dark wood hull—no one should ever ask me what kind of wood—with teal accents that make it look like it matches the ocean. When they first got the ship, I asked Eli about the flag, what they wanted to design. I was informed that, for the most part, they're required to fly flags that state where the ship berths at 'home' and their association with the merchant's league. Apparently, there's a stigma around flying a personalized flag and being extremely stuck-up. I remember *Sunbeam* has a personalized flag.

Things get even busier after that. Some man who is standing up at an unnaturally straight angle comes onto the deck with a clipboard and asks about a million questions that Eli, Dava, and Tevin seem to anticipate and answer quickly, easily. Meanwhile, they're all moving crates around, and I have no idea what's in any of them or where they're supposed to go. Or why. I choose to stay quiet and stay out of the way because it seems like the best bet at the moment. And no one makes me move crates. I want to help but not like that.

"Have you ever been here, lover boy?" Yen asks, whipping out the new nickname she seems to delight in. She grins at me now when I look up at her, and I can't help a laugh.

"No, never. Haven't been most places honestly."

"Well, not yet," she adds.

I like that. Because sailors can travel. "Exactly. Not yet."

"There's a very cool old bookshop in this town," Dava informs me, pulling a map out of her back pocket. I only need a glance to realize that it's a map of this town, Wind Falls, oriented to show a path around the city if coming off a ship and approaching from the docks. She points to a block of shops a little ways from here. "It looks like nothing from outside, but the dwarf who runs it has been collecting old titles forever."

"That sounds amazing—I'm definitely gonna check that out." I look between her and Yen, growing more excited by the moment. "Any other suggestions? I was kind of just planning to explore, but I'm open—"

"We'll hit everything we can," Eli interjects, giving me a confident and kind smile as they appear, fixing their ponytail. I'm more distracted by the look on their face than their biceps for once. They don't look nearly as excited as I feel, and I know they've been here before, but Eli is usually the type to be happy for me when

I get to enjoy something. At the moment, Eli looks like he'd have to force himself to enjoy anything at all.

"I'm ready," the person with the clipboard announces, pulling Eli and Dava away to look over inventories and sign something. Or maybe it's none of that, but I don't much care. Even if I were to spend the next twenty years of my life on a ship, I'm confident I won't be foolish enough to make that stuff my job.

"This town is a little rough," Yen tells me, motioning for me to head off the ship and down the ramp toward the dock. I glance toward Eli, a little weird about leaving with them but confident too that I'll be just fine. "Most of the people who live here are merchants used to dealing with pirates and treasure hunters, and most of the people who visit are those pirates and treasure hunters. You're not…"

"I'm a little bit of a target at least," I finish for her instead of making her go through the discomfort of actually saying that. "I've been in a wheelchair most of my life, Yen, I promise that doesn't offend me. But I'll be okay."

"You've managed for this long," she agrees with a grin, but then she pops one of the five daggers off her belt and holds it out to me, handle first and her fingers comfortably holding the blade. "Take this with you. Just put it in your bag, and we'll both assume you won't need to use it."

I kind of want to reject it, but I take it from her anyway. It can't hurt, and she's only looking out for me. "Thank you, Yen. I'm sure I won't need it, but you're sweet. And I'll take good care of your blade."

"Okay, well, the thought of you losing it or dropping it or something never crossed my mind 'til now," she informs me, grimacing playfully.

I laugh. "You'd be okay with me stabbing someone with it, but dropping it would be a problem for you?"

"Very much so," she quips, falling into laughter. I've always loved that her laugh is so feminine, high-pitched and sweet, when I'd bet money on her to take down this whole port with a dagger if she needed to.

"We're all good," Eli announces, joining us on the docks. I look around to realize that the whole crew is here now, waiting for final instructions. I guess no one leaves 'til that whole inventory thing is done. I still don't understand why Tevin and Jak brought crates off the ship or what could possibly be in them. Did we pick up something to sell along the way? How did I miss that? "Everyone has a shopping list and a time to check in. Otherwise, have fun."

Dava and Yen head off right away. Ros squeezes my hand and says, "I'm gonna find you for lunch. I know a place."

"I'm sure you do. See you then!"

She goes too, Jak heading off a moment later and leaving me with Eli and Tevin. I smile up at both of them, easing my wheels back so I don't feel quite so small and don't have to stare up at the sky. "I was informed about a bookstore, so I'm going there first. What time is that check-in, and do you want me to have a shopping list, too?"

"I..." Eli frowns and blinks at me. They look completely confused, then shake their head a little. "You aren't going off by yourself, Max."

"Eli," Tevin says softly, and I almost laugh until I realize that Eli looks serious—and still confused, too.

"I thought you knew that," they press, tone tense like they're imploring me. "This place isn't great. Lots of shady people doing shady shit here. You shouldn't be alone, not your first time."

"But...everyone else is allowed to be alone?" I confirm, cocking my head at them. I don't want to challenge them, but this is starting to feel very bad very quickly.

"You've never been here before."

"No, but I'm shockingly good at using a map."

"It's a dangerous city."

In response to that one, I just hold up the knife that Yen gave me. Eli scowls at that, less pleased that I have it than I expected—apparently because they want an excuse to keep me with them. "If I thought you were lonely and wanted to hold my hand all day, I'd be okay with that. But you want to babysit me, Eli, and I'm not going for it."

"That's not true," they scoff, but they wilt a bit when both Tevin and I give them a sharp look. "It's not fucking babysitting to want to protect my partner in a place like this. I'm being careful—why is that a bad thing?"

"Because I'm the one who should be careful," I retort. "It's my business to take care of myself *and* to ask for help if I need it."

Eli crosses their arms over their chest. "Maybe you just don't know you need it."

"Okay, alright," Tevin interjects. "I didn't realize I would hate it this much when you two argue, so you have to stop right now or I swear, I'll cry in public."

Eli barks out a shocked laugh, and the mental image that threat brings on makes a forbidden giggle escape me. It helps, the tension between me and Eli easing, and I even manage to smile genuinely up at the big butthead who wants to play overprotective. "I just want you safe," they remind me. "I'm not sorry I love you."

"Well, I don't want you to be sorry for that part," I laugh, and they echo me when I roll my eyes. "But I need you to remember that I live alone the majority of the time, and I have for... What is it now? Six years?"

Eli glances down at their boots—leather and heels and sexy as hell, of course—and scuffs the heel against the ground a bit. "Seven."

"Seven years that I have been taking care of myself, and aside from one very regrettable haircut, I have never been hurt." I throw my hands up a little, my frustration boiling over. I have to stamp down the urge to just go back onto the ship and hide instead of dealing with confrontation, instead of pushing either of us to face this. Eli would follow me anyway, so then the merchant meeting would also be a moot point, and it'd ruin everything. So we're doing this right here on the docks. "I'm going to be just fine on my own today, and I need you to respect that."

"*You* are not what I'm worried about," Eli groans, rubbing both hands over their face. "Look, I promise that after the meeting this morning, we can go to the bookstore and everywhere else you want today. I'm not trying to trap you, but I just don't want you out here alone."

I cock my head at them. "So if I was with someone else, that would be okay?" They narrow their eyes at me, questioning, until I look up at Tevin. "Tevin, would you like to hang out with me today?"

"You know what, Max? I would love to." Tevin beams at me and stands up a little straighter, and he looks so adorable at the thought of spending time with me that my cheeks flame. Eli can't manage to completely hide the smile they're desperately trying to turn into a scowl. "You'll be fine with Magnus, right?" He kisses Eli's cheek and murmurs, just barely loud enough for me to hear, "You need to figure out a balance before you push too hard."

Tevin heads off a little, waiting for me to join but obviously giving me space with Eli. It's kind of hard for someone his size to be subtle anyway, but the way he's staring up at the sky—more gray than blue but not even cloudy in an interesting way—makes it a little more than a little obvious.

I hold a hand out for Eli, and they don't hesitate to take it, stepping closer but now I don't really care that I have to look up at them. "You have to know I don't want to be watched all the time, whether or not you call it babysitting."

"I know. I...I knew you wouldn't like it," they admit. "I haven't always been around to protect you for the last few years—seven, apparently. I know you haven't needed it, but that doesn't mean it feels good. Doesn't mean I haven't worried."

"You? Worry? No!" I tease. Eli laughs and rolls their eyes at me, not insulted but not able to deny it at all. Eli could overthink anything at all, and their brain tortures them by actively finding things to overthink and worry about. It's not like anyone can hold that against them, considering everything they went through growing up. Their entire childhood was spent either being abused in orphanages or fending for their own on the streets—they had more than a few things to be worried about. Unfortunately, it's not simple to just stop worrying once things are better. And I never, ever want to be a source of worry for them. I pull their hand to my mouth and kiss it. "Would you like me to bring a bigger knife? Seriously. I'd carry a broadsword for you."

"Much as I'd like to see you trying to navigate a broadsword in the chair," they laugh, "that's okay. I know you really would if I asked...but I know you deserve to be independent, too."

"Do you know that I love you too?" I flash my cheesiest smile and then offer my mouth for a kiss. Eli doesn't hesitate to lean down and kiss me; their lips taste even more like the sea while we're on the ship, and I think I've become addicted to it. When they start to pull back, I follow and steal another kiss. And then a second. Eli is smiling for real—finally—when we part. "I'm gonna be fine. I need you to work on believing that."

Eli pulls in a deep breath, chest lifting dramatically and holding before dropping in a rush. "I'll work on it." And I can see how much even working on it is weighing on them.

We part then, Eli going one way for the meeting with Magnus in a location I forgot to ask about and me going toward the port's shopping center with Tevin. I can only make it a few feet, though, before I have to ask: "This is going to get much worse before it has any chance of getting better, isn't it?"

Tevin can only answer with a comforting squeeze on my shoulder. If Eli is this worried when I haven't faced any actual danger or anything close to a threat…what are they going to be like as my ride on *Tempest* continues?

Chapter 21

Eli

I don't know much, but I do know that if a rich guy offers to buy you a fancy dinner, you accept the offer. Especially when the offer is extended to your partner, your cartographer, to celebrate the successes you've had so far.

"Ooh, you look pretty, Cap!" Yen teases from the doorway of my quarters. I definitely shut that door, and it definitely makes a noise when it opens, but of course, Yen managed to sneak in here. Damn elf.

"I always look pretty, thank you very much," I quip, but I do appreciate her noticing the effort. My hair would be much more manageable if I kept it short instead of letting the thick waves capture all the salt water around us constantly, but I'm too shallow for that. I love my hair—especially tonight when I have a reason to put more effort into it, smoothing it back into a braid that hangs over my shoulder. I catch her eye in the mirror and motion down at my body. "Too much? Too femme?"

She purses her lips and cocks her head, her thinking face, walking toward me slowly while studying my outfit. My top is corset style, dark blue and tied up over a black lace piece that only covers a thin strap of my shoulders. If I had cleavage, I could make this obscene; it's showing off a lot even without breasts. I went for one of my favorite skirts, black leather to match the top, buttery soft, and it shifts perfectly when I move.

"You're wearing heels, right?" she asks. I give her a look instead of dignifying that with an answer. "If you want slightly less femme tonight, swap the skirt for pants. Oh, those black ones with the ties on the sides—your ass looks fantastic in those, especially with heels."

"Yeah?" I glance down myself in the mirror again. "Slightly less femme might be the right call. Less chance for distraction or nonsense around Magnus."

She gives me a sympathetic look I appreciate. I'd love to be able to dress and act however I want no matter where I am or who is around. I have the privilege of being big and scary enough that most people have the good sense not to comment about my appearance or their inevitable confusion around my gender—or lack of gender in my case—but it's not guaranteed. More than one business deal or potential job has blown up. Magnus hasn't had a single thing to say, even when we met alone earlier, but we'll be in public tonight.

"Yeah, slightly less femme. Okay." I head for

my dresser while tugging through my belt, and Yen sits down on my bed. "You mind?"

"Never have."

It's permission enough for me to strip from the waist down since I'll need new underwear with the pants she suggested. It's far from the first time she's seen me naked—or half naked in this case—since life on a ship is what it is, but still seems polite to ask. "Did you just come down here to help me get dressed, or do you need something?"

"I need to tell you that you *must* go with a thong in those pants, and *Sunbeam* is here."

I turn to her, looking over my shoulder instead of giving her a full frontal but just barely. Too surprised to stop completely. "You saw them?"

"Just before we came back on the ship," she confirms with a nod. "Figured they might be just stocking up here but—"

"But Cross Fields is too good for this place," I finish for her, rolling my eyes. The captain of *Sunbeam* may technically be a competitor ship in the treasure-hunting world, but he's a privileged, stuck-up jackass who was born with a silver spoon in his mouth. He often just pays other ships to turn over the treasure they acquired so he can take the glory, and he's hated me ever since I told him where he could shove that offer. He doesn't come to places like this, to pirate ports, like the rest of us for supplies; he has his own channels, and he makes sure the rest of us are aware of it. So if he's here... "You're thinking it has something to do with Magnus?"

"You know I'm a big fan of jumping to conclusions," she notes, pulling her feet up under her. She frowns and bounces on my bed a little. "This is way too firm."

"Get a softer one when you're captain," I retort, finally dressed completely again. I only realize then that the door was wide open, but it doesn't bother me. We've all seen everything that there is to see, and even if Max came in to find me naked with Yen, he wouldn't be worried. "I also like jumping to conclusions, and I wouldn't be surprised if Magnus called us and our competition here, but it is what it is. Gonna go to this dinner, gonna let some rich guy feed me and stroke my ego, and that'll be the end of it."

Yen smirks at me. "Yes because you're excellent at controlling yourself around people like Cross Fields."

"Worst thing that happens is we learn who we're up against," I press on, choosing to ignore her entirely correct jab. I'm less likely to start a fight with Max around at least. "Thanks for the heads up. Won't stop us from finding all the elements and changing our lives forever."

"There's my captain," she chirps, hopping up. "You look super hot, by the way. Just femme enough to still be you, but I'd fully expect you to kick ass."

"Exactly what I was going for." I motion her out ahead of me and follow her toward the deck, leaving the door open still behind me. She grabs the railings on either side of the new ramp leading up to the deck and swings herself to the top before skipping away. I laugh and follow her like a normal person. Or at least like someone who is over six feet and wearing heels; I would have no shot at landing her little move.

"Hey, I was starting to wonder if you'd be late," Max calls. I open my mouth with a retort, but I'm cut off at the sight of him. He's waiting near the ramp down to the docks, bathed in the golden glow of the sunset, and he looks *amazing*.

"You're fucking gorgeous, do you know that?" I inform him, aware of the rest of the crew but not about to censor my feelings for the love of my life. Though Rosleigh's high-pitched 'aww' does make my cheeks feel a little hot. At least Max is blushing, too. It makes him even more beautiful somehow. "Ready to go, baby?"

"A rich guy wants to feed us. Of course I'm ready!" This is why everyone should fall in love with their best friend.

We say a round of goodbyes, everyone demanding we bring back leftovers. No way am I leaving anything leftover, but we make the promise for peace anyway. I kiss Tevin, so does Max, and I happily accept his smack on my ass before heading down to the docks. Max sets the pace so he's not trying to race to keep up with me. One hand resting lightly on the back makes me feel closer and makes sure I don't start moving faster by accident. More than once, I've made Max race, and he's too sweet to complain.

The restaurant where Magnus asked us to meet him is on the private end of the docks where it costs more than a year of maintenance on my ship to even make berth. We make the walk down there in companionable silence, Max's head on a swivel the entire time while he takes in the sights. I mostly just take him in. He's curious and interested and excited to be seeing new things, new places. I love that he's enjoying this, and I'm glad he basically told me to shove it before heading off earlier. I can't control him, shouldn't want to. Can't stop wanting to protect him, though.

Tonight, at least, I get a night off. The restaurant is expecting us. Not sure I want to know how Magnus described us for the host to immediately know who we're meeting, but the two of us might not have been welcome on our own, so it's for the best. It's not a suit-and-tie establishment, but it's definitely not a local tavern either. Magnus, of course, is wearing a suit and tie; I've never seen him in anything else.

"Gentlefolk!" he greets us, the word coming totally natural and not with a stumble like he almost called me a man. I kinda like the greeting and mentally pocket it for later. "Thank you both so much for joining me this evening. Please sit, sit."

Magnus has already had a chair removed for Max, and he motions me to sit so Max will be between us. We're attended to almost immediately, and by the time we both have drinks—a whiskey I would never have tried without someone else paying for it for me and a glass of wine for Max—Magnus is just about bursting at the seams. He can't say enough about how thrilled he is that we brought him two elements already, and he rightfully credits Max for the advantage.

This is about as great a night as I could have asked for. Excellent food and drink, and I get to sit back and listen while Max gets all the credit for his magic and his genius he deserves. Magnus has tons of questions, the usual ones that people want to know about Max's abilities, and he gushes over what Max has accomplished. He actually knows more about previous maps and clients than I realized, which might be creepy if I didn't know that Magnus is familiar with Max's family. They brag about his achievements and the business that he's built, too—as they should. I wish I could.

If other ships learned about Max's abilities and that we use his maps on *Tempest* to give us the competitive edge other ships have been chasing since we first set sail, Max would be in danger. And that's why my stomach sinks, the whiskey and fish inside it quickly souring, when I look up to spot Cross Fields approaching with a cocky smile on his clean-shaven, pale face. I almost throw up right at the table when Cross pats Magnus's shoulder and greets him like they're old friends.

"Good to see you, Magnus!" Cross greets him, angling his body toward Magnus and so I'm slightly behind him. Intentional, for sure.

"Oh...Captain Fields," Magnus replies, forcing a smile for the first time all night. He looks surprised, maybe even uncomfortable. "Apologies for my surprise. I believe we were scheduled to meet tomorrow morning."

They were scheduled to meet... *Fuck.*

"You can understand I wanted to make sure my friend Eli here knows who the competition out there really is." Cross turns to me with a wide smile that only highlights the cocky hate in his blue eyes. He shoves a hand out between us; I fucking hate that he works on a ship and is so pale—it's proof that he doesn't actually work with his crew. "Good to see you, Captain Rose."

"Sure," I answer, not bothering to make a single move to accept his hand. He knows he's bullshitting as well as I do, but I'm not going to pretend. I look to Magnus who couldn't be more uncomfortable. "So, the original ship you hired to find the elements was *Sunbeam*. And when they couldn't do the job well enough, you came to us."

"Eli," Max says softly, not a scolding or even really a warning but a request. He doesn't want me to be responsible for anything that escalates from here.

"Oh, don't worry about them, Max," Cross says. The familiar way he speaks Max's name sets my blood to a simmer and puts me even further on edge, muscles tensed and ready without any conscious command. He grins at Max. "You're the real prize, after all, aren't you? Quite a reputation you have. I'm not at all surprised that Eli has kept you a secret. Until now."

Max opens his mouth without speaking, eyes flashing between me and Cross. He almost always knows what to say when talking about his work, but I seriously doubt anyone else has ever walked up and made it sound like a threat. But before I can tell Cross how I feel about him threatening my partner, Magnus jumps in and says, "Captain Fields, we have a meeting scheduled over breakfast tomorrow. I look forward to seeing what you have for me."

I'm not sure Magnus meant that as an insult, he just doesn't seem the type, but I delight in watching Cross Fields wilt a little. He hasn't found any elements of the gods yet...because he's been trailing us. I knew I saw a ship before the dive for the first one, and now, I know who. He was coming in behind us the warehouse the other night, too.

It's so like Cross to try and take from someone else instead of putting the effort forth himself. He's going to try and beat us to the elements that we find through Max's maps. And he's going to fail.

"We don't mean to be rude," I lie, reaching for Max's hand and covering it on the table—comfort for him and a claim I want Cross to see, "but we're here to celebrate our achievements so far. You understand we'd rather keep this private, I'm sure."

Cross huffs and manages to turn it into a low laugh, adjusting his gloves that I'm sure are some fancy sort of leather from an animal that no one should have killed for clothes. "You do love your secrets, Eli. I can't help but wonder how you'd celebrate if you didn't have this particular secret anymore, hmm?" Before I can retort, he turns back to Magnus. "Enjoy your meal. I'll see you in the morning."

He leaves with that, Magnus quickly filling the table with apologies and Max trying to soothe them away. Of course, Cross is pissed. He played a good verbal game here, but I could see it in the rapid rise and fall of his chest, the tightness in his shoulders. I've had no choice but to be good at reading people, especially when those people are angry as fuck at me. Cross was hired for this job originally, and Magnus brought us on to create a safety net and some competition; now, we've had success where he couldn't.

I'm not surprised he's failing, and normally, I wouldn't be worried. But Cross's final words are sticking.

He made a threat, I'm sure of it…but against what? Is he threatening to expose the secret about our relationship with Max, that *Tempest* has a magical cartographer on our side and now on our crew? It's not like we're doing anything illegal, and he'd even have trouble making the argument we're doing anything immoral. Everyone uses whatever edge they can get, magical or otherwise—Cross himself has a crew member who can add wind to their sails, making his ship faster than most.

Or is he…

I don't want to let the thought in, don't want to give it room in my head or in the chasm that threatens to open in my chest whenever I think about Max being in danger. I've had my concerns about Max being on *Tempest* and working on the sea, dealing with the places we need to go and the people we need to be around. But if Cross is threatening Max directly… That changes everything.

Chapter 22

Max

I have no idea what's going on. Last night, din-ner almost turned around after that very rude introduction to the captain from the ugly yellow ship. Eli managed to talk me up the way they always do, and they sounded confident about what we've achieved so far, but they were off the entire night. After dinner, they didn't want to talk about Cross Fields or what he said after, and then, they left. No idea where they went or who with because they didn't explain or leave room for questions, just kissed me in their quarters and left. This morning, I woke up alone, and now, I'm equal parts annoyed and worried. And confused because I have no idea what's going on!

Treasure hunters and their nonsense, I swear...

We're still in port, based on the view through the window over the bed. I guess that's a bit of normalcy at least. I'm pretty sure it's unusual that we would leave in the middle of the night. I can hear activity on the deck above me, though, so I quickly throw on clothes and grab my crutches before making my way to the deck. I even forgo worrying about a binder for the moment because I just want to get up there, get to Eli, get some understanding of what really happened last night. There's no way this is just about that other captain being a bag of dicks in the restaurant.

On the deck, the whole crew is on the move. Dava and Jak are both bringing crates of supplies onto the deck while Yen, Tevin, and Eli are all doing things with the ropes. All of which have their own names apparently, along with the sails. If I thought I was going to be around or pulling rope for a while, I'd learn them. Maybe someday. Or maybe Eli is in full-on panic mode and will have even more trouble letting me out of their sight.

That's a little harder to believe when they spot me and smile. "Good morning, Max!" they call from across the deck, then make their way to me. Their smile softens when they get closer. "I'm sorry for how I acted last night and just disappearing on you. I had a lot to take care of before this morning so we could get moving."

"You slept the last time we were leaving in the morning," I note, cocking my head at them. The emotions that I can read on them are all over the place; there is mischief in their sea-green eyes, genuine regret in their smile, and tension written all over the rest of their body. "Eli, what is going on? You really freaked out about that guy last night. I half expected to wake up and find us out to sea because you're racing him."

"Cross Fields is a problem, and he's still here, too," Eli tells me, motioning down the docks further. There are a bunch of ships there, but the bright yellow sails and red flag with a sun painted on it stands out. There are people moving around on the deck over there, too. "He's got enough money to be a threat to everyone around him, including the people trying to work on his own ship, and I'm... He threatened you."

I frown, thinking back on last night. "He did? When?"

"Max! He made it clear he knows what you can do, how you help us out on Tempest, and then he said he wants to see what I can do if I don't have you." Eli throws their hands up a little. "How am I supposed to take that if not a threat?"

"Well, I took it as a rich guy trying to make himself sound tough to intimidate someone else," I note, shrugging. "That's kind of what rich guys do. I've had more than a few guys like that come into the library and try to intimidate me into all sorts of shit." I know it was a mistake the second the words are out of my mouth, and Eli's eyes go wide. "Okay, let's pretend I made that up."

"I'd rather," they laugh, rolling their eyes at me. "I don't want to get into it again about whether you can handle yourself because he crossed a line when he threatened a member of my crew right in front of me. That makes it my responsibility to take care of it." They flash a grin that I've seen on them just before things are about to get wild or they need to make a run for it. "And I have taken care of it."

"What does that mean?" Instead of answering me, Eli leans down to kiss me quickly and then heads up the stairs to the helm. "Eli! What does that mean?"

"You'll see. Get somewhere stable because we're about to start moving."

I'd love to chase them up there and demand answers, but half a dozen steps are at least a few more than I can actually handle, and if they're warning me about movement, I need to take that seriously. The deck is kind of rough on my crutches anyway, and the ship moves an awful lot when we're coming out of a port. Fortunately, the crates nearby give me an option to sit down, and neither Dava nor Jak seems to mind as they finish up.

Everyone starts moving around faster on the deck, Eli shouting out orders that I assume the others are following. A loud crack echoes off the buildings facing the docks and makes me jump so high, I nearly fall off the crate. My heart starts racing, and I look around for the problem, for the cannonball or the fire that follows an explosion or... Why doesn't Eli's crew seem concerned? Something definitely just broke, and for some reason, they're smiling.

"Hey." I look up toward Eli's voice and find them grinning down at me over the rail. "Told you I took care of it."

They point, and I follow the direction of their finger. As *Tempest* moves out of her dock and starts to leave the city behind us, I spot another ship with a huge beam across the deck and people scrambling all around it. Not a beam—a mast. Even I know that much. A mast with a

bright yellow flag hanging off the end and now
dangling toward the water so that the sun looks
like it's going to drown.

Well then. I guess they did take care of it.

Chapter 23

Eli

"Would you slow down? You're embarrassing me."

"You embarrass yourself, Eli Rose."

I kick Dava's boot with my own more because she's correct than for any other reason. "That's *captain* to you."

"You're an embarrassment, Captain," she amends, giving me a shit-eating grin that reveals enough of her tusks to make the sunlight catch on the tip. No point in bothering to pretend I don't find that funny.

I lean over to reach the cup of water I have sitting on the railing and use it as an excuse to look over the rail and check on Yen. She's sitting on a board connected to the ship with ropes tied through holes on either end and then lowered over the side of the ship. Scraping barnacles is one of the ship chores I've always hated, one I would avoid as hard as I could when I was just a crew member. It's a necessary task, though, and one we draw straws for on *Tempest*.

In theory, Yen drew the short straw. In reality, she's down there kicking her feet and singing softly like she's having the time of her life. Wonderful little weirdo.

"You'd be sewing faster if you weren't distracted every ten seconds," Dava notes, giving the section of the sails in my lap a pointed look, eyebrows raised. She has another piece of it in her hands, both of us taking on the task of repairing and reinforcing while the ship is anchored until we get another map. Seems like a good day for chores since *Sunbeam* will take a bit to get back on the water and then find us again—and I picked a chore I like.

"Hey, you're the one who taught me how to do this, so really, my process and failures are your fault," I remind her, throwing raised eyebrows right back in her direction.

Dava laughs and shakes her head at me. "You were a horrible student, you know."

"Oh, I know." I met Dava not long after meeting Tevin when all three of us were hired as hands on the same merchant ship. It was very hard, very physical work, and at the time, I'd only really beed hired for very hard, very physical work. No one but Max had ever encouraged me to chase my dreams of owning and captaining my own ship. Until I met the orc twins who became my best friends almost over night.

Dava became determined I needed to learn how to do everything around the ship, get as much knowledge under my belt as possible. She pushed me to charm the ship carpenter into giving me tasks, and to this day, I swear she conned our captain at the time to teach me his tricks for navigation. I thought I knew a lot before that voyage, but I was wrong, and more than anything, it prepared me for constantly learning something new.

And poor Dava took it on herself to teach me how to sew. I'm capable of a lot, but tiny tedious and repetitive tasks? My brain doesn't want to tolerate those. I was a horrible student and ending up bleeding from my fingertips more than once. Got yelled at my fair share, too. I can sew the sails now, but I can't keep up with Dava's much more nible fingers. Even though her fingers are bigger than mine.

I finish up my last stitch, knot it up, and cut the string. Not pretty, but pretty isn't the goal. "Finally," I huff, and she laughs at me.

"Go find something else to do," she says, waving me off. "I'll string 'em up myself or get Yen to help when she's done."

"Yen is enjoying herself down there, so it might be a while."

We both go back to the rail and look down, Yen further away than she was last time I looked but still swinging and scraping and singing like she has not a care in the world. I've always envied people who can just dive into a simple task without their mind dragging them into a swirling vortex of what-if terrors. I can't be alone like that, can't do tasks like that on my own. Can't be left alone with my own brain. I envy her. And I'm grateful she's doing the task so I don't have to.

"You want me to lie and tell you I'm gonna go find something else to do or admit that I'm gonna go grope Max for a while?" I ask, leaning my head on her shoulder. "Maybe your brother too."

"Eli, you know I'd prefer lies over your fantasies of my brother," she drawls, shrugging the shoulder under my head to jostle me just a little. I laugh and hand over my sewing kit along with an apology I only mean a tiny bit before cutting across the deck.

It's beautiful today, sunny but breezy so none of us has to be sweating out here. Below deck should have the windows open, the wind moving through, so I'm not dreading going down there to discover thick heat. Down the ramp, I hear a thumping coming from the bathing room, where I know Jak was making repairs today; I could go in and fuck with him a little, entertain both of us with a playfight, but maybe later. Ros is almost definitely in the kitchen, but I'm not hungry enough to con her into giving me a snack. I know what I really want, who I really want to see, so I turn toward my quarters.

The door opens to reveal a sight that stops me in my tracks. Tevin and Max are on the bed, laying on their sides, hands all over each other, soft but needy moans filling the room. For a second, I almost back up, almost shut the door and pretend I wasn't here. They haven't had a lot of one-on-one time, and they've never had sex without me, so maybe I'm interrupting.

But I've only managed to turn halfway before I hear Tevin murmur, "Uh-oh. I think my captain just caught me lying down on the job."

I laugh and turn back to find them both looking at me, Tevin still propped up on his side and Max on his back now. "Don't worry," Max says, his face flushed and lips swollen in the most perfect way. "I'm very good at finding ways to earn your captain's forgiveness."

"Oh, is that so?" I head toward them, kicking off my boots on the way. "Does that mean I get an invite?"

"Do you really have to ask?" Tevin counters.

Max shifts up a little, elbows underneath him, and asks, "Yeah, were you really just gonna leave?"

I shrug and pull my shirt off. "You two are allowed to have alone time. I didn't want to interrupt."

"You could never," he informs me, holding both arms out to me. I still have my pants on—extra grateful now I wasn't responsible for s craping barnacles today—when I crawl into my bed with them, moving into Max's arms and diving for his mouth. Max kisses me back and lets me lay him down flat again, and when I turn to kiss Tevin, too, Max starts working through my belt. "You're at a bad angle for this."

"Pardon me," I quip, sitting up and kneeling instead, one foot on the floor.

"No, no," Max argues, though, sitting up in front of me and going right for the clasp again. "Let me."

"Let us," Tevin chimes in, also sitting up. He takes a handful of my hair in his big hand and pulls back, exposing my throat to him and running his tongue up the length of it. His tongue is cooler than a human's, and while that was a surprise at first, it's always been incredibly pleasant. After being in the sun for the last few hours, the contrast his mouth brings now sends a shiver down my spine. And heat follows it when Max shoves through my pants to take hold of my cock.

"Let you?" I realize what's going on when Max pushes at my chest and then Tevin starts to guide me down in front of them—both of them.

"We did say that we wanted to earn your forgiveness, didn't we?" Max smiles brightly at me, mischief written all over his painfully handsome face. "You go ahead and let us know when we're forgiven, Captain."

With that, Max has his perfect mouth wrapped around my dick, tongue fluttering and hand jerking and *oh, fuck, he's perfect*.

Tevin comes up beside me, his pants also still on but unbuttoned, his own cock in his hand which is stroking the length. I'm panting when he leans down to take my jaw in hand, kiss me briefly, and then sit up over me. He's almost in reach; if I lift my head or he shifts forward, I'll have that thick cock in my throat, and the thought makes me throb in Max's. "You'll have to wait a little while to tell us, though. Your mouth is gonna be busy for a while."

Oh, fuck. My life is perfect.

Chapter 24

Eli

I love storms at sea. The sky and the ocean go to war against anyone who dares face them, a tandem effort to make the very world around us thrash and seize. The sky is every bit as murderous as the waves, lightning striking directly into the water. In the seconds before those strikes, there's a deadly stillness sailors learn to notice even on land. The hair on my arms and the back of my neck stands, my heart flutters uncomfortably, and then…

There's a storm to the east. Above me, an expanse of inky blue and twinkling stars unmarred by anything except the glow of the moon. Over there, the clouds are already bruised and battered by the chaos brewing inside them. Part of me is jealous of anyone who gets to take their ship through that, battling back against the water and winds to prove your merit out here. The other part of me isn't foolish enough to take us that far off course even if I know our competition is going to be delayed by at least a few days.

The thought makes me smile. The memory of the fantastically loud crack of *Sunbeam's* mast makes me almost giddy. Neither of them begins to compare with the arrival of curly brown hair on my ship's deck, Max gliding into view before turning to look up at me. "You up there planning more sabotage?"

"Unfortunately, no," I laugh. "Not yet anyway."

Max didn't want to celebrate my vandalism at first. He worked hard not to smile while we sailed out of port and left a very pissed-off Cross Fields behind. He even tried to scold me. And he failed fantastically 'cause it was an excellent plan that went off without a hitch.

After Cross's thinly veiled threat against Max, I knew I had to do something more than just spiral. I was sitting on the deck after dinner, tumbling into the never-ending hole of anxiety always waiting to swallow me up, when it hit me that I had two options. One, I could eliminate the threat by taking Max home and working on the elements without him. It would hurt Max and screw my crew, not to mention my own future. Or two, I could let Cross know I heard him, and no matter how much power he thinks his money gives him, I'm not going to roll over and take it.

Dava, Jak, and Tevin came with me, the former with a few protests about doing something so illegal but endlessly loyal to me as her friend and her captain. Yen played lookout. With Jak's expertise as a carpenter, a few select toys, and brute strength from the rest of us, we created a big problem. The second Cross gave the order and his crew started to raise their mainsail, they were screwed.

It occurred to me while we were doing it, while we were committing a crime in public, that it might piss off Max. He and I grew up in very different situations, and when he knew I was stealing or something as a kid to get by, he never judged me. He pushed me to accept help from his parents, of course, but he never made me feel like he looked down on me for doing what was necessary. That doesn't mean he loved it, though, and he always made me promise I'd be careful. And then promise again and promise some more. If I'd been arrested last night, Max would be devastated with worry for me. But he still doesn't judge me.

And he's still doing his best not to smile about what I've done.

"It's my fault," he says, throwing his hands up a little. "This is the life I get for falling in love with a pirate."

"Okay, now we're hitting below the belt," I growl playfully. We both know I'm not a pirate, not a criminal without a purpose or someone who causes problems just for the sake of it. I only do that to myself. That, of course, is why Max said it. I'm not letting him get away with it.

I set the lock onto the ship's helm, the wooden piece designed specifically to keep the currents from turning the ship without our permission or control. We're not going to even be in sight of any landmasses for almost twelve hours, and we need to keep going in this direction. Besides, I'm captain of this ship. If I want to be a tiny bit irresponsible and step away from direct control to take care of something much more important and much, much sexier, I'm allowed.

Max is rocking his chair back and forth and grinning at me when I approach him on the deck. His hair is tousled enough I can be sure he was asleep at least for a little while, and he's wearing a baggy pair of gray sleep pants and a black t-shirt. No shoes, no socks, no binder. He looks comfortable and absolutely edible. Made to be ruined.

"Come here." I don't give him a second, swooping down to slide my arms behind him and pull him up into me while capturing his mouth with mine. His lips are always so soft, so warm. I love that he's starting to taste like the sea, too, the salt permeating absolutely everything out here already becoming an ingrained part of him. I love that it makes me feel like he's going to be here, to stay here. Even if that's nothing more than a fantasy.

Fantasies aren't always a bad thing, after all.

Max wraps his arms around my neck and squeezes, a signal we've long since solidified between us, a request I pick him up and a promise it won't hurt him. The smell of vanilla and mint all over him is stronger than usual, meaning he probably got a handle on his pain earlier, and I'm hornier than usual, so I don't hesitate to slide my hands behind his thighs and pull his legs carefully around my waist. When he doesn't so much as wince, I can't help smiling against his mouth. I'll get to make him scream instead of his pain tonight.

I start carrying him with me, a destination in

mind, but Max pulls back and protests, "Lock my chair!"

"Oh, you'll go around the ship with it unlocked, but the chair needs to be cared for when it has no precious cargo. Makes perfect sense." I roll my eyes, but I still lean down to set the locks on his wheels. I know how much the chair means to him even if I tease. I'm grateful Max weighs next to nothing so I still look tough, carrying him once it's locked. Max doesn't ask questions about where we're going, kissing me deeply and threading his fingers through my hair, already pulling himself flush up against me and writhing a little. Nothing turns me on like making him hot for me.

I set him down on the lid of a barrel up against the main mast; it never moves, secured to the deck, so I feel safe with him standing. And I feel like I've wasted way too much time not taking advantage of Max being on my ship. We could have some real fun.

"I think it's about time you learn the ropes around here," I tell him, surprising Max by stepping back a little. I reach out to grab a rope hanging near his head and say, "Literally."

"Oh, please let that be a sex joke," Max groans.

I just kiss him in response, breaking it only to pull my shirt off and toss it to the deck. I realize somewhere in the back of my mind that it could end up in the ocean, that all of my clothes could if I drop them casually up here, but I can't quite bring myself to care. Especially not when Max's hands start running over my chest, my shoulders, squeezing my biceps, tugging the ring in my nipple.

That's all it takes for him to get me hard, my erection straining against the cotton pants I'm wearing. I tug his hips closer, only careful enough, and rock against him, desperate to make him know the effect he has on me. Max moans and pulls himself closer, arms wrapping around my waist. If that storm came right now and swept us away, if these were my final moments, I'd be more than pleased with the life I lived. But somehow, I'm lucky enough that the gorgeous man in my arms is going to make my life even better. He's going to make our future better... even if it remains apart.

We are not apart right now, though. Time to take advantage.

Max and I learned everything about sex from each other. When we were teenagers and starting to get curious, to explore, we did it all together. Eventually, we both figured out that other people had something to offer too, and involving other people in our beds or our hearts can't do anything to separate the two of us. But even then, whatever we gained and learned from other people, we brought back to one another. After all these years, after more than a decade of getting to know each other's pleasure and needs, Max is well beyond asking questions or resisting whatever I seem to have in mind when we're getting naked. I'm going to take advantage of that, too.

"How are your shoulders, Maxy?" I ask, leaning down so I can punctuate it by kissing the curve between his neck and shoulder. "Think you can put your arms behind your back at all?"

He considers it for a second, jumping when I nip to make sure he stays grounded instead of getting too lost in thinking about his pain. "Behind my back is okay but not up. Not above my head."

"Got it. I can happily work with that." I slide my hands under his shirt, teasing the sensitive skin along his waist and smiling against his neck when he can't help but jump at the sensation. He swats my arm even while pulling me closer, encouraging me, and when I cup his chest in my hands, Max moans deeply. "Wanna keep the shirt on?"

I don't look up so I don't pressure him, but I can tell he's looking around a little, making sure the door to the deck is very much behind us. Intentional on my part, of course. "No, take it off."

Max's shirt joins mine on the deck. Since he's in sweats, I don't need both hands to deal with them; I use my free hand while undoing his drawstring to continue teasing, torturing, pleasing him—my mouth staying just as involved. Max leans back against the mast, giving me more access to all of him and making it easier for me to slide his pants and shorts out from under him. I realize in that moment that I'm going to make him sit on rough wood and almost freeze.

"Wait, here." I lift him a little, my arm around his back, and set his sweatpants back underneath him. Max tugs me in to kiss him again when I set him back down, and I smile against the kiss but have to move to continue with my plan. His wary look when I grab the rope again makes me laugh, but I know he's only worried I might try to teach him or quiz him. I very seriously doubt Max will ever care that this is the end of the buntline, and I think we're both good with that.

Now, I take my time.

Chapter 25

Max

I wasn't ready for my partner to act like a pirate.

It's not like they've hidden this part of their life from me. Even if they tried, I read, and I listen, so I know what pirates are out in the world doing. But when it's Eli who is off the ship, putting themself at risk for things I don't even want to give thought to, I suddenly have trouble breathing.

"Okay, boy!"

I nearly fall off my wheelchair and flat to my face on the deck; I've never been so off-balance while sitting, and that's really saying something for me since I'm off-balance almost all the time. But Jakgrout comes stomping right up beside me, planting his hands on the rail and staring out at the sea. I can't tell if he's scowling or not; he always looks unhappy, but he doesn't always act unhappy. Unless he's with Eli, and then he makes a point of being unhappy.

"You need a task? Is that it?" He turns toward me, hands on his hips now, and looks me over from head to toe. "You ain't useless, and you know it."

"I… Thank you," I reply, mostly because I don't know what else to say. It is kind; plenty of people have looked at me and assumed I am useless, so I'm grateful to someone who thinks otherwise and is willing to say it. I just wish I knew what this conversation was and how I'm supposed to interact.

"So? Do you need a task?"

"Um. I mean…no? But do you need something?" I quickly add. "I'm happy to help, Jak, and—"

"I don't need nothing!" he shouts, throwing his hands up. It might startle me if I wasn't so used to him now; Dava swears that since Jak has always lived and worked around humans, not dwarfs, that makes him convinced he needs to be loud since he'll never be tall. I'm sure Jak would set the ship on fire if he ever heard her share that theory.

I am still completely lost, though, and now I'm getting yelled at for it.

"Jak, do *you* need me to have a task?" I finally ask.

I'm still surprised when he answers, "Yes!" I just stare at him, and he sighs like explaining is a burden. "I can't just watch you sitting here pining. Worrying. It ain't right. If you have a task… maybe you'll feel better."

"Oh, gods, Jak. How can you say something that sweet and not expect me to share it with Eli later?" I throw my arms up just like he did a moment ago. "And you know Eli will never let you live down being so nice to me—especially if you're looking out for Eli."

"I am not!" he practically screams. "I'm looking out for you, and I'm starting to regret it."

"Well, yeah, but looking out for me is looking out for Eli," I note. "I don't mean to brag, but they kind of like me, and they want me looked out for so..."

"Boy, you keep it up, and I'm gonna give you a task that will involve answering your questions about how sewage works on a ship." I pull a face at that, and he instantly laughs. At least I hope that breaks his worry and any concern between us.

"I don't need a task," I tell him, "but I'd really like some company. And maybe a snack. I eat when I'm..."

"Worried." He nods and motions behind us, which I assume is supposed to mean inside the ship. "I won't ask you to come inside since I know you're gonna be set on staring out there like they'll pop up any second...and that ain't the direction they'd come from by the way."

"Wait, what?"

"So, I'll go and get us something to...snack on."

I'd be more entertained by the way he says 'snack' as if the word and the concept are foreign to him if I didn't just learn that I'm looking in the wrong direction to watch Eli come back. They left in this direction; why wouldn't they come back this way? And how does Jak just know which way they're going to come back from?

"Tea? Or coffee?"

"What way are they going to come back from?!"

"Oh, fuck," he mutters, heading off. "And you're making our maps."

He has a point. "Jak, bring back chocolate, or I'll throw myself overboard. And tell me where to look!"

"Look no further!" This voice is louder but so much more familiar that it doesn't actually make me startle—a good thing since I'm not sure how much more I couldn't handle tonight in the way of anxiety and surprises. I didn't expect to be this wound up about Eli being off the ship, but now I get to turn around and find them leading Dava and Tevin back on board, the latter tossing a new orb—the one yellow—from hand to hand.

"For the love of my mother, is that an element of the gods you're throwing around?" Yen does startle me again, appearing from the shadows like she just melted out of them. How long has she been there? "Do you want to drop it and ruin us?"

Tevin laughs at her and waves it off. "Dava, take this mess below deck and store our new treasure please."

Yen launches a very colorful stream of swear words and foul language at Tevin while Dava takes the obr, wraps an arm around her girl-friend, and leads the still-swearing elf off the deck. She gives me a sympathetic smile on the way. I think she should be taking sympathy in-stead of giving it, but I'm too happy to see Eli again to think much about it. Tevin being here too is a lovely bonus.

Eli slaps Tevin's chest and then aims for me, their smile huge and gorgeous ."Please tell me

C. Knight

you're both ready to celebrate tonight. We just got back a piece of treasure that isn't even supposed to exist, and if I'm not hard for the next fortnight on the rush, it'll be a miracle."

"I, for one, vote we go handle that right now," Tevin announces, also giving me a charming smile.

"I'm in. But we have to wait for Jak." Tevin and Eli both gape at me, exchange a glance with each other, and then look back at me with their mouths open a little. I shrug and explain, "He's bringing snacks."

Chapter 26
Eli

"You wanna race?"

I have to bite my tongue to keep from barking out a laugh and ruining Max's plan.

The first time I accepted Max's offer to race, we were twelve, and I thought he was kidding. He was in a wheelchair then, too, and while I was a scrawny thing, I was still pretty tall. It felt like he was joking, maybe testing me, and since I was already head over heels for Max, I was very nervous about being tested—and failing the test. I didn't know Max well enough then to know that he would never test me and that he definitely was not kidding.

Max has won more than a few bets and successfully diminished the egos of many in these races. His trick is the wheels underneath him and his exceptional knowledge of the world around him. He has no choice but to be that aware, to know things abled people don't have to know, and Max has figured out a couple ways to use that to his advantage. Specifically, he's very good at picking up an incline or decline in roads.

Whenever he's on any sort of decline, unless there's a real risk of flying off the end of a dock into the ocean or slamming into a wall, Max is going to release his wheels and zip down, usually while shouting, "Weeeee!" People watching this get all sorts of horrified, and I've been endlessly entertained by the screams and people covering their faces so they don't have to watch. But if Max gets a chance to race someone unaware, he's going to take it.

The races scare me since he'll go faster than normal even when he's enjoying a downhill opportunity, but I've seen him do it enough too know I can relax. Mostly. As much as I'm ever relaxed, especially when Max's safety might be in question. I can't help but turn toward him now, though, more eager to watch than to finish buying coffee with Dava.

It's Yen he's challenged this time. Yen will take a loss well, but she'll definitely be expecting to win. She looks around the street around them and doesn't see the decline any more than I do, but if Max asked, I know it's there. He doesn't need much for the chair to really get going, especially with a few well-timed pushes. I nudge Dava and motion in their direction. "Wanna see your girlfriend get thrashed?"

"You're okay with him racing on a street but hound him around the ship?" she teases, handing over some coin to the merchant and turning with me to watch while we wait for the crew's order.

I scowl at her and argue, "I do not hound him. And I'm okay with this 'cause I've seen him do it—and I've lost to him more than once." She gives me a surprised, skeptical look. "Just watch."

Yen has never needed much convincing to get a competition going, whether or not she thinks she can win. So long as she gets to try. The two of them line up at the edge of a cart that's selling cinnamon-apple flavored donuts— why the fuck don't I have any of those donuts yet?—and decide on the lamppost at the end of the street as their finish line. There are people around, but most are near the carts, so there's an opening right down the middle of the street.

"You think it feels weird to bounce around on stones like this?" I ask, nudging one of the stones under our feet that forms the street. They're wide and mostly in shades of gray; I would guess they were white at some point, probably intended to make the town look fancy but likely didn't last long. This is not a pirate port, definitely a more upclass market coming here, but people getting off ships can only keep their shoes so clean.

"Probably," Dava notes. She cocks her head. "Might feel good. I had a massage once where the woman was used magic to make vibrations in my muscles. It was pretty fantastic."

"Bet she wasn't half bad either, huh?" I tease. Dava laughs and shoves my shoulder, but the blush on her cheeks gives away the truth. "I might ask Max to borrow the chair and give it a try. Or I might end up landing on my balls."

"That does not seem worth the experiment," she notes.

"You're up!" the dwarf manning the coffee

shop calls. We half turn toward her to gather our drinks and rejoin the crew, but I'm mostly distracted by Max and Yen counting down the start of their race. When they're off, it's obvious in a second that Max isn't about to lose this. Whatever downhill momentum exists on this street is pulling him well ahead, and Yen is left sprinting and laughing behind him.

"Go Max!" Rosleigh shouts, and a few others on the street join in, applauding and cheering on the spectacle. Max hates attention from strangers, so leave it to him to be so good at attracting it.

"Wow, you were not kidding," Dava notes.

I laugh and finally manage to retrieve our drinks in the little cardboard trays that the dwarf shoved the cups into. "I never joke when it comes to how incredible my partner is, thank you."

Dava says something else; I know she's talking, and I can vaguely hear her voice as I turn away from the coffee stand and toward the end of the street again. I can't get my brain to process what she's saying, though. Not with people approaching Yen and Max at the end of the street. People I recognize. People who shouldn't not be anywhere near my Max.

The coffee cups hit the stone with a dull thud, and if they splash, I don't care or notice. I explode into a sprint, moving as fast as I can to get to Max. Yen is standing between the three humans who joined them and Max, blocking him from Cross Fields and his two biggest crew members, but I need to be there. I'm still twenty feet away when one of the big guys lunges for Yen while Cross and the other go for Max.

I don't bother slowing or bracing myself before crashing into Cross Fields. The impact makes a sound like a bat hitting the hollow hull of a ship, and he cries out in pain when we slam into the stones. "Get away from him!" I punctuate that by punching Cross in the face, my knuckles crunching against his jaw with Cross on his side underneath me.

Pain erupts against the side of my own face, confusing since Cross didn't move. I don't manage to remember he had friends until someone grabs my shoulders and throws me off him. I turn and scramble up, ready to face his crew, but then mine is there. Tevin gets between us, bigger than the brute of a human, and shoves him back. Yen and Dava have the other one cowering, and since Cross is still down, I whirl for Max.

He's on the ground.

Max is on the ground. His chair is on its side, and Max tipped out of it. He's sitting up, Ros and Jak with him—Ros helping him and Jak clearly serving as a final line of protection. But Max is on the ground, and it makes me want to throw up. Especially because I'm pretty sure that's my fault.

"Hey, hey, look at me," I breathe, throwing myself to my knees in front of him. The sharp stab when I land is nothing. I cup Max's face in my hands and search his deep brown eyes. "Are you okay? Where are you hurt?"

He shakes his head. "No, I'm okay. Just… banged up." He looks past me toward the others, toward the fight still happening. "Eli, make them stop. All of them."

I think to argue. I want to get Max back in

his chair and then beat Cross bloody. I want to stomp all three of them into the stones until they can't so much as think about coming near Max ever again. But I know he's right, and I know he's a better person than me. I know the crowd watching all of this is going to start problems, too.

"Stay right here, okay? Don't move yet." Max nods, but I still look at Rosleigh and press, "Make him stay down however you need to."

"On it," she promises.

I stand and turn back toward the mess, Cross now on his feet and acting like he might come for me. He's shouting all sorts of names at me, most of them revolving around me being queer because he lacks creativity, but he's not that brave or that foolish. Unfortunately. I'd like an excuse.

"Alright, enough!" I shout to my crew. Tevin has to ignore one final shove from the jerk who hit me, but he steps back to come by my side, ignoring his own pride for it. I squeeze his arm gratefully. Yen and Dava join me, too, all of us keeping an eye on the three humans from *Sunbeam*. And Yen is holding one of her arms oddly. She's hurt. If it wasn't for Max and witnesses, I'd kill all three of them for hurting my friend and threatening Max. "The fuck are you thinking, Cross? You thought you'd just walk off with a member of my crew, with my partner?"

Cross's eyes flash between me and Max; I don't think I'd admitted before that we're in a relationship, and I wish I hadn't now. Especially now that I know Cross's game. He's after my Max, and I might have just given him more reason.

"What's wrong, Captain Rose?" Cross asks,

crossing his scrawny arms over his chest. The guy doesn't look like he's actually worked a day in his life; how is it that he's been on a ship—supposedly captain of that ship—for years? "Are you afraid you won't be able to find anything at all without your pretty little map maker?"

He just said at least four things that warrant me breaking his nose, and it takes every bit of self-control I have not to lunge at him. The only thing holding me back is the need to keep my body planted firmly between the three of them and Max. My crew is here, and I know they'll fight for Max—they already have, but I'm not about to make that anyone else's responsibility when it's my honor.

"I don't need to fear that," I tell Cross, grinning at him. "You can't just steal Max from me, and I don't have to wonder if he'd rather sail with you. Max is a member of *Tempest*, and that *pretty little map maker* is going to make sure you don't get a damn thing from Magnus. You'll be lucky if I ever let you find anything again. Except maybe a couple more broken masts."

Tevin barks out a laugh from beside me, and that only makes the goons turn an even deeper shade of red. Cross's hands fall to his sides now, fists clenched so tightly that his knuckles are a stark white. It just makes him look like a pissed-off child instead of a threatening captain.

"I'm gonna go ahead and guess you're here to try and take Max 'cause you don't have anything to offer Magnus?" When Cross can't answer, I laugh. "There are only four left now. The reward and the bonus are ours, and everyone is going to know it was *Tempest* who discovered the elements of the gods. My ship will become legend just like those stones. You'll have to try much, much harder. Let's go."

I turn to Max first, of course, sweeping my gaze over him quickly to make sure he doesn't have any obvious injuries now that he's been helped back into his chair. Jak and Ros got him back in the chair. He looks a little less put together than usual, but there's no blood or anything obviously painful. At least not outwardly more painful than usual. And he's always in pain. Fuck, I hate that someone hurt him more than he already has to deal with, especially when they did it because of me, because of Max being on my crew.

"Alright, alright!" a voice booms, deep and cross. The city guard has arrived, three of them in dark red uniforms with shiny boots; apparently, they manage to keep their shoes clean. "What exactly is going on here?"

Cross flashes me a smug grin, aware of how we both look and which one of us is more likely to get beaten by jerks in uniform. But before he can tell a single lie in his own defense, a old woman who doesn't look strong enough to yell shouts, "That one started it!"

She's pointing right at Cross and his goons, and he's not the only one. The apple cider donut merchant gives Max a box, and the dwarf at the coffee stand brings us replacements, all while witnesses from the crowd tell the city guard what happened. The guard is appropriately horrified that three grown men attacked someone in a wheelchair, and Max doesn't hesitate to play it up a little. He won't cry, but he points out new bruises and scratches.

For the first time in my life, city guard let me

know without even a warning. Cross isn't getting so lucky this time, and if I know anything about dealing with guards like this, I know they're about to be held up. When the guard pulls out a set of chains and Cross practically screams at the sight, I'm pretty sure we've just been granted at least a few days' lead on Sunbeam.

Instead of sticking around to give the guard a chance to find a reason to hate me, I turn and lead my crew back up the street. Not just to get back to the ship and into those donuts, but it's a factor. A bang and a shout has me whirling back around only to find Max smoothly maneuvering off the curb while issuing obviously fake apologies. Behind him, Cross is swearing up a storm and hopping up and down on while foot while clutching the other one leg desperately. He's just about howling in pain, and since I've had that chair hit me accidentally, I don't need to wonder what happened. Or that it really fucking hurts to get hit on purpose.

"Oops," Max offers with an innocent smile up at me, and I recover from my shock enough to give him a kiss in appreciation, the crew and crowd laughing and only making the whole thing better.

"Let me," I say, taking the back of Max's chair once he smiles and agrees. "You deserve a break for being fucking incredible."

Protecting Max is only going to get more complicated from here on out. I know Cross and rich people well enough to know he's not going to let this go. Max is going to be in danger until this whole thing is over and maybe even after that. But I can protect him. Nothing is ever going to take my Max from me.

Chapter 27

Max

When I first came on board *Tempest*, Ros warned me not to spend too much time below deck, away from the sunlight. She also makes me eat an orange every day, and I know she's piling extra veggies onto my meals, so I've been assuming she's protective of me. I don't like being babied or even being protected, but someone choosing to give me a few extra health benefits is just kind. I have to admit, I haven't taken her warning about the deck and sunlight all that seriously.

And now I realize I haven't actually seen the sun in days, not more than through the windows in the captain's quarters. I set my mind to working out the final four maps all at once, and of course once I decide it's happening, I have trouble focusing on anything but. I've stopped to eat and drink the meals Eli brings me during the day and the dinner they practically drag me to, showering and sleeping when necessary, and not much else. Well, Eli has managed to distract me for fun a couple times, too.

This happens to me without trying. My brain gets all excited about something new, and by the time I come up for air, I've lost days. I don't even realize it's happening until it's over or until I get so stiff or sick that I have no choice but to stop. Today...I finished up the last of the four maps I've had my mind on. It's like being released from a fog, and I'm always a little disoriented after. But the most disorienting thing today is the fact that it's daylight, and I can't remember the last time I was in the sun.

I...slept last night. And I think two other nights. Has it been three days?! Oh, that can't be good. Ros was definitely right, and I'm definitely feeling that disorientation now.

At least I've been moving around enough that I can still move without too much stiffness, shifting off the almost too-comfy chair at Eli's desk and into my wheelchair without excessive pain or issue. There's been more than once that I needed days to recover physically from one of these days-long brain freezes, the focus on a project overruling my body's needs somehow. Thank the gods I've had Eli here feeding me and keeping me hydrated this time at least.

I don't think I've ever told them about these fixation periods, though. They probably would have tried to help me come out of it sooner if they knew this is an issue for me. I tend not to tell them things that I think will make them worry about me more than they already do...and the way they've been acting about my safety on our little adventure so far isn't really convincing me to do otherwise. If I'm going to be on the ship, though, I should be honest and let them help when I do need it.

Especially if I'm going to stay on the ship beyond this little adventure. I still haven't decided whether I should bring that up with Eli. Maybe I want them to bring the idea to me first; it's their ship after all.

And maybe I should work on clearing out my brain so I don't prove to them that I'm at risk here. Sunshine. I need sunshine. I'm gonna take an extra orange today, too. That halfling knows what she's talking about!

I turn around and scan the room to try and remember where I put my crutches, but the door swings open and distracts me. Eli striding in distracts me even further, especially when they're smiling at me. "Look at you, away from the desk in daylight hours! I was starting to wonder when I should be worried about you," they admit.

"Only truly worry if I stop eating. Can you bring my crutches over? I want to get up to the deck, get some fresh air."

"Probably a good idea." Eli heads for my crutches; they don't have to look around to know that they're leaning against the side of the bookcase. I have no memory of leaving them there. My forgetfulness for anything not related to my maps gets worse when I fall into these periods of intense focus. At least I knew where the chair was when I needed to get up.

Eli pauses just before wrapping their hand around the crutch, though, and then looks at me with a grin. The sort of grin that they only get before they're about to do or suggest something that's less than responsible, usually a lot of fun, and often ends up getting naked. And those suggestions are usually even more fun when they involve getting naked.

"I think I should probably bathe before we take our clothes off for whatever idea is making you smile like that," I note.

"I like getting dirty with you," they quip with a wink, "but my idea doesn't require taking our clothes off. I was thinking... You want a piggyback ride?"

Eli used to give me piggyback rides all the time. When we were kids, I was on my crutches much more often than my wheelchair mostly for pride and other nonsense reasons, and they exhaust me a lot faster than using the chair. Instead of making me get worn out, Eli would suggest a piggyback ride, and it was always a lot of fun. There were a few times that we decided to get more creative, too, though I'm not sure either of us would be willing to repeat the 'Eli is a sled dog' idea that ended up with both of us covered in snow and freezing cold. I hate the concept of being carried, but something about a piggyback ride with Eli has always just been about fun and sparing me, not making me a literal burden on their back.

I raise my arms to them, and Eli practically runs to me, making me laugh. They turn and kneel in front of my chair, letting me use their shoulders to pull myself close enough. Eli reaches back, confidently but carefully tucking their hands under my legs and standing. I know my weight barely affects them at all, but they're cautious while pulling my legs apart and guiding them around their waist. I plant a kiss on their cheek in thanks when I'm secure.

"Let me grab my crutches on the way so I can get around on the deck." Eli stops by the bookshelf, and I grab the crutches to hold in one hand while anchoring myself with my forearm across Eli's sternum. "Remember when we did this as kids?"

Eli laughs. "You mean do I remember the first few times when I was terrified I would somehow hurt you and only offered because I was so desperate to make you smile? Or do you mean later when I realized you're not all that breakable, and I really enjoy having you on my back?"

"I forgot that you were so scared at first! I never understood that when you offered...though it's really cute you wanted to make me smile." I squeeze them a little tighter and nuzzle their cheek with mine, tickling my skin. "Your beard is amazing these days."

"Jak says that I spend more time taking care of it than the ship. Don't tell him which one I love more," Eli tells me while climbing up the six steps to the deck level of the ship, sun-soaked and open air and smelling of the sea; it's amazing how much of that scent is lost even below deck, and it's a lovely bonus to coming outside. Especially since the sea smells much better on the open water than it does near the docks where the water is significantly less clean. And the people sometimes, too.

"Oh, that's so much better," I admit, exhaling as far as I can. "I don't think I want to know exactly how long I was down there."

"I won't tell you. You seemed productive, though?"

I appreciate that it's a question, so they aren't suggesting any sacrifice I made for who knows how long is worth it if I was productive. They're only asking whether I feel like my time was well spent. But they are the captain of this ship, and I am here for a reason, so I'm proud to be able to give them an answer - the answer they want most.

"I've made a ton of progress. I have maps for two more pieces. Two more, and you'll have directions to everything." I let him ease me down onto the steps leading to the upper deck and then get to my feet on my crutches. It feels weirder than it should to be standing since I haven't in a while, but it's kind of nice for a chance to stretch a bit and even put a little weight on the limbs that won't hold me up completely. Fortunately, they don't have to for me to get more comfortable. "Well, you'll have directions to everything, assuming nothing is found first and moved."

Eli waves that off. "We'll be ready if it happens, but we're way ahead. You're the magic, Maxy. "

Something dark passes over their face even though their smile looks pretty genuine. They're troubled by something but also happy, and I can see them fighting off whatever it is, so when they head to the railing and motion me closer, I join them instead of pressing for what's going on. I have to trust that they'll tell me things I need to know or that they're struggling with. Eli's a good partner; we're just around each other a lot more now than usual and we're adjusting to that.

But when that adjustment includes getting to see just how well Eli's green eyes match the sea almost perfectly, I have very few concerns or complaints. They've always kind of astounded me with their beauty, from the moment they plopped down on a library table in front of me, too thin and soaking wet. I've never had a chance before this trip to admire them on their own ship, the thing they worked so hard for, and I think it makes them even more beautiful.

"I'm very proud of you, E. You know that, right?"

They just make a soft sound in their throat and stare down at the waves gently lapping at the ship's side. "You tell me all the time, baby. Thank you."

"Are you okay?" I move closer to them, ducking my head to catch their gaze. "You seem worried about something."

They take a breath and look like they do when they need to tell me that they're leaving for a long time, like the words are getting stuck inside them so it's hard to get them out. "Cross is gonna keep following us."

"Yeah, but *Sunbeam* should be days behind us now, right?"

Eli shakes their head. "Maybe, but he's following us because he wants to take you."

"That's an unpleasant thought," I quip. Eli doesn't laugh, and it makes my stomach feel sour. "We're ready to deal with that if they catch up, right?"

"Of course," they answer, but I'm not convinced that's the whole truth. When I frown, they smile softly and reaches out to cup my jaw. "Sorry, Maxy. I'm just stressed out about it, that's all. But I am dealing with it."

"I know you are. And you told me what's going on, which is good progress, right?" Their face falls again, any semblance of smile—real or fake—completely gone. "Eli?"

I'm distracted by a gust of wind blowing their loose hair across their face and shoving mine out of order. I love being near the sea, but I've always hated getting smacked in the face by my hair—especially because my hair in my eyes makes it hard to see where I'm going, and taking my hands off my crutches or my wheels to clear my vision is pretty dangerous...or at least it's really inconvenient. I thought coming on deck today would work in my favor since we should be heading into the wind, which would blow it back off my face, but...

Wait.

We should be heading into the wind.

"Eli..." I turn around to find who is at the helm. Tevin. And he's absolutely glaring at us. At Eli.

"Did you tell him the truth yet?" he calls down to us, and Eli lets out a sound like they just got kicked in the nuts. "Take that as a no."

"Tell me what?" I ask, not turning back to Eli yet but also not shouting loud enough that they could assume I'm talking to Tevin. But they still don't answer me, so I turn back to face them. They know how much I hate spinning in circles on my crutches, but I'm apparently going to be forced to do that for answers today. When they reach out to steady me, a hand aiming for my elbow, I risk falling by jerking away; I'm damn glad I don't fall, but I'm happier that the point clearly lands. Those sea-green eyes are in a storm now. "Tell me what, Eli? What's the truth?"

Eli is holding their breath when their eyes dart rapidly over the rail and out toward the sea before snapping back to me. Too late, though. I saw it, and I turn in the same direction.

There's more than just empty sea awaiting us out there now, but instead of the mountainous coastal area I was expecting, the one that I directed us toward with my last map, there's a port city skyline approaching. A familiar one.

"We're going back." My stomach flops so violently, I have to swallow for fear of throwing up all over myself. "You're taking me home."

"Max..."

"Were you going tell me before got there?" No answer. Which is an answer.

I've been wondering if I can do this, if Eli and I can make living together in this way work, if we're done with being apart and...and if we get to be together all the time again. Now, I have my answer.

It won't work. Eli doesn't want me here anymore; no matter the reasoning that they give, they're taking me home. So that's it.

Adventure over.

"Max, I—"

"I'm gonna go back down and finish up. You'll have the rest of the maps before we get to port." I force a smile this time. "You'll be able to finish your job, find your future."

I head for the door to take me back inside, wishing I could go faster, that there is any chance of me outrunning them. A loud thump comes from behind me, and then a huge hand pushes the door open for me before I get there. "Go steer *Tempest*, Eli. I need a break," Tevin informs them.

"Knock it off, Tev."

"Fine, crash your ship. Your problem."

I get through the door and halfway down the ramp before Tevin lets the door shut, darkening the hall enough that I have to pause and readjust. The tears rapidly filling my eyes aren't helping me see, and even though Tevin's hand on my back is comforting, it's not what I want. "I'm not gonna follow you. I'll just make sure they don't either for a while. Go."

"Thank you, Tevin, but I don't want you to get in trouble." I hate that my voice cracks.

"Max. Go."

I don't waste the chance or another second, dragging myself down the long hallway and into the quarters that have never felt less like mine. All the work we did to put the books on the shelves and unpack my stuff, everything on the desk that we reorganized to make room for me, all the little pieces around that belong to me and made me feel welcome here. None of it matters if Eli doesn't want me here.

All I asked was to be allowed to make decisions for myself, for my own safety, and now...

Eli's bed just feels wrong, especially when I hate that I'm crying, but that's where I find myself, blankets over my head to block out the orange glow of sunset, legs and back aching from stress more than anything, the port getting closer by the moment.

I cry until my cheeks itch and my eyes are sore. The only win is that Eli doesn't come in and find me like this.

I'll eventually drag myself out of this bed and back to work. I'll finish enough maps that Eli and *Tempest* can keep their advantage and their headstart because even while I'm pissed at them, I want Eli to have their dream. But right now, all I can do is lay here and know that going back to my life on land will never be the same. And I don't think anything about my relationship or my friendship with Eli can be the same either.

Chapter 28
Eli

I've never had so many storms brewing all at once.

There's an actual storm on the horizon, the clouds bruised, purple and angry and heavy. They're a ways off still for now, but that's only for now. Usually, a storm coming excites me. My heart beats harder, more life flows through my veins, when I can feel the crackle of the atmosphere against my skin.

Right now...it just feels like one more attempt to drown me.

The rest of my storms are all metaphorical. At least I think that's the right word. Max would know, but Max isn't talking to me. No one on the crew is speaking to me at the moment more than is required to operate our ship; Ros informed me that we're low on oranges just before proving we still have enough to spare because she threw one at my head, Jak updated me on a fix for the canons before unlocking one to let it roll over my foot, and Yen told me she's making sure our blades are as sharp as possible in a way I'm certain was a threat. Oh, and Dava warned me that if I get caught in a small room alone with Tevin, I should find a way out of it very, very quickly.

The crew has never been upset with me like this before. We've always had an easy time getting along, effortless teamwork and a lot of fun and shared passion driving us and *Tempest* through the waves and around the world. Even when I make decisions they aren't sure about, I have their trust, and I have their friendship—and they know I value them as friends. I try pretty hard not to upset them, actually.

It's all made so much worse by Max. Usually, when something is going on during a trip that has me worried or stressed out, I'm aching to see Max, to talk to him. It's always been that way, ever since we met. If there's something bothering me or weighing on my heart, I want Max to help me hold that burden and work through it or even just comfort me. I need him. And for all the years we've known each other...I don't think Max has ever actually been angry with me. He's needed to smack me upside the head once or twice when I've been foolish but never angry with me. I don't think I've ever done anything to earn that. Not until now.

Max and I grew up very differently. He has a family who loves and supports him; they communicate regularly, and if Max was to show up at their door asking for help, it would be offered no questions asked. His mom and dad are such kind people that they've afforded me the same care and safety. They've been there for me whenever I needed them over the years even though I don't belong to them; it's always been enough that I belong to Max. I don't know who my parents are or even exactly where and when I was born. Someone brought me to an orphanage when I was a baby, and that was home until I left at thirteen. I made my own home after that, finding a living and getting by until Max and I moved in together after his training ended.

But as different as our lives were, we both had to fend for ourselves in significant ways. I had to scrape by and get creative—sometimes in illegal ways—to survive. No one was going to feed, clothe, or house me if I didn't make it happen for myself, if I didn't find opportunities to pay, if I didn't build skills people would pay for. Max has to navigate a world that isn't accessible to him. He has to get creative and sometimes put up a real fight to be able to go places and do things that people who can walk don't struggle with or even have to think about. He has to constantly manage his energy levels, his pain, his flexibility; if I had to think constantly about all those things, I'd be exhausted!

Max has to take care of himself every day of his life. He lives alone for the majority of the year, he goes to work and does his job so well he's earned a reputation across several continents, and he keeps up the home we both fell in love with the moment we walked through the door. He manages his symptoms and his body, and he's responsible for his own safety.

Max is more than capable of taking care of himself, and all he asks of me as his partner, the person he wants to spend his life with and has supported endlessly, is that I listen to him and trust him with his own life, his own safety.

I know he thinks I'm failing at that now, but Max isn't seeing the big picture. None of them are. If Max is hurt—or, gods forbid it, worse—the treasure and the reputation and all the things that we're supposed to be chasing will mean nothing. If going after my dream means losing my heart, it will never be worth it. I'm just not strong enough to balance both, to the chase the dream and handle the risk to him. I'm not as strong or as brave as Max is.

I'm a huge coward. Such a big cowardly coward, in fact, that while Max is saying his goodbyes to the crew and everyone is bringing his bags onto the docks, I'm standing at the helm and watching from a distance. Too scared to listen to all the things they might be saying about me, all the reasons they might be pissed at me, all the names they're probably calling me—and not for fun this time. Too scared to hear Max tell me he doesn't want me to walk him home today...and that he doesn't want me to visit again.

I can only be a coward for so long, though. I want to walk Max home because it'll feel normal and because I hate that I'm leaving him again. It's been amazing to have him on the ship, to have him with me every morning and every night. I need another chance to explain, and I need to believe there is some possibility I'll have those mornings and nights again in the future.

My ship is completely docked, so there's absolutely no use for me to be at the helm anymore. I finally pull myself away and head off the ship, joining the crew and Max down on the dock. I let my boots fall heavily the entire way so they can all hear me coming, maybe put the insults away for the moment.

Ros doesn't look at me, sniffling back her tears and hugging Max before she rushes past me and back onto the ship. Great—that's another heart I broke.

Yen and Jak take off after Ros. At least Dava gives me a look before going, too. It's not a kind look by any means, but it acknowledges my existence. I was starting to wonder if I disappeared.

I may prefer disappearing to standing here with Tevin and Max. Neither of them has spoken to me in more than a few words and terse moments for the last week. I'm endlessly grateful Tevin is here to support Max and that Max trusts him so much, but there's also part of me that is jealous. Unfairly, disgustingly, terribly jealous. They have each other, which makes it easier for them both to keep me out.

"You want me to walk you back?" Tevin asks, a kind offer that feels like a smack in the face. I always walk Max home. I always get that chance for one more private goodbye, a quiet moment together before we separate again. *Again.*

"I'm okay, thank you," Max answers. "Go ahead and get back to the ship. I'll...see you."

Wow, that's not awkward. Tevin is smooth, though, smiling brightly at him and then leaning down so they can hug. I look away, finding it too hard right now to see them finding solace in one another while shutting me out. Or while I shut myself out, I guess.

It's hard to be rational about it at the moment. I've never had a second of doubt about Max or Tevin, but while I'm doubting myself and my career choice and my life and everything I've ever done...

I'm grateful when Tevin walks away, and I can't say I've ever felt that before. It's not much better to be alone with Max at the moment, and that's an even more unusual feeling.

Once, Max and I got into the sort of overly dramatic and ridiculous fight that only sixteen-year-olds can muster up, and we broke up. It happened about twenty minutes before an event his family was hosting which I was invited to, so I had no choice but to go. For four hours, Max and I were forced to pretend we were a happy, young couple with eyes on the future while we weren't even speaking to each other. It was torture, and we both only used it to get more dramatic, more emotional.

This? This moment right now is worse than that. And not just because this is a real problem, not teenage drama.

I gather Max's three bags, slinging one across my chest and another over one shoulder while carrying the third. His case, of course, I pick up and carry in my hands; this case holds his most prized possessions, including the compass his grandfather gave him before that sweet old man died and the custom quill set I got for him in what feels like another lifetime now. I would never just throw this into one of Max's bags, no more than he would. He'd probably prefer to carry it himself, but we both know things on his lap in the chair tend to end up as things on the ground in front of the chair.

"Ready?"

Max doesn't answer the question, just turns away from the ship and heads off the dock, aiming for home. Or the apartment. His home. My brain is fucking mess right now.

"Do you want me to do any grocery shopping for you before we leave?" I ask, walking a step behind him. It's unusual—I'm not even sure I've noticed the back of his chair like this before since I've always walked beside him. I don't know if this is the irrational part of me again or what, but I don't feel like I deserve to walk with him.

Or maybe I'm still just the biggest coward on all the seas, and I don't want to see the way he looks at me.

"No, I'll be fine until tomorrow when I can talk to the kid upstairs," he says. There's a long pause, and then he adds, "Thanks, though."

"Of course."

"Are you leaving tonight or in the morning?"

The question makes me draw up short, catching me off guard. Even with Max being this angry with me, I didn't think further ahead than the next step. I always walk him home and then I always spend one final night with him. We always leave in the morning, after I get at least a little more time with him. Tonight...

"I don't know," I answer because it's the truth. He doesn't respond, but I don't know why.

It's a little later than we usually get in, and unless there's some sort of seasonal event going on, this port is a quiet area. It was one of the reasons Max's parents relented in their arguments about moving him inland, moving him closer to home. Max hated that they were so over-protective when we were trying to find the right home for us; he's always hated people who try and make decisions for him based on what they think is best.

Does he hate me now?

The quiet streets mean the silence between us is thick and heavy on the walk from the docks to the apartment. It's only a couple blocks, but it feels like it stretches on forever. My brain takes every second as a new opportunity to wonder whether Max will yell at me before he ends our lives together, to question whether he'll let me stay tonight or ever again, to go through every single thing about my life that would change if I didn't have Max. And maps are nowhere near that long list. I don't care about the maps; he matters so much more. That's how we ended up here, with me silently following him into our building and to the door that's been home for years without saying a word.

Max has his keys, which is a good thing since I only realize I forgot mine right then. I have to restrain myself from moving while he unlocks and then pushes open the door, letting himself in without me needing to hold the door for him. He gets home to this apartment every single day while he's here alone, and on a normal night, I wouldn't even think about doing that. On a normal night, I'd probably be on his lap or groping him, making opening the door difficult for reasons other than the wheelchair. But tonight, even though I know I'm in trouble for forcing my decisions about his health and safety on Max, while he's angry with me, I can't help wanting to do more, more, more.

I restrain myself, only stepping in behind him, waiting for him to turn on the gas lamp near the couch to brighten the room, and then setting his bags down near the table. The cozy little apartment is cold and forbidding tonight; I never noticed how dark the shadows just outside the reach of the lamp can get. I swallow the feeling, too aware that it's me and not the environment.

"Here." Max goes to the largest of his bags, the one that carries his books and his other supplies, and he pulls out a small satchel I recognize as mine; Max had been using it around the ship, and now he's holding it out to me. "The remaining maps are finished. I numbered them; I'm sure you could have figured out the best path but… just doing my job."

Ouch. We both know the treasure hunt and *Tempest* were more than just a job to him—and not this time, not just on this hunt. Max always puts special care into what he makes for me, for my ship, for my crew because it matters to him. None of it would even be possible without him. I turned it into a job when I decided it had to end, and now, I've basically fired him. I take the satchel and flip it open only for an excuse to hide my shaking hands and the burn in my eyes.

"Four more?" I shake my head a little, a laugh escaping me. "You finished four maps already."

"I didn't want to leave until you were ready to keep going. That should do it for you."

"Impressive," I tell him; he knows I've always thought that. "Thank you for this. I appreciate you doing it even while being pissed at me."

"I was hired for a job; I wasn't going to leave it unfinished," he says. "Especially not this job. I know how important it is to you—to all of you."

Of course he does. Max made it all possible. For years while I was saving every coin to put toward buying and then rebuilding *Tempest* and the crew, Max was the only one responsible for things like rent and food. He made sure we had somewhere to live, something to eat, warm clothes, and tools. He worked his ass off to do that so I could keep saving, and he never complained for a second. Whenever I suggested getting another job to contribute, he shot it down immediately. He's been as fierce about my dreams as I have. *Tempest* wouldn't be mine and wouldn't be afloat without him.

"Max, can we talk about this? I don't want—"

"I'm tired, Eli," he cuts me off, already heading toward the bedroom. "I heard everything you have to say, and I don't have it in me to hear it again."

"You want me to go?" I ask, the dismissal like a knife to the gut. He's never sent me away before; when I didn't have any other home in the whole world, I had Max, and I knew he'd always make space for me.

But tonight, Max only hesitates for a moment before he answers, "Yes. You should go."

I watch, dumbfounded and shattered, as he disappears through the bedroom door. A second later, the door shuts behind him. Shuts me out.

I don't realize I'm crossing the room until I'm standing in front of the bedroom door, staring at the dark wood, not daring to so much as touch it. I'm not going to invade his privacy. I just upturned his life by bringing him onto my ship, and then I cut that short and threw him off again. We both knew it was a temporary arrangement, but not like this.

No one is hearing me, though. I have to try and make him hear me before I go.

"Maxy, I know it's not right that I'm making a decision for you. I know I promised I wouldn't do that when we were still kids. But Max, this isn't kid shit." I take a breath, forcing myself to keep my voice level. I have to speak up to be heard through the door and wherever he might be in the room, and it's a little too easy to make the jump to shouting from there. Yelling at him sure as shit isn't going to get me anywhere. "There are people who know about you now. They know you're the edge to a race like this, and if we're carrying you around on the ship, we're only making you a target. You came on to help me with this treasure hunt, but the hunt isn't worth risking you. I can't stand the thought of you being hurt. I know you'd rather make that call for yourself but...not this time. I know this is the right thing, and I know that even if you hate me for it forever, it'll be worth it because you're safe."

There's no noise at all on the other side. I don't hear him moving around, can't hear him breathing or—gods forbid—crying, and he doesn't make any effort to respond. I'd stand there all night if I didn't think he really wanted me to go...but he does. He wants me to go, and despite what he believes at the moment, I do respect him.

"I'm gonna come back when we can, and I hope you'll talk to me then. I love you, Maxy." I leave his new turtle on top of his case, and then, I have to go.

It's never been so hard to leave that apartment. It sucks to leave Max here even under normal circumstances, and I often have to practically drag myself out to actually achieve leaving. Even with the ship waiting, even with my life on the sea, there's a huge part of me that wants to be here at all times. A part of me that wants to be wherever Max is. Tonight, leaving without one last kiss, without Max saying he loves me, without his warning to be safe...I don't want to go.

I choose a method of one foot in front of the other, never stopping and never so much as lifting my head. I can't risk something drawing me back to the apartment, back to Max. He wants me gone, and I have to go.

The walk back to the ship is even longer than the walk to the apartment. I feel like I'm walking through swamp mud, every step heavy and my feet unwilling to lift. Every inch of my body knows it's wrong to leave Max like this, to leave things like this between us, but I don't have a choice. I didn't have a choice to bring him on the ship, I didn't have a choice to send him off the ship, and I don't have a choice if Max finally decides he's had enough of me. My only option is to get back onto the water and get back to our hunt. At least when we win the prize at the end of this treasure hunt, I can make sure Max has what he needs for a secure life even if I'm not part of it.

I never should have come back here. I should have trusted my gut initially and just asked Max for maps, taken our chances out there like everyone else. I never should have put him at risk like this—and I definitely shouldn't have bragged about our edge when I got the chance and just a tiny taste of confidence. All of this is my fault.

But the one thing I didn't do wrong is putting Max's safety first. Cross and *Sunbeam* have gotta be days behind us, and they have no reason to know where we live. He'll be okay here, and whatever storms lie ahead of me, I'm willing to weather knowing Max will be safe.

I step back onto the ship and look at the crew, all of them on the deck and waiting for work. We should stay the night, do some maintenance, restock. But if I'm going to survive this, I need to be out on the sea.

"We're all hands. Let's get out of here."

Chapter 29

Max

Eli can't have been gone more than an hour before there's a knock at the door. I roll my eyes and don't get off the bed. They forgot something, I'm sure. Including the key that would let them inside without disturbing me. They'll go find the key and figure it out, and I won't have to try and face them again. Not tonight.

But then the knock comes again. And again. It continues, getting louder. Eli is forgetful, and it wouldn't be the first time they showed up here without a key, but Eli also is not patient and knows that I'm disabled; if I don't come answer the door quickly, they're more likely to run back to the ship and get the key than to just keep knocking, keep waiting. And much as I want to avoid them for the rest of the night, if that is Eli—and who else would it be?—they're starting to sound urgent.

"I'm coming!" I call. The knocking stops.

I didn't bother getting undressed or unpacking or anything when I got home; I just went to the bedroom, got into bed, and hugged my pillow. I thought I might cry, and I still might later. Or maybe I'm all cried out. But at least I'm still dressed, so getting back into my chair and heading for the door isn't too much of an ordeal.

"You have a key," I note as I pull the door open. My biggest concern as I'm saying the words is that it'll sound playful; I'm not ready to be playful or even very nice to Eli, and I don't want them to be confused by it. But that concern disappears the second the door is open.

This is not Eli.

"Hello, Max. It's a pleasure to see you again." The person on the other side is completely unfamiliar to me for a moment, which makes the way that they're smiling at me especially unnerving. It's the smile that eventually makes me realize who this is, memories of the person who reminded me of a shark but much scarier. The bruise making his right eye and cheeks swollen and purple helps, too—I remember Eli putting that bruise there.

Cross Fields.

I instinctively roll back a little, trying to get more space, but Cross takes that opportunity to step further inside.

"Stop!" I snap, my brain firing off a thousand different alarms at a virtual stranger walking into my house. Did he really just walk into my house?! "You need to leave."

"I don't plan to stay long, Max," he says, emphasizing my name again like he wants to drive home the point that he does know me. "I just have an offer to make you. A job I'd like to hire you for...and an opportunity. I thought I'd have to get more creative to take you from *Tempest*, but Eli was foolish enough just to abandon you here."

More than his intrusion into my home, more than offering me a job with him, I *hate* that someone like Cross Fields knows what went down between me and Eli. I have to fight to keep my face calm and give nothing away. I don't let him know how I hurt.

"We were not properly introduced when we last met," he announces. His affected accent makes me want to ram my chair into his legs. "My ship is—"

"*Sunbeam*," I say, and that makes him smile broadly.

"I'm honored you've heard of me."

"I remember you trying to kidnap me," I correct.

Cross isn't phased. "And as I said, I have heard quite a bit about you, Max. So much, in fact, that I'd like you to join my ship and help me complete this treasure hunt ahead of your sweet little partner." He grins, the smile showing too many teeth and never touching his eyes. It's just as fake as the gold in the buttons on his jacket in a shade of yellow that is flattering on absolutely no one. "Think about it, Max. Captain Rose thought they were ahead of me, but they underestimated me. And you. Won't it be satisfying to defeat them after Eli decided they don't need you?"

I want to argue it. That's not what Eli decided, and it's not why they left me here. But the word 'abandoned' is still echoing through my mind, and the only thing louder is the alarms. This is a stranger—able-bodied, a sailor, someone with physical advantages over me—standing in my home when I have no real defense. And he's still smiling at me.

"Besides," Fields continues, "you are much, much too handsome to be left on land."

Ew.

I swallow, determined to sound brave and calm. This isn't the first person like this I've had to deal with, the kind of person who wants to throw their muscle around. The kind that believes they don't really need muscle to deal with me. That doesn't mean I'm unaware of what he could do to me, though. "If you're making an offer, that means I have the right to say no."

"I suppose that's true. But…" Fields snaps his fingers, and his smile grows when two other human men come in behind him, these two even bigger than Fields, as muscular as Eli. My throat tightens, the mental alarm bells screeching at full volume now. "If you say no, I'll be forced to convince you in other ways. Everything will be easier if you agree to come work for me, Max. Let me be your captain."

He punctuates that with a wink, and I almost gag.

I mentally run through my options. I can make a pretty tight turn with my chair, so I could spin around, race to my room, and shut the door. It locks from the inside, but there's no doubt in my mind that these three could break it down. So I could run, and then get caught. Once I'm caught, I could go quietly, or I could scream and fight the whole way out of here, maybe draw some attention from someone who could help. But I also don't have any doubts in my mind that Fields will shut me up; he's not going to kill or maim me since he needs my help, but what does he care if I'm hurt or knocked out for a bit? And anyone who does come out to help could end up hurt, too.

Eli is too far away by now to help.

On my own, I only have one real option, one actual path ahead of me.

Knowing that it's the only choice doesn't make this any easier, though.

"I can go with you," I manage, my voice strangled like my throat is trying to keep the words in. I swallow and force myself to look Fields in the eye when I say, "I'll go with you. Can I bring my things?"

"You're not a prisoner, handsome," Fields laughs. "What do you need for maps?"

I turn and go to the case on the table, tucking it upright between my legs to carry because I don't trust any of these people with my most prized possession. If they break these pens, it'll be much more difficult and time-consuming for me to build maps, but I can't trust that they wouldn't find that out after being reckless. I have to look determined to get the job done.

"I can't carry my bags," I admit, closing my eyes against that confession. I know who I am and what my body is like. I know what I'm capable of, and I don't hide my disability—I can't, but I also don't want to. But having to admit what I can't do in front of strangers who are effectively kidnapping me is hard, painful, almost even shameful. If even Eli couldn't respect my strengths and my weaknesses on a ship enough to keep me around, and they're my best friend who loves me, what are these people going to think about me? What are they going to do with me once the maps are complete?

One of the big guys marches past me and yanks open the buttons on the larger bag. "Books," he scoffs, saying that word like it's the most ridiculous thing ever. "And whatever this is."

My turtle.

"Oh, you won't be needing any of that," Fields laughs, the condescension thick. He drops my new turtle on the floor and crushes it under his foot. And then much, much worse, he comes over, grabs the back of my chair, and uses it to turn me around. I have to clench my fists and my jaw to keep from lashing out with either; nothing is worse than people grabbing my chair like it's not part of me. This asshole doesn't even realize that he just assaulted me because, to him, I'm barely a person. Which is further proven when he says, "You're not a prisoner, but we aren't going to pretend cripples belong on ships. You're coming to do a job, little Maxy, and you'll do that job. No more luxury cruise." He laughs harshly. "Eli took a while to figure that out, but what can be expected of an urchin playing pretend pirate?"

"Unlike a spoiled noble playing pretend pirate?" I retort before I can help myself. He can assault me, talk shit about my body and about me, but I'm not going to be quiet when someone is trashing Eli. Not even while I'd like the legs to kick Eli in the balls. No one gets to degrade them.

Fields' first reaction is to look toward his crew, to see if they heard and if they're reacting. He doesn't care what I said or how it makes him feel, only how it makes him look. I've known so many men like him, and I've hated them all.

When he does look back down at me, I get another smile. Nothing like the first—and I thought that one was unfriendly. "You're about to learn all the ways you've been spoiled, Max. Now, are you going to come to the ship real nice and quiet in your chair, or are you going to make me have one of my friends here carry you back and leave the chair behind? I don't care if you have to crawl around my ship like a dog, but I'm thinking you might."

He says all of that with the smile on, and it makes me certain that he means every word of it. If I want to follow that one path I see ahead of me, I'm going to have to bite my tongue... even though I hate how smug Fields looks when I don't answer.

"Let's go!" he chirps, acting like we're heading out for a picnic. And he takes it upon himself to push my chair for me instead of letting me function on my own. It makes the walk to the docks and to his ship even more shameful than it already would be just by agreeing to go with him—whether or not I have a choice.

My only hope to stop all this right now, to free me from this path, is if *Tempest* is still at the dock and I can get their attention. But we get into view of the docks, my eyes go right to the berth where I know we left *Tempest*...and it's empty. She's gone, and so is Eli.

I didn't tell Eli that I love them before they left.

I let Fields take me to a smaller ship that will apparently get us back to *Sunbeam*, and I let him threaten me about the work I'd better do, and I just nod over and over to accept it. The entire time, I'm praying to whatever gods will listen that Eli will somehow learn of what happened and then go to the treasure sites in the right order. If I can stage a run-in between *Sunbeam* and *Tempest*, I'll have a chance of getting out of here before Cross Fields decides that he doesn't need me anymore.

My prayers quickly shift away from the gods and to the only person I really believe in.

Eli...please come get me. They're my only hope. I need *Tempest* to take me home.

Chapter 30

Eli

I watch the purple gem, semi-encased in a rough, light gray rock, float through the air and hang suspended for a split second before it tumbles back down and lands in my palm. I toss it up again, idly wondering if I could catch the moonlight on the precious fucking rock to make the ocean look purple for a second.

I also wonder, slightly less idly, what would really happen if I just missed it. I watch it suspend in the air again and think about moving my hand, listening to the plop when it hits the water, watching it float slowly into the ocean.

We found this one in the mountains, part of a witch's crystal collection, whatever that means. She was kind and amenable to selling it to us. She knows what she had whether or not any of us admitted it, not a foolish woman, but that also means she knows she can do more with the gold we offered in exchange. I don't think she'd care if I dropped it in the sea now.

This fucking rock was so important to me so recently. I need the money that'll come with winning this hunt, turning over the elements of the gods, collecting the rest of the massive prize. All that gold for rocks. Enough gold to change our reputation and our lives. More gold than I've ever had. More gold than I'll need, meaning I can give it back to my crew, my ship, people who need it. My Max.

I can't quite bring myself to care as much about treasure or the future when I think I already threw my whole life away.

It's been eight days since we left Max. The first map he made for us—a number 4 written neatly inside a tiny circle in the upper right-hand corner—included everything we needed to make excellent time. Of course it did. Hiring Max was never just about being so close to him. I could have hired other cartographers, but none of them are nearly as talented. If any sailor or ship captain—pirate or treasure hunter or otherwise—wants maps for things that would be almost impossible to find without it, there is no one better than Max. And it's not his magic alone; Max has an incredible understanding of the world despite having seen so little of it first-hand, so the paths he recommends on his maps are just about flawless.

He got us where we needed to go for this element very quickly. He got us away from him very quickly.

Eight days since we left. I wonder what he's doing right now. He's probably gotten himself some new clients already, so if he's gone home from the library yet today—and that's unlikely—he's probably on the couch at home still working. He has an old record player he sometimes uses when he works at home, humming along to the music, but more often, he opens the windows and listens to the city outside.

Max won't often admit he feels like he's not really part of the world around him; between his disabilities and his pain, the way he can explore and connect to the world is different than everyone else. He likes to hear about the adventures the ship has been on, the things that his clients have seen, and he likes to listen to the city because it makes him feel closer.

I wonder if now, after his chance to do his own exploring ended so quickly and abruptly, the sound of the city is making him bitter. I hate that thought even more than the idea of him being mad at me.

If Max was still here tonight, I'd be celebrating this gem with him. Purple is his favorite color, so I bet he would love this one especially. I miss the regular sex with him a little, but I miss the chances to hold him so often more. We could just lay in bed together...or I could go down there and lay in bed alone. And that's why I keep tossing the rock.

Max isn't the only person I have to miss right now. Usually, when we leave Max behind and I get a little depressed about it for a few days, I have my crew to rely on. Ros misses Max terribly too, so she always makes comfort foods and reminds me to eat. Jak is harder on me during those times 'cause he knows doing battle with him helps both of our moods. Yen and Dava are there with distractions whenever I need it, one pragmatic and the other ridiculous and both in the right balance. And Tevin is extra snuggly, even though snuggling isn't really his thing. He lets me be clingy and never holds it against me for clinging to him while missing Max; he knows it's never a replacement thing, just that I miss one of them and need the other.

This time... I caught Ros crying this morning, and she hasn't done more than make the basic meals necessary. Jak has his head down, doing his work, but he's not giving me more than a glance. Yen and Dava are talking to me as much as they need to for work, but there's been no play or support or heartfelt talks. And Tevin hasn't come to me once. He's staying even busier than usual during the day, and at night, all I can do is stare at the door and wonder how long I'll have to be so lonely.

I can't blame or even be upset with any of them for the behavior. They're still doing the work they need to do and supporting the ship, so as their captain, I don't have any room to speak on anything they're doing. They're performing like the great crew they are.

Which means if I do complain about how they're acting, I'll be doing it as their friend, and that means they're going to talk to me as my friend too. Right now, I know that means they're going to voice just how much they dislike me, and I don't have the courage to deal with that. I feel badly enough about myself as it is. Even though I still feel confident I made the right choice, running back there and back to Max is damn tempting.

I want last week back. I want to be happy again.

I really want to drop this gem into the water, so before those thoughts can take over and make me do the incredibly foolish and wasteful thing, I step away from the bow and stick the rock in my pocket. The wind ruffles my hair; that's not nearly as freeing a sensation as the wind on my legs, but I'm not in the mood for any of my skirts. I don't care if I feel good about my body when nothing else feels good.

I wince at my own pathetic thoughts. I've been through worse than this; I've been through enough to kill most people. I never just sat around and moped. Okay, I absolutely have, and anyone dealing with hard shit who doesn't admit to misery sometimes is a liar. But I've never let it keep me down for so long, and that's got nothing to do with mental strength or determination. It's always just been out of necessity.

When I wanted to cry about being hungry or cold as I kid, I often did just lay down and cry for a while. But then the hunger and the cold got worse, and I had to go do something about it. The same is true now. I've grieved what feels like a loss, whether or not that loss is permanent, and if Max is really done with me, there will be much, much more grieving in the future. But I don't have a choice just to lay down and cry any longer. I have a ship to run and things to do.

I check once more that the legendarily godsent chunk of rock is secured in my pocket and head across the deck. "How long?" I call to Jak at the helm.

"Coming up to the docks now." And he doesn't comment on my ability to somehow miss that the docks are clearly in view now. Any other time, Jakgrout would have jumped on the opportunity to tear me apart for the misstep. Nothing now.

I duck through the door below the deck, taking the new ramp down. No one has so much as thought of taking out the adjustment we put in for Max, even if his presence on the ship was always intended to be temporary. I know better than to think Max being around is ever really temporary; he leaves an impact that lasts, and it's left this ship a hollow shell of what it was.

In my quarters, I secure the new gem with the others in the satchel Max should be using. The maps we've already used and the ones he made for our future are also tucked into the satchel in neat little rolls, standing sentry over the elements hidden at the bottom. We're halfway through this treasure hunt now, and we've barely faced more than inconvenience on our way. We're constantly a step ahead, and I plan to stay that way. But since we didn't stay in port after dropping Max over, when I ran away like a coward, we need to dock and get some supplies now.

Two quick raps and then the door opening behind me without pause tells me that Tevin just came in before I turn around to face him. He glances down quickly, allowing only a quick flash of surprise. It takes me a second to realize the reaction is for my pants, and I manage a laugh. "I wear pants sometimes. It's not that surprising," I say.

"It's absolutely a surprise because you very rarely wear pants—especially off the ship," he says, almost smiling. Almost but not quite. "You're coming off the ship, right?"

I nod. "Yeah, I could use a meal someone actually wants to serve me. And a stiff drink."

"Solid coping skills," he teases, but we can both feel there's no heart in it. It's habit, nothing more.

I haven't just lost Max. Looking at Tevin on the other side of my quarters and feeling the stark difference in the relationship between us—not only the romantic one but as captain and first mate—is a knife to my gut. I made one choice, one I still believe in, and everything is different. I haven't even begun to grieve everyone else.

"You don't have to come off the ship," I offer. "Not tonight anyway. You don't have anything to deal with in the morning, so."

I can't look at him while saying it, staring down at my desk even though absolutely nothing interesting is there, but my head snaps up when Tevin says, "I'll come have that drink with you."

But I'm still me, stubborn and anxious and a fool, so instead of just being grateful and quiet, I blurt out, "Don't do me any favors. I said you don't have to leave the ship, and I meant it. You've had plenty of work to keep you busy away from me the last few days."

"You've been more than worth avoiding the last few days," Tevin retorts without missing a beat; the way he's never backed down to me is one of the things I've always liked most about him. "You're a whiny pain in the ass, and I'm pissed at you for making a decision like that without any input—not from me or the crew but especially not from Max. So I've been avoiding you. But now I want a gods damned drink, and you're gonna buy it for me instead of working on your sad puppy act."

"The only drink I'll be willing to buy you is something extremely fruity and pink," I inform him. "Or ogre piss."

"Let's hope they sell some then. You gonna help with docking or what?"

"Alright now, don't push your luck," I grumble, tucking the satchel under my pillow. It's not a safety measure but a sad one; it makes me feel closer to Max, especially since the satchel still smells like his vanilla and mint salve.

Tevin waits for me by the door, and I almost pause in front of him, almost steal the kiss I've snagged for years. I try to keep moving, but he catches my arm to stop me. "We all want things back to normal, too," he tells me. "Especially me. But it's...Max."

"I know. I've always loved that you're all as loyal to him as you are to me. Means the world to me." I shake my head and look him right in the eyes so I know we understand each other when I continue, "But I can't really apologize, and I won't pretend I think it was a mistake. Max was at too much risk. The storms, the ship, we could deal with all that, but Fields was on the hunt. What if they came after us for him? *Tempest* isn't prepared for that kind of thing."

"Eli..." He sighs and rubs his face with his hand like he's dealing with a child and frustrated by it. By me.

I want to be insulted, but I also kind of want to just keep talking to him, to anyone. This is the most conversation I've had since getting back on the ship without Max, and it's easing some very traumatized, lonely part of me I don't need to feed. Let him yell at me.

Of course, he just gives me a disappointed frown, which isn't as helpful as I'd like. "It's not the decision you made. It's that you made it alone."

"Yeah, as the captain of this ship."

"No, you dick, as Max's *partner*," he counters.

I blink at him, wishing I had a retort or something to counter with, some way to make it better...but he's right. I've been so worried about getting everyone to see I had to make the choice, that it was the right choice to make. I've been so focused on Max's safety it was the only thing I could see or think about. But I didn't so much as have a conversation about it with Max. I assumed he would argue and fight me on it instead of giving him a chance to see what I saw, to at least have a say. And I did that to the rest of the crew, too, forcing my decision on them.

"You would have agreed with me?" I ask, though I'm not sure I want the answer at this point.

"It...took me a little while to get there," he begins, giving a side-to-side, noncommittal bob of his head. "And I still think we might have found another way, another solution. But with some time to think about it, to think about that rich, coiffed, asshole coming after Max... Yeah, I get why it was necessary. And I think Max could come to that realization too."

"That's worse," I groan, running my hand back through my hair. Some piece in the back of my mind registers that my hair feels greasy, stringy; I haven't managed to bathe nearly enough since Max left. I've been too emotion-ally exhausted to care for myself physically... and now Tevin is telling me all of it was unnec-essary. That if I'd taken the time to talk to the crew and to Max, we all could have made the right decision together. "We don't even have time to go back and make it right...if it's not too late."

"It's not too late," he says. There's no way he could know that. It could all be too late. When I frown up at him, he offers a little smile and squeezes my shoulder in his huge hand. "You'll be more irresistible when you're rich. Let's go get that drink before you spend yet another night overthinking."

"We both know I can drink and overthink si-multaneously," I answer, though I let him push me through the door and then make my way back up to the deck.

This place isn't a proper port, like the city where Max and I live. Or, well, where Max lives until I know if I'm welcome back there. But in that city, the port includes actual rules—people who care about what you're bringing into the city and who want to know basic things like the name of our ship. There are pubs and seedier places in all cities, of course, but the proper cit-ies tend to hide them a little further back from the port so tourists can escape that. And so can the rich folks who make cities survive.

Here? The first pub is loud enough to hear from the ship, smells like the wrong end of a dead goat smeared with all the fluids anyone could hope to find in an alley, and it's about ten feet from the docks. And tonight, I can't say I mind.

We manage to find a table in the back corner where the barmaids notice us—admittedly, we're hard to miss—but where we can hope the crowds leave us alone. Except we're hard to miss by them, too, and while *Tempest* is still up-and-coming, me and Tevin have worked on enough ships we're familiar faces to most pirates, sailors, and other treasure hunters. And places like this are always full of people like pirates, sailors, and other treasure hunters.

"Oh, if it ain't the prettiest crew around," a voice only vaguely familiar calls. I'm nice to people until they give me a reason not to be, but I've always struggled recognizing faces or voices. Once I get a name, I'm good, but the smiling face approaching and saying both of our names might as well be a complete stranger. These belong to a dark-skinned half-elf, evidenced by the pointed ears but human build, with a bright smile and eyes that are brown, golden, and green all at once. He's striking—he'd be familiar if my brain wasn't broken.

Fortunately, my good friends know this about me, and Tevin quickly rescues me by greeting him, "Laurence! What brings you this way?"

Oh, Laurence! I definitely do know him and definitely should have recognized him; this is why I don't like to go anywhere alone. Without Tevin here tonight, I would have been completely embarrassed and hurt the feelings of an old friend. Well, an old acquaintance. Still, it makes me feel like shit, and I buy Laurence a drink along with our orders to make up for a slight he doesn't even know about.

"My old lady is knocked up again," Laurence tells us, sitting at the end of our table so he's facing both of us. "Whenever she's pregnant, she starts to hate me a little for getting her that way, so she told me to stay away for a while. Signed up with a crew making the rounds."

"How many kids does this make now?" I laugh. "She was pregnant last time we saw you, but it can't be the same kid."

"Nope, different one—and this'll make five!" He gives us a broad, proud smile. "I get her going with a new one almost every time I make it home."

"Poor lady should just stop letting you come home at all," Tevin jokes, and Laurence laughs louder than any of us while a barmaid who looks much too young to be working in a place like this delivers our whiskey. It's going to be the cheapest whiskey ever, but the burn will be welcome.

I remember taking any job that would come my way, any means of getting fed or getting out of the cold, when I was far too young for it to be fair. When I finally have some coin to spare, I'm coming back here and getting that poor girl out of this job. I'll buy her a fucking house and a private tutor so she can make something of her life if that's what it takes.

Yeah, the burn of this horrible whiskey is a good thing tonight.

"You two look in better spirits than I figured you'd be," Laurence is saying when I remember to listen again. "You're here licking your wounds and all, ain't ya?"

I frown at Tevin, completely lost and wondering if that's just me. His returning frown does not make me feel any better. Laurence couldn't possibly know about me and Max, so I can't imagine what else he'd talking about.

"Why would we have wounds to lick?" Tevin asks, laughing the question to keep it casual. Meanwhile, my stomach is already churning up the whiskey; it's almost worse not knowing what he's talking about if it's related to us and our ship.

"Oh, I ain't mean to insult you or nothing!" Laurence protests. Great, we made him feel bad, too. "Just, *Sunbeam* was around this way yesterday, and you know Cross Fields ain't one to keep his secrets. He was bragging about getting some magical secret on board that'll guarantee him the win in that big treasure hunt y'all are on." He whistles a little and shakes his head. "Man, I wish I'd been around to sign on for that! Missed my chances."

"Wait, wait, hang on." The room has tilted, and it has nothing to do with the whiskey. I have to press my palms against the table to keep from falling over or letting out the scream I can feel building in my chest. "Cross Fields said he had a magical secret on board *Sunbeam*?"

Laurence nods, frowning at me and glancing at Tevin like he's trying to get answers on what's wrong with me. Get in line. "Uh, yeah, that's what he said. Said it was some edge he stole from you and—"

I can't hear the rest of what Laurence says. I can't hear the chaos in the pub or anything except the blood rushing past my ears. I don't know when I gave myself the mental order to get up and leave, the cold sea air smacking me in the force and forcing a breath in. I stumble back, too weak to even withstand the wind, and crash into a hard but familiar body behind me. "I know, I know," Tevin murmurs, sounding like he's talking underwater.

I shake my head and press a hand to my chest, trying to tell him, to explain somehow that even though I'm gasping for air, I can't breathe. The night is getting darker and quieter, no competition at all for the roar inside my head and the throbbing pound of my heart, all of it creating one sound over and over again: *Max Max Max Max.*

I stumble again, losing control of my body when I can't focus on anything but the building panic, the failure of my body when I need it more than ever, and Tevin grabs me more firmly. He steers me, arm around my waist, ignoring the clumsy steps and falters. "Just get to the ship," Tevin murmurs, rushing me onto the docks. "Just get on the ship, and then we'll figure it out. Don't fall apart until you're on the ship, Eli. Just get to the ship."

The ship. My ship. *Tempest.* Where Max is not. He's on another ship now, and it's all my fault.

Everything goes dark, and my last thought is that I have no idea if I made it back to my ship.

Chapter 31

Max

Every inch of my body hurts. It's like an intense, bone-deep, horrible bruise everywhere that I exist. My skin doesn't fit right, everything that touches me makes me feel like screaming or gagging, and there's not a single thing that I can do about any of it.

Fields wasn't worried about my medications, including the ones to stop my monthly cycle, which is going to become more of a problem if I'm on this ship for a few more weeks. The immediate problem, though, is that I have no way to resolve my own pain and no one around who cares about it at all. That's more than clear by my sleeping arrangements—on the floor, since I can't get myself into the hammocks that everyone else sleeps in. And my working arrangements, which are also on the floor since there's no desk on offer, and there's no real way for me to move around this ship.

Even if I wanted to get around now, I couldn't, and I wouldn't. I have to reserve what little energy and life are left inside me. I have to hold onto the remaining dredges of functioning body parts if I'm going to get through this for as long as I need to. It'll be over soon if I manage for a little while longer.

I close my eyes and inhale as slowly and deeply as I can. It's been harder to eat with my pain increasing, and after twelve days on this ship, that's started to take a heavy toll. Every time I shift my body position, I get dizzy and nauseous, and I can feel my heart skipping around awkwardly inside my chest. My whole body is falling apart on me, and the humiliation of not being able to get properly cleaned is adding insult to injury...but I'm clinging to hope and my magic. They're all I have right now.

It's a good thing that I've already made this map once, so I'm using memory for a good deal of it instead of my magic. Can't spare the energy. It's an even better thing that Fields has no idea how this process works or what to expect from it. That means buying time, even when it'll keep me trapped here longer. And it means he doesn't notice the corrections I make when also using my magic to find *Tempest* and make sure that we're avoiding her...at least for now. Until the moment is right.

My shoulders and back are screaming at me to change position, even though I got into this position, hunched onto the floor, to take strain off my legs and hips. If my body could get into agreement about what it needs from me, my entire life would be easier. No such luck. And shifting means smelling myself again. I don't know why the other people on this ship haven't complained enough to make it possible to get some actual soap instead of the bucket of cold water and the ratty rag I've been tossed three whole times. My curls are hanging flat at this point, and if I smell this bad to myself, I'd hate to think what other people are smelling.

Eli won't care. It'll be embarrassing to see them like this, but all that matters is knowing that I will see them again.

I find another position that I can stand for at least a minute and get to work. I have to do my part too if the timing is going to be right. Fields thinks he's taken an advantage away from Eli, but he underestimated exactly what I can do. Secret weapon indeed.

Chapter 32

Eli

I make my life reading maps in the same way Max makes his in creating them. No one can live at sea without being a master of maps, and with a lot of extra years to dream of this life, I did a lot of extra study to make myself better than any other treasure hunter. It helps that I've had Max in my life for so long, and he has such an incredibly intimate knowledge of maps and cartography. It's quite literally in his blood.

So when I look at a map now, as an adult, I can think back on all the impressive routes I've found and all the boons it's given me and my crew. All the storms I've successfully avoided, all the races for a reward I've won. But tonight, staring at a map Max created and marked a '6' in the corner of...I've never felt like I understand maps less. I've never felt less adequate.

"I don't understand why we're going from number four to number six, though," Ros presses. She's practically shaking where she sits across the long dining table on our ship, and she hasn't stopped shaking since Tevin and I broke the news about Max and Cross Fields. Well, since Tevin broke the news. At the time, I was locked into my own mind from the sort of panic that hasn't seized me since I was a child. Now, though, I need a plan, and my crew needs to know that there are answers.

"If we go to site number five, we might miss *Sunbeam* if Max already made their map, and we might get there right at the same time," I explain, pointing to each of those maps. "Max is going to make those maps for Fields in that order, five and then six. Let them go to five while we head for six, and we'll be waiting for them when they arrive."

"And you're sure?" Yen asks. "You're absolutely sure that's what Max is going to do?"

Fortunately, the news of Max's kidnapping isn't making Yen shake because she hasn't been without a blade in her hand in the last twenty-four hours. She keeps throwing them at things too, which would be unnerving if I didn't know she has so much control. Even still, I damn near duck whenever she turns in my direction.

I can nod to this question at least, even though it makes my throat feel tight again. "I'm sure. I know Max, and I know he'll be thinking two steps ahead."

I know Max will be expecting us. He'll expect *me* to be there and to get him home. And I know if I fail, I'll never forgive myself.

"Max is thinking ahead," I repeat, "and we

need to do the same if we're going to find them. We can't play catch-up."

"And we can't get into a situation where we're fighting them at sea," Tevin chimes in, giving me his most confident nod. He hasn't stepped more than a foot away from me; I think he's waiting for me to panic or pass out again, and he might be right. Never felt less connected to my body, not even when panic attacks were an everyday thing for me. "*Sunbeam* has cannons. We're faster, but we can't outrun a cannonball."

"That was deep," Dava quips, and Tevin flipping her off at least creates a moment of levity. A very brief one I feel hollowly. There's a fucking bucket of dark, horrible, tentacle and poison-filled water deep inside me, and that second of laughter doesn't even make a ripple on the surface. And those aren't the hot kinds of tentacles, either.

Max would laugh at that joke. If I could tell him. If he wasn't still being held captive on some rich dickhead's ship. If he wasn't gods only know where, too far from me. He was already too far the moment *Tempest* left the docks, and I have nothing in me now except dark water and regret.

No, that's not true. I also have a plan based on faith in Max, faith in how well I know Max. I need to hang onto that.

I need to do better than I have been.

"We should reach the site tonight, late," I tell them all. "It's an island with a lagoon—not a place I've ever been. Max has a chest drawn here, so we can probably assume shipwreck, and it washed up here. I want to get on the ground right away, get a good look at the area and our options. We'll figure out the rest from there. We know where the fifth site is, too, so *Sunbeam* should show up at our lagoon tomorrow night after going to the fifth one first."

"It's just...a lot of assumptions," Yen mutters, rubbing both hands back through her hair and then tugging on her newly-finished braids. That's about as close to her own panic attack as Yen ever gets, her eyes stormy and dark when she looks at me again. "You're sure? Because if you tell me you're sure, Cap, I'm with you all the way. I just need to hear it."

"It's Max," Ros breathes, shaking her head and staring down at where her hands are folded in her lap. "Max is in trouble."

"And we'll do whatever the boy needs from us," Jak chimes us, voice full of gravel and determination. He takes a breath and looks at me too, and for once, I don't think he's about to berate me. "Tell us you're sure."

My heart skips and finally feels like it might fill up again a little. They all love Max so much. And they trust me enough to follow whatever I say, so long as I'm sure it's going to make Max safe again.

I don't know how I got lucky enough to end up with a family on board like this; I've never had any real flesh-and-blood family, but even without experience, I know this is exactly that. A family.

"All of you listen to me," I say, looking around to meet each of their eyes and making sure I have their attention. It's sharp and focused because nothing means more to them than this. "I failed all of you, not just Max. I fucked up, and

I'm sorry. I don't deserve your trust right now, and I know I didn't prove it, but I trust Max more than I trust myself, and that's what I'm doing here. Trusting Max. He gave us these maps to use, and his maps are going to lead us to him. We're going to find him and get him back. I'm sure."

Ros's whole little body straightens up, and she slaps her hand down on the table—maybe the loudest sound I've ever heard her make. "That's enough for me, Eli. Let's go get our Max back."

The others agree, neutralizing just a tiny bit of the poison in that dark bucket. Tevin kisses the side of my head, then presses his forehead against my hair. "We're gonna get him, back," he says softly. "You can do this. But babe?"

"Yeah?" I ask, more than a little cautious about anything that includes a 'but' right now.

"You have *got* to wash your hair before that poor sweet man has to hug you. Gods only know what he's going through on that ship; he deserves a partner who smells nice."

I laugh and roll my eyes at him, though I know he's right. Max won't care, he's smelled worse on me, but maybe bathing is a good way to distract myself for a bit at least.

"Pull the anchor. Jak, you're on the helm. Get us there as quickly as you can for the sake of my sanity."

"Fuck do I care about your sanity?" he grumbles, sliding out of the bench seat and marching off. It's the first time he's treated me normally in almost two weeks, and I never thought I'd be so grateful for that grumpy old dickhead to sass me. Not that I'll ever admit it.

I let Tevin herd me toward the bathtub, and Yen makes it extra hot for me. I try my hardest to relax. I really do. I'm bad at relaxing even at the best of times, though, and this is not those. All I can think about is the last time Max was in here with me and where Max is now. Tevin didn't mean to make me feel worse when he mentioned what Max might be going through on *Sunbeam*, but I know Cross Fields and his crew well enough to know he's a threat. There's no way Max is being treated the way he deserves, and the thought of the physical pain he might be in at the moment makes my stomach cramp.

Gods, if I get Max back hurt, if Field did something to him, I'll burn everything he's ever built or loved or cared about. I went into this whole job to further my own crew, our future and our reputation; it was never about defeating anyone else. That's changed. I'm going to destroy Cross and that horrendously ugly ship.

The bath is a waste of heat on me, so I quickly wash my hair and get out, heading for my quarters. Of course, this entire place reminds me of Max now. It didn't always. Max visited the ship when I first got it, but it's changed a lot since then, so it used to be that we could leave him behind, and even though I hated it, I didn't have reminders everywhere I turned. Now, Max's living ghost haunts me on every inch of this ship, howling constant reminders that this is my fault, that anything that happens to Max is because of me, that if I don't save him, he'll—

"You're gonna stop breathing again."

I startle at Tevin's voice. How fucking lost in my own mind was I that I didn't notice him sitting on the couch in my quarters? Not like he's small or easily hidden—and he's right in front of me!

"Gods. Fuck. Sorry."

He laughs. "Considering you just jumped three feet off the floor, maybe I should be saying sorry instead. I'm here because the crew is demanding you eat dinner."

In response to the mere suggestion of food—a real meal instead of jerky and whiskey—my traitorous stomach roars more than growls. I glare down at my body and then assert, "I don't want to eat. I'll throw up if I eat. I'll eat when I see Max again."

"You can't even choose one excuse because you're so hungry," Tevin counters, glaring at me even though there's no heat to it. "E, if you don't eat and sleep tonight, you're going to have one hell of a time trying to execute any plan tomorrow. If we get into a fight, you need strength. If Max needs help, you need strength. Don't eat for yourself; eat for Max."

"Oh, that's a low fucking blow," I growl, though I lean into him. He wraps his arms around me, the first time he's done that when I'm conscious in way too long, and I can feel that realization flow through him too when he lets out a breath and softens his entire muscular, stone-built body. I'm a big person, but Tevin's hand is massive, and having it rub slowly up and down my spine is comforting as fuck.

When I tell him that, he answers, "Eat, and I'll rub your feet after we go explore that little island."

"I'll eat after we get a look at the island and I have some proof we might be able to hide *Tempest*." I bury my face in his chest. He smelled better when he'd been hanging out with Max and both their scents were combined. "I'm sure this is the right path, but there's so much that could go wrong. If they spot us before getting close enough, if we can't get onto *Sunbeam* and grab Max, if they decide to hurt Max because of us..."

"Your poor little brain must be so exhausted with the number of 'what if' paths you take it down," he murmurs, squeezing me tighter. "There's nothing you can do to fix every possible scenario tonight. All you can do tonight is explore, scout the island, use your amazing crew to build a plan, and get some fucking sleep."

"Tevin, I can't." It comes out like a whimper, and even in front of my best friend and first mate, shame stings my eyes, and I have to shut them tight. "It's Max. He's too important. He's...everything. And it's all my fault."

He lets out a slow breath. "I'm not gonna lie and tell you that you haven't messed up. But you couldn't have known where Cross was or even that he knows where you live off-ship. You aren't at fault for this."

"I should have known," I argue. "I should've figured it out somehow. Whatever Cross does to him, that's my fault, too."

"You know what? I'm so confident we're going to find Max and be back with him by tomorrow night that instead of arguing with you, I'm gonna wait, tell Max, and let him argue with you about it."

I huff out a laugh, a couple tears spilling and catching on Tevin's shirt. "I kinda hope he's mad at me. It might help."

"Let's hope Max goes into a rage for the first time in his life, then." Tevin kisses my head, pats my back firmly, and then steps back while holding my shoulders. "Food and then sleep. I'm not taking no for an answer anymore. We both know that Yen can find ways to force-feed you if needed."

I grimace at the thought. "Fine. But not a single vegetable. Nothing healthy."

"It's a meal made by an emotional Rosleigh," Tevin notes, turning me toward the door and then steering me out through it like he doesn't trust me not to make a run for it—or like I have anywhere to go if I did run. "We both know there won't be anything healthy available."

Good. Maybe the rich foods will kill me before I can make things any worse.

Chapter 33

Eli

I went to bed last night feeling sick from stress. I could barely eat anything for dinner, I didn't keep it down anyway, and I think I only fell asleep from exhaustion. And grog. Too much grog, more than the crew wanted me to drink.

This morning, sunlight coming through the window over my bed woke me up. Max loves that window—he's the one who talked me into putting the bed underneath it in the first place. Every morning he was on *Tempest*, he sat up and looking out that window. Happy just to see the ocean, the sky, the horizon, the world out there. This morning, I wake up ready to go. Ready to get Max back where he belongs.

I go over Max's map again. Not that there's anything I could do about. Or that I would do anything even if I could. Max isn't just an expert at his job—he's a master of it. We're already well on the way to where we need to be, following his planned route. And Max *will* be on the other end of this map.

Barely dawn and still cold outside, I make my way around the ship, looking for everything that could possibly wrong, that could even maybe slow us down. We aren't a warship by any means, I have one cannon because Tevin and Jak pushed me to install cannons, and that was the compromise. I think there are cannonballs somewhere on the ship, but I never wanted to use it. And if I have to go to battle on the ship against Fields and *Sunbeam*, who had pretty much endless pockets and could equip his ship for more, I won't stand a chance. So that's not how I'll do my battling.

Relief sweeps over me when I step into Yen's room. The armory, as she calls it and not actually her bedroom, but it's the space where we keep all of our weapons. Thanks to Yen being Yen, we have more than we probably need. More than we needed before now anyway. I'm not relieved for the weapons, though. It's the company. Tevin, Dava, and Yen are already here. Waiting, ready.

"We figured you needed the time to check out the ship but you'd be here eventually," Dava explains, a kind smile on her face. Yen is jumpy, rocking back and forth from ball to heel, fiddling with the knife in her hand; anyone else, I'd worry she might cut herself. Tevin isn't looking at me, though, and the only thing lower than his shoulders is his mood.

"I wanna go through what we have available, just in case. Wanna know what we have if we need it." I smirk at Yen. "I figure you've been waiting for a chance like this."

"You have no idea," she quips, and then she proves both of us right.

There are enough blades on the ship for all of us to have at least one when we need it. I take one of the three pistols we have. I hate these things and never wanna fire one at another person, but if it's the difference between getting my Max back on the ship or not, I won't hesitate to take a shot.

I can't say I really feel better once I know we can all be armed. *Tempest* isn't that kind of ship; my crew didn't sign on for this kind of work.

"Hey, uh..." I clear my throat. I like attention, but I've never really been one for speeches or big moments. That's why it took me more than two years to tell Max I love him even though I knew it the first time we met. Not a mistake I want to make, leaving something so important unsaid. I won't get another chance for this one. I look at all three of them, my closest friends. "Thank you. For all this, for doing so much."

"We love Max," Yen notes, and I nod.

"I know. And I... That really means a lot to me. Thank you."

"Max knows you're coming to get him, Eli," Dava reassures me. I look at her with a grateful smile and a nod, but she gives me a meaningful look and then tilts her head toward her brother. Tevin hasn't moved.

"Tev, will you come with me?" I ask. Not about to call him out here, and I seriously doubt that's what Dava was hoping for either. Tevin signs hard enough for me to hear it, the sound almost more exhausted than anything else. I didn't think he was still mad at me. No way am I going into our rescue with anything unresolved or hanging over us.

I lead Tevin down the hall and into my quarters where he shuts the door behind him. I pause halfway to the bed, trying to remember that other things and other people exist, and reach back for his hand. He takes it but doesn't squeeze, and we just sit beside each other on the bed, feet flat on the floor, shoulders pressed together. It takes me a minute to realize we're still holding hands.

"I feel like I barely got to know him," Tevin mutters. "I should have tossed you off the ship and let him stay."

I bark out a laugh, relieved for the joke and even more for the threat. I know it means he's not made at me. But I don't miss what he said, and I turn toward him.

"Talk to me," I breathe, but Tevin shakes his head. Not sure he's ever just shut me down before—Tevin is a talker in general, not shy about sharing his emotions. It's one of the things I love about him, one of the things that made me so interested in his company when we first met. I reach for him now, leaning against his side and wrapping my arms around his shoulders even though I can barely reach my hands together again at this angle. "Tev. Please?"

"No, I can't," he presses, huffing out a heart-breaking mix of a sob and a laugh. "You're chasing down your partner, the guy who has been your best friend since you were little kids. I know what he means to you. I can't...dump my shit on you too, Eli."

"Ah, Tev, you know that's now how this works. That's not how we work," I argue. He still doesn't look at me, staring down at his lap. I have to swallow to tell him, "It'd help me. Nice not to be alone in how I feel, you know?" I wince when he finally turns his head toward me. "I pretty much just said I want you in pain too, didn't I? Gods, I'm a dick."

"No," he laughs, "I know that's not what you meant. You've always had a way with words, Cap."

"My specialty."

He laughs again and leans his head over slowly. I rest mine on his shoulder and he leans on top of me, lifting a hand to hold my arm where it crosses his chest. He shifts, and I feel him press a kiss to my head. "I love how much faith you have that we're gonna get him back."

"I do. We are. There's no other option." He squeezes my arm, and I close my eyes, trying to take in his presence, let him ground me. Trying to find the words when I've never been very good at that. These don't need to be perfect, at least. "I know we'll get him back. I have faith. But I miss him so much. I missed him the second I left him behind."

There's a long pause, neither of us moving or saying anything. Both of just acknowledging that we're sad, that we miss Max. Our Max. Tevin's voice is much softer than before, softer than I've ever really heard it, when he asks, "Do you regret taking him back home?"

That's a loaded fucking question.

"I regret how I did it," I answer, thinking out loud more than answering. He's never judged me before, and he's seen me do a lot of stupid shit, so I feel safe enough to talk this out. "I shouldn't have gone behind his back. Or yours or anyone's but especially not his. And I regret putting him in a place where he got fucking kidnapped. I should have considered that *Sunbeam* had found us again or they were waiting there—fuck, I don't even know how they knew when to find him. I regret letting that happen."

Tevin shifts to wrap an arm around my waist, but he says nothing yet.

"But if I could go back and redo all this, if I could make the decision again..." I don't have the answer to that yet. Not even inside me. There is no clear answer in my brain, and I have to laugh at myself. "I don't know. I have no fucking clue what I'd do if I did it again because all I wanted to do was make him safe, and it blew up on me. I just wanted Max to be safe, I wanted him to be—"

"Eli, Eli, it's okay," he breathes, turning and pulling me against his chest. I don't realize I'm crying until my face is pressed against his chest and I feel it. I don't realize Tevin is crying too until he sniffles, and I wrap both my arms around his back, sitting up enough to let his head fall on my shoulder.

I don't know how long we stay there like that. I know I could be preparing, finding something to improve our chances with Max. But this is exactly what I should be doing. This is where I'm needed, supporting the pieces of our partnership until we can be whole again. Tevin needs me right now, until we get Max back. I need Tevin right now, to see me through until we get Max back.

And we will get Max back. I'll hold things together until then, and then I'll make damn sure
of it.

Max is coming home.

Chapter 34

Max

I am painfully, sickeningly aware of how much I'm taking on faith. I'm basically running entirely on assumptions and hope, and that's very much *not* my style. It's Eli's style—they've always been a lead-with-the-heart person. They let their heart be the deciding factor in which ship they were going to purchase when the time came, and more than once, they changed directions on the water because of their gut. I don't know if it's another disability or if I was just built differently than Eli, but my stomach and my heart have never had quite that much to say.

The only reason that I feel okay with this right now is that I'm relying on Eli's heart and Eli's gut more than my own. The only thing of mine that I'm depending on is the way that I trust Eli, and nothing that's happened recently changes that.

I know Eli better than I know myself, and I have to believe that I know what they're going to do. I have to believe that I can be the other half of whatever their plan is without even knowing their plan. I don't need to know the details to know where Eli will be and that they'll do whatever it takes to save me. And I'll be damned if I just sit around and wait for that to happen.

"The pretty cripple has a problem," Jacko shouts as he dumps me unceremoniously into my chair. Being carried up to the deck by Cross Fields' first mate, a human brute who smells almost as bad as I do despite his regular access to bathing, is incredibly humiliating, and being dropped into my chair is even worse. The poor thing is going to break with the way these people have treated it, and the rest of the night is only going to make things worse for my very expensive, familiar, important wheelchair. Replacing these things isn't exactly easy, so if the brute breaks it, I'll be forced to accept getting carried everywhere for far too long.

After tonight, it might be Eli who would carry me. Maybe Tevin, too. Okay, so there might be one tiny upside to the possibility of something as precious as my chair breaking.

"You think he's pretty?" another member of the crew asks. I haven't had a chance to learn all their names. I haven't actually tried to learn all their names. The first two days on the ship were the only two days I wasted hoping for sympathy from anyone. I should have known better than to even try for that long, but I'm naive and like to mentally pretend that the world isn't even worse to disabled people than folks whose bodies behave.

I block out the conversation about whether or not I'm pretty and focus on Fields and Jacko. It's time to sell this or kiss my freedom goodbye.

"What's the problem, Maxy?" Fields asked, grinning at me yet again. I want that smile beaten off his face, and I no longer even mentally cringe at that thought.

"The gem that I tracked here is either in water or underground or both," I explain. Lie number one. "I only know which side of the island we should start on, but beyond that, there's one hundred square miles to search." Lies number two and three. "If I'm going to get a better trace, I need to actually get onto the island." Number four. The biggest one. And the big one is leaning on all the other ones. So if I screwed any of those up...

Fields is studying me, watching me closely, searching for cracks. I have no idea what I look like when I'm lying since I don't do it very often—apparently, I should work on that as a life skill. All I can do now is try to look natural, and trying to look natural, of course, makes me extremely aware of my face and how unnatural it feels to even have a face. I can no longer remember how faces work at all, and I am very seriously wondering what would happen if I just burst into hysterical tears about needing to get off the ship when Fields finally nods and smiles again.

"Whatever our magical map man wants, he gets," he tells Jacko, slapping the larger man's shoulder. He winks at me and adds, "Especially since he is so pretty."

I've never heard my brain go 'ew' as many times in my life as I have since meeting Fields and coming onto this ship. He hasn't done anything outwardly gross, and if I knew him better, maybe I could assume that he's joking or flirting or something more charming and less disgusting. Maybe if he hadn't kidnapped me, talked so badly about Eli, and referred to me like I'm a tool to be used instead of a person.

And if Eli heard someone on their crew—or someone else anywhere in the world—call me a 'pretty cripple,' they would start burning the world down. They cringe when I call myself a cripple, though they'd never correct me on it.

Everything about Fields is like the antithesis of Eli, and it's making me realize just how lucky I am and have been. It doesn't let Eli off the hook for deciding that they make the rules for my life and my safety without my input at all, but it definitely shines a brighter light on all their good points. And it makes me miss them even more desperately. I didn't even get any proper time to sob and wallow at home! That's definitely part of the crime Fields committed.

But at least I've done something right so far. And at least I've become disliked enough by the rest of *Sunbeam*'s crew—mostly just by existing—that I'm left on the deck alone. Otherwise, they'd have to coordinate getting me back down below deck. It's easier to forget about me. And forgetting about me is exactly what I need them to do.

I have my map supplies with me thanks to the lie I told. I can manage to look like I'm sketching the map while we approach the island instead of silently thanking the gods that I spent so much time with Eli when they were still doing all sorts of unsavory things to get by. I find a few more gods to thank that I got to know

Yen, too, since that elf has some terrifying skills.

I'll get off the ship. Eli will be there. Eli and *Tempest*'s crew will help me. I'll help. I'll get to go home. Whether that means the apartment or the ship... I don't know if I actually get the right to complain either way at this point. No matter what, not being on *Sunbeam* anymore is all I need. Whatever happens after that, I'll deal with it. I might still want some time to wallow and cry, but I'll be safe. Eli is going to help me get out of here, and I'm going to help myself get out of here.

And I have to believe that even now that we're in view of the island I mapped out—for Eli and for Fields—and I don't see *Tempest*. The island isn't as big as I made it sound, but only the eastern approach is a clear one, the rest of the island covered in a thick, evergreen forest that comes right up to the waves. The path between the fifth site on the gem treasure hunt and the sixth site brings the ship following that map to the east, so that's the approach we're making. I'm trusting that Eli came right here and skipped the fifth site, meaning that they came from another direction and they could be hiding *Tempest* on another side of the island. I want the ship hidden at this point, but that doesn't mean I don't desperately just want a glimpse of those blue sails and the gorgeous person at the helm. Or Jak at the helm.

I almost smile at that thought and have to hide my face. If anyone on this crew sees me smiling, they're going to know for sure that something is wrong.

I stay near the cannons while the ship is prepared to anchor and discussions are had without me about how I'll get onto shore. I hear at least one use of the world 'drag.' Whether or not I want them suspicious of me, if these assholes try to drag me anywhere, I'm going to throw an enormous fit. Toddler-level tantrum. And just in case that's necessary, I shove my pens and compass, my precious map kit, into my pocket. They barely fit and are going to push against my leg to the point of pain, but everything left on this ship will be lost to me soon. At least I hope so.

No, I believe it. I have to. It has to happen. If it doesn't, the only other option is either no life or a life without Eli. Same thing, really.

I'm going to kiss them very, very hard...and then probably whack them in the nuts once or twice for all of this. I don't know if I blame them—it's not like they could have predicted what would happen when they dropped me off at port, and none of us guessed Fields had my home address. But I need to hit someone, I'd get killed for hitting Fields, and I could also kiss Eli all better so...

"Can you swim?" Fields shouts to me—at me—from across the deck where the crew is preparing the small boats to drop into the water. "Or at least tread water?"

"Arms work just fine," I answer, rocking my chair back and forth a little to prove my point. Swimming by using my arms almost exclusively isn't ideal, but moving my legs underwater is much, much easier and more pleasant than on land. All told, I can swim pretty well. Well enough to stay alive...not that I ever want to have to prove that. And the smug way that Fields nods in response is not making me feel confident that I won't have to prove that.

"Perfect. Here's what's going to happen."

Fantastic. I love being told what other people are going to do with my body like there isn't a person in here. I'm his magical map.

Fields is oblivious to any wrongdoing, of course; with the details of his money that Eli gave me, I can bet no one has ever told Cross Fields that he's wrong.

"We're going to put you and the chair, the whole deal, in the middle of this rowboat. It has no middle row. You'll need to hold still or you'll need to swim. Do the wheel lock?"

"They do but..." I want to tell him that this is a terrible idea. Even locked wheels aren't going to stay completely still in the middle of a floating, rocking, moving rowboat. I'll be off-balance, off-kilter, completely unsafe. And if I do tell him that, he might just decide to leave me on the ship. Or just to leave my chair on the ship. Neither option is acceptable. Not if things go the way I need them to. "Yeah, the wheels lock. I'll hold still."

"That's a good boy."

EW. Gods, I hate this guy.

The only thing I want more than to get off this ship and back where I belong is to watch everything explode on Cross Fields.

Chapter 35
Eli

Max's safety is all that matters. I know *Sunbeam* has a bigger crew and bigger weapons, and I just don't care what happens to any of us if Max gets away. I'm sure that means something is wrong with me, and I'm sure Max would be pissed at me if he could read these thoughts, and I don't care about any of that either. Max is all that matters.

I damn near bite my tongue off when I watch that tree-sized first mate Fields has lift Max and his chair as one and then unceremoniously plop them both down in a rowboat that should never be used for the purpose. But Max doesn't react. He sits perfectly still, hands poised on his wheels like he might be able to run, managing to keep the chair mostly steady while the rowboat is brought to shore. And then, of course, the chair is plopped just as unceremoniously on the sand.

Fields reaches the beach in another boat. Including him, there are six of them. He probably has at least twice as many people still on board; big ships need big crews. We had to leave Jak, Dava, and Ros on the ship to make sure *Tempest* is ready to go as soon as we get back and make as quick an escape as possible, so there's only three of us. Our advantages are two-fold, though: surprise and good hiding places. The forest on this island is thick and starts suddenly, so the trees butt right up against the beach Max's chair is being shoved over. I know it's got to be killing him, the treatment that his chair is getting. It's not only expensive and hard to replace but a part of him.

We aren't going to make that a problem for him. I'd never even consider rescuing him without the chair. Tevin is going to grab the chair while I grab Max, and Yen will cover us with fire as needed. As soon as we fight our way through to get to Max. And that's the hardest part.

I force down mental images of Cross grabbing Max, threatening him with a blade or a gun because of our attack. If I think too hard on that, it'll trap me here. My heart is already racing, hands sweaty around my sword. It's a wonder my fucking knees aren't knocking.

Get it together. Max is all that matters.

I know we didn't leave it all up to force or numbers. We didn't leave any of it up to chance. All I have to do is wait for the right moment, and then...

The half-scream and half-yelp *thing* one of Fields' crew lets out when the sand under his feet gives out and he collapses into a hole is incredibly satisfying. It might be funny if I had enough breath in my lungs to manage a laugh. The scream he lets out when he lands on the sharpened wooden posts Yen set up in the bottom of the hole—with some help getting in and out safely—isn't funny, but it might actually be more satisfying.

It freezes everyone else in shock and terror, eyes wide and flashing around like any grain of sand might launch its own attack. Considering three of them are less than a step away from traps of their own, they should be suspicious. But we don't have to give them time to figure that out on their own.

I nod to Yen, and she ups both the shock and terror by launching one of her throwing daggers. It buries itself up to the hilt in the massive right shoulder of Fields' first mate, debilitating the biggest weapon on the beach. When he shouts in pain, he's not the only one shouting, all of them realizing this is an attack—which means there's not much more point in staying hidden.

"Congratulations, Cross," I call stepping out of the tree line and approaching slowly. I can't pretend I don't hope I look kind of cool since this is the first time Max has seen me in a little while. Plus, it's a rescue; who doesn't want to look cool while staging a rescue? Maybe I should pay more attention to where I'm stepping in the sand so I don't trip. "You created the one problem Mommy's money can't buy you out of."

"Eli," I hear Max breathe, his entire body straightening up and almost glowing. He looks too thin, too dirty, too exhausted, to convince myself he's completely okay. His body is tense and oddly angled; he's hurt. But he's so, so beautiful.

Cross barks out a laugh, pale face growing redder by the second. "You think you've achieved something here, do you?"

One of his crew gets their courage and goes running at Tevin, also now revealed and closest to them at the moment while we each approach from a different angle. That was my brilliant idea in case anyone started running away. But running *at* someone the size of Tevin is just foolish. Tevin gives absolutely no wind-up to the punch that lays his attacker out flat on the sand.

Max barks out a laugh, and though he claps a hand over his mouth to try not to draw attention to himself in the moment, it fails. I can't breathe when Cross turns to look down at him, only then remembering Max is there at all. But when he remembers, I know what he's going to do next, and I cannot let Max become a pawn.

I take one full step, unable to even start running, before the blast from the ship comes with no warning, strong enough to make me stumble back. Yen comes much closer to falling, stumbling in the sand, and a few of Cross's men aren't lucky enough to catch themselves at all. But that's it for a long minute. A huge boom, the sand and trees rattling, and then nothing while we all just stare at the ship. At *Sunbeam*. Which is on fire.

All hell breaks loose all at once, like everyone watching is simultaneously freed from the shock and tossed back into the real world where the ship is burning from an explosion. The cannons, I realize somewhere at the back of my mind. One of them is floating in the water, still on fire.

"Eli!" This time, Max shouts my name, and it's what I need to snap back to myself.

Cross is shoving at one of the rowboats and screaming at his crew, all of them in chaos, either leaping off the burning ship and into the water or trying to get back to the ship. All with their captain screaming at the top of his lungs. They aren't going to need long to remember we're here or who to blame. We have an escape window, and we can't miss it.

"Tevin, chair," I snap, already moving as quickly as I can while making sure I don't end up in one of the traps we set overnight. It's nice to be this big when it means I can carry Max so easily, but I sink right into the loose, hot sand— kind of a nightmare to run through. My legs are going to burn when this is over no matter how small the island is. Worth it.

"I knew you'd be here," Max says when I reach him, slumping forward a little like the release of a weight on him has doubled him over. We have barely seconds before Cross or someone else notices what's going on, but I slip my fingers under Max's chin and lift his face to look at me. His brown eyes are a little reddened, and he looks more drained than I've ever seen, but they're still the best sight in the world. "My turtle is broken," he blurts.

"Your...what?"

"The turtle you gave me. Fields broke it. I'm sorry."

I almost laugh. "Maxy, I'll buy you a million turtles. Are you hurt anywhere?"

"Just get me out of here please." He reaches for me, and I don't resist or make him wait another second. It's already been too long.

I pull him into my arms and stand with him against my chest, my arms carefully under his knees and behind his back. I know he'll be in terrible pain, probably worse when this is over and his adrenaline comes down, but there's only so much I can do to keep his body stable at the moment. This is gonna suck for him. Fuck, I hope I don't fall.

"Any reason I need to get on that ship, Maxy?" Yen demands as I start moving back toward the forest, Tevin right at my side with the wheel-chair in hand, holding it at his side like a purse. Yen is walking backward to keep an eye on our potential pursuers, but another blast tells me the flames reached their weapons and ammo stores; they're going to be busy for a while. And I'm jealous Yen can walk backward on the sand while I'm stumbling forward. Fucking elves and their lithe fucking bodies.

"No," Max answers. "They didn't bring most of my stuff, and I got what's most important before setting the charges."

When I stumble this time, hard enough to make Max grunt—though he's sweet enough to try and make that quiet—it's because of shock, not sand.

"Wait a minute!" Tevin laughs, maneuvering the chair and his big body through tight trees and sinking even further into the sand than I am. "You set those cannons to blow?"

It had to have been Max, of course. But it's so not like Max, it didn't even register 'til now. Max blew up *Sunbeam*.

"I had to do something," Max mumbles, blushing fiercely and somehow embarrassed about doing something so incredibly badass. He's the reason we got away without a fight or even any major threat. He's the reason *Sunbeam* can't give chase. He's—

"Oh, fuck," I mutter, wincing when Max looks up at me; I didn't mean to say it out loud. "You took them to the last site, right? That means Cross still has one of the elements."

Max gives me the most beautiful smile. "Really, Eli? I think I can find it."

Chapter 36

Max

Yet again, Baybridge's port is looming on the horizon. We'll be home tomorrow.

Home.

I used to think I know what that word means. I had a home with my parents growing up. It was a warm, safe place. A little strict and too focused on who I would become than what I was at the time, but still. A home, and I have fond memories of it and emotions associated with it.

I had a home at school too, a home in all the libraries that I frequented, spent hours in. I've had homes with Eli. We moved a few times, but we always made a home, and the most recent—the one waiting for us now—is the home that Eli gets to return, so it's special. All of my homes have been special in some way.

I don't think I ever believed a ship could be a home, though. I realize now that I believed

C. Knight

home has to be a building. A place with a roof and doors and a wall. Maybe some of that is from meeting Eli so young, seeing what a life without those things was like. I brought Eli to my parent's home as often as I could to give them a place to rest, a warm meal, safety. All of that within a home. But I realize now, after only a couple months at sea, that I was wrong about what makes a home.

Tempest is home. The entire crew is at home here. This isn't just where they work and the thing that they sail on. They aren't pursuing their treasure hunts, this wild adventure, just for the money or what it will bring to them individually. The success of this treasure hunt is important to the crew because they want to make *Tempest* famous. They want to improve not only their lives individually but as a crew and for the ship. For their home.

And for me, it's so much more than that. For me, it's not just the ship that is my home. I've realized on the waves, while we worked and lived together, while we got to wake up together every day, even while we've fought and made mistakes...

Eli is my home. I don't need a building or a ship or any specific place. All I need is them. And that's been true since we were twelve and they dripped rainwater on my book, mesmerized me with their eyes. Since they made me feel seen for who I am and not what I do.

Eli is my home, and with the port approaching, I now have to figure out how to live without a home until the next time Eli and *Tempest* come back.

I didn't expect this when I signed on. I thought

310

I could come here, have a great time onboard, help the crew accomplish their goal. I thought I was okay without Eli all the time, that we'd both come to accept our lives. But now...

A blue orb hits the desk in front of me with a thump, startling me. "I didn't hear you come in," I laugh, tilting my head to look up at Eli.

"That's the last one," they announce, motioning to the element. The sun isn't bright today, hidden behind gray clouds, but the little light available seems drawn to this thing, clinging to whatever is inside it and throwing shards of rainbows all over. "That is the last element of the gods, the last legendary piece of treasure, the final impossible-to-find thing that we found. Now we just make a drop-off and...we're done. We did it."

Eli looks...bright. They're thrilled. This ship and taking part in adventures just like this are exactly why they wanted to do this, why they wanted to get a ship in the first place. It's what they've always dreamed of doing, and now they're accomplishing it on a new scale. This success will change all their lives and change what they can do with *Tempest* from here forward. Eli's achieved their dreams, and I'm here feeling sorry for myself.

I reach up and scratch their beard lightly; that always gets them to nuzzle into my palm and hum happily. "I am so proud of you."

"So you've told me," they laugh. "But you know we couldn't have done this without you." They shake their head a little. "We could have lost people. Even the ship. You prevented all that. I'm proud of you, too, Max. We all are."

"Thank you. It's been...so much more than

I could have imagined, so really, thank you for bringing me here, E." I offer my mouth for a kiss that they lean down and take, and when they pull away, I know I have to say what comes next. "Do you think you'll stay for a bit after we reach port? Or come back soon?"

"Well..." Eli turns to sit on the desk; as soon as their butt touches the desk, they pop back up and pull something out of their back pocket, which then goes on the desk beside their hip. Eli is constantly carrying a million things in their pockets—a practice picked up when they didn't have anywhere else to keep all their belongings, I think—so I don't bother to ask what it is. "We need to stop in port to restock. Ros mentioned needing more chicken feed, salted meats, and fresh fruits, and all that can take a while for us to get."

"So I get you for a while?" I ask hopefully. At least if I don't have to say goodbye immediately, I can prolong the inevitable pain and loneliness.

"Kind of depends on you, baby." When I just stare at them, they smirk a little and cock their head. "How set are you on working out of the library? Because I know it won't be totally the same, but I know you're worth seeking out, and people will. They'll find you when we stop in ports, and there are lots of ways they could reach out. Even a letter can find us. You can still work."

"I can still work...from ports." I have to say it slowly, trying to work the words out. A spark of hope ignites at the back of my mind, and I try my hardest to squash it. I don't want to get my hopes up, can't risk that. Not again.

"Right. You'd *have* to work from ports."

"Why would I have to work from ports?" I press. Eli's eyes are sparkling in the way they do when they're teasing me, and this is a horrible thing to tease me about. "Eli!"

"Hey now. You can't go yelling at your captain. I'm going to add that to the ship charter." They retrieve the mystery pocket item again and then drop it on the desk right in front of me, a scroll well-taken care of and rolled with caution. "Right after you sign it."

The ship charter.

I'm going through my mental bank of everything they told me about the ship charters. It's rules for living on the ship, an agreement about how they'll split up any profits or treasures, a promise for loyalty to one another and to *Tempest*. Someone who wants to be part of the crew must sign the ship charter—by agreement of the majority of the crew. And once someone signs the ship charter, they're a part of the crew for life in spirit even if not physically.

"You want me to sign it?" I ask, still trying not to get my hopes up. I unroll it in front of me, staring at it like what it says might personally matter to me. But if I get hopeful and then it doesn't matter, I'll be lonely and bored *and* heartbroken when they leave.

"We all want you to sign it." I look back up at Eli, and they nod behind me.

I turn in the chair to find the rest of the crew standing there; apparently, it wasn't just Eli I didn't hear come in. Ros is holding Jak's hand and bouncing like she needs the tether to keep her from floating away. Jak is making a poor attempt at scowling, and Yen is schooling her features as best she can lest anyone suspect she's not the coolest person on the ship. Dava is grinning at me, though, and Tevin is all-out beaming. He looks like he might start bouncing too.

"We all want you to stay, Max." When I look back up at Eli this time, they start blabbering, speaking rapidly. "You can keep working on your own, like I said. Your own clients. In ports, right? But you'd be our ship cartographer too, a full part of the crew...though you'd still get as much of the profit cut as you always have through me. But...but maybe if that's not okay since you might not work on your own as much... Okay, we could work it out, and I —"

"Help me up." It gets them to stop talking, though they don't move until I hold out my hands. I use their hold and stability to pull myself up and then just launch myself against them, throwing my arms around their neck. Eli laughs and hugs me to them. "Thanks for inviting me onto the ship, Captain Rose. I'd love to sign."

They pull back, their sea-green eyes searching mine. "Yeah? You'll stay on the ship, Max?"

"I'll stay with you, Eli. Wherever *Tempest* takes us...we're home."

The End

Acknowledgments

Writing a book is not a solo-venture. Every book finished and published is built on the shoulders of an entire community, and I am endlessly grateful to my community.

Ry, you've never made me feel capable of less than galactic takeover. Your willingness to read any nonsense I write, whether or not it's anything close to a realm you enjoy, and to give me space to write whenever I need it are the reasons this book got finished. I'm lucky you're my best friend.

Monkey, everything I do is for you. You're my little adventurer, and you inspire me to take on my own adventures fearlessly. Knowing that you think it's cool I write books has made this whole journey worthwhile, no matter how it turns out. I love you and I like you. But please don't grow up and read my books—we'd both be mortified.

Monster, Bear, and Pebbles, the best dogs in the world. Thank you for snuggling with me into the wee hours of the night while I wrote.

Team Free Will! I never would have started writing again without you two, Eva and Cas. Traveling 300 miles to meet two complete strangers who I only knew online is one of the best decisions I ever made. You've both loved me unconditionally and taught me so much. I don't know what I'd do with you.

Felix, thank you for supporting me as much as you support my stories. Thank you for loving my characters, loving me, and never letting me get away with hiding from the world when RSD reared its ugly head. There's something priceless about knowing you have a friend you could say anything to, drop any idea on, and you'd still get their support.

Sam, I don't know if you knew this, but you gave me the courage to even think about publishing something original. Having someone with your talent and your passion for all the awesome things in the world take an interest in my work, in me, changed everything. It's an incredible bonus that you've turned into such an awesome friend (and future co-author).

Thanks to Felix for my cover and Archer for perfect formatting. Thank you to the best beta team anyone could ask for! To the Draft Your Heart Out Discord server, to the still-shocking number of people who have read and commented on my fanfics, to the original #Smorewords group, and to all my editing clients: you made me feel capable of doing this, and I can't put into words how much that means to me. R.M., Addy, Ant, Z, Kayleigh, and the mountains of people on BookTwit, BookTok, and Booksky, too many to name, who have always cheered me and Butt Pirates on: I hope you know how much I appreciate your support, your love, and you screaming at me to hydrate.

I hope I do you all proud.

And thanks to YOU, my reader, for taking a chance on my debut and the messy little dorks in love within these pages. I've been working on this book for 6 years, but I wrote this version when my family and I were being forced to leave our home because of hate crimes. My found family—found through social media—got us out of that house and into a newer, safer one. This story was born of that love, of that protectiveness, of that community. It means the world to be to be able to share it with you, and I truly hope you enjoyed getting to know Max, Eli, and the crew of *Tempest*.

About the Author

Charlie Knight hates talking about themself.
Please don't make them do this.

https://cknightwrites.carrd.co